DORMANT ROOK

A.B. COHEN & JP RINDFLEISCH IX

To Claudia, Chris & Nissim.
Our beloved Beta readers.

Tree of Life

Divine One
Keter
Holy
Timekeeper
Binah
Time
Traveler
Chochmah
Space
Elemental
Gevurah
Nature
Lover
Chesed
Heal
Seer
Tiferet
Vision
Invulnerable
Netzach
Sheild
Pacifist
Hod
Hold
Bonded
Yesod
Link
Warrior
Malchut
Push

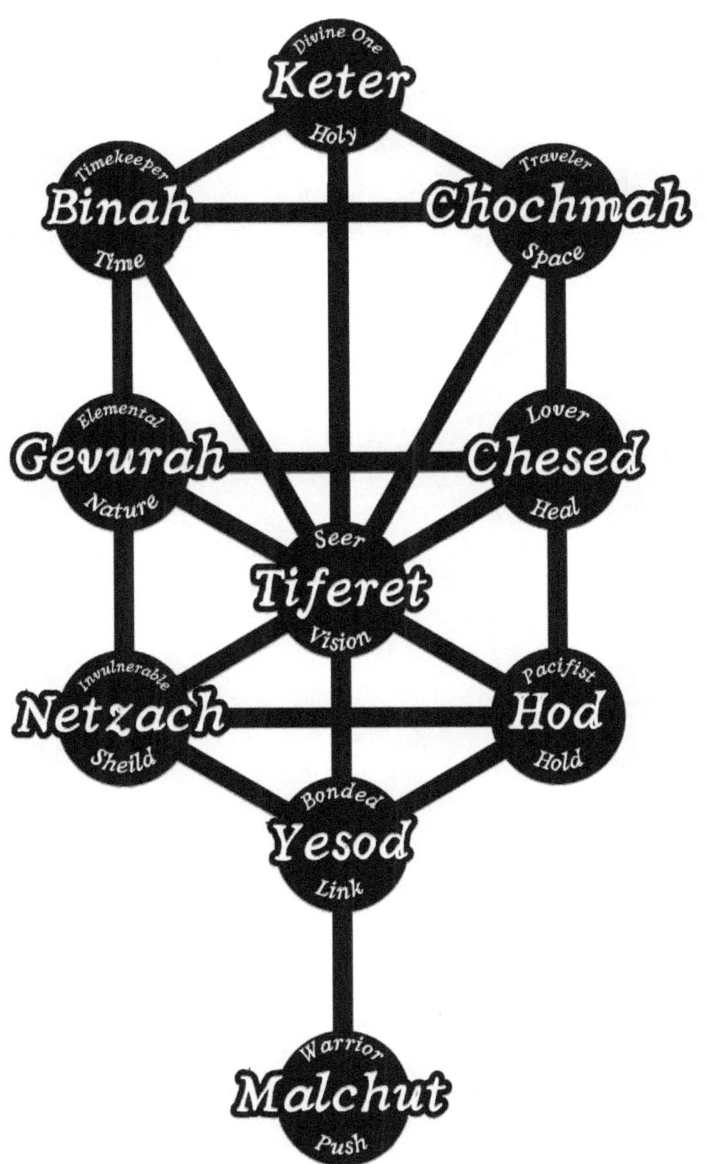

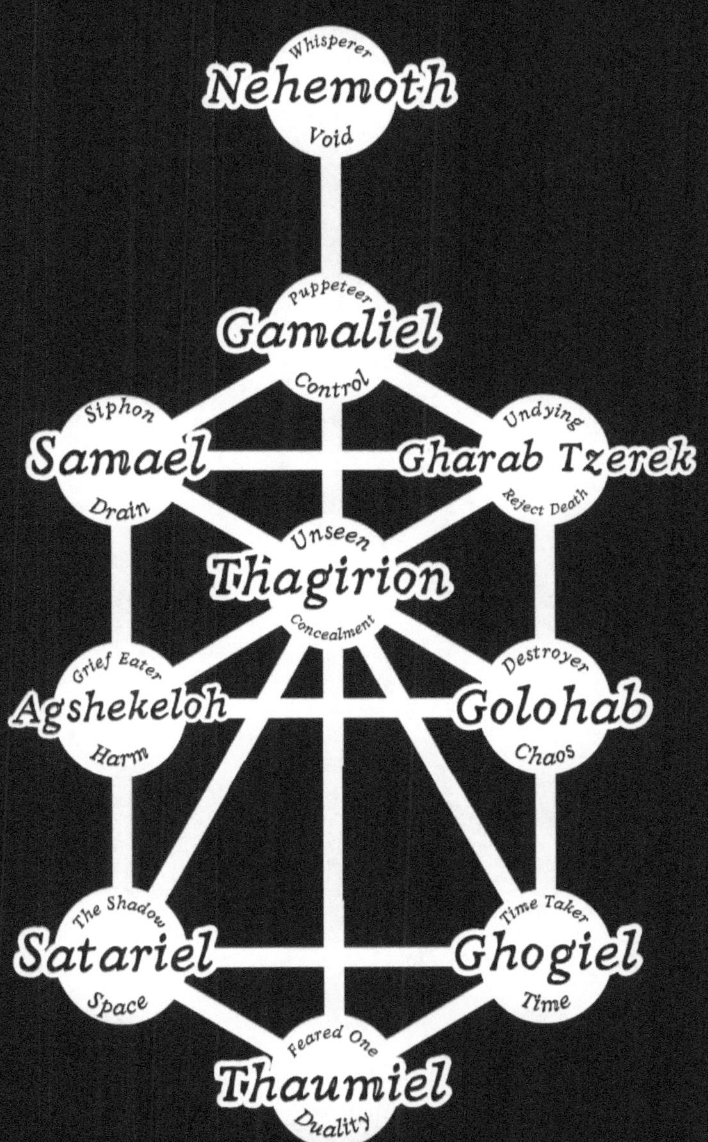

Tree of Death

The Infinity Board

 King

 White Queen

 Black Queen

 White Rook / Sage

 Black Rook

 White Bishop

 White Knight

 Black Bishop

 Black Knight

 White Pawn

 Black Pawn

 Square

CHAPTER 1
A DARK PLACE

"Please, stay with me," Leah whispered.

Exhaustion washed over her like lapping waves, pulling her deeper into the darkness. She blinked and nuzzled at the fabric against her cheek. Sleep was the only thing she wanted, or better yet, needed. As she moved, exhaustion clung to her skin, some kind of sticky residue stealing her comfort. She pulled away, her eyes focusing on the Queen's trench coat and the pool of blood settled in the bottom of the boat.

Leah winced as beams of light flooded the Jon boat, spilling onto her friends, casting three dark silhouettes. Isaac and Sarah leaned against each other at the stern of the boat. The third silhouette stood up, waving his arms.

"Over here!" Gabe yelled, his voice hoarse.

As it echoed across the water, the pull into darkness grew stronger. Color faded from Leah's vision, and she looked down at Helen, the woman's pale face and high cheekbones offering no solace or comfort.

"Please, stay with me," Leah whispered again as she clutched Queen Helen's coat.

Her chest ached as if a hole had torn through her. She

took in a breath, feeling the pain in her lungs as an image of her uncle Eric formed in her mind. He looked just like her mom, with the same amber eyes and chestnut hair. She'd never see him again, just like her parents.

The pain consumed her thoughts, a darkness wrapping around her like a blanket, threatening to smother her. She didn't fight back. Why would she when it was an option to fall into this void? Fall into darkness. Darkness. Nothingness. No blame. No guilt. No pain. No sorrow.

The sounds around her muffled, and the Jon boat melted beneath her as she slipped into the void.

A familiar voice, deep and with a hint of malice. "How many times do you plan on replaying this?"

Leah let out a breath. Of course, even here Asmodeus would find her. "Leave me alone. I'm done."

Asmodeus laughed, an echo that reverberated in Leah's hollow chest. "I think not."

Fingers snapped, and gravity pulled on Leah, dropping her onto solid, smooth stone. A light above her flickered. She groaned and opened her eyes, glaring at the familiar marble table as she righted herself.

Asmodeus straightened his suit jacket and crossed his arms. Aside from his extremely pale skin and elongated fingers, he looked almost human. He intertwined his fingers and stared at her, dark eyes peering right through her.

"What do you want?" Leah asked, keeping her eyes on the table.

"I've grown bored with this memory. When do you plan to move on?"

She could see it replaying in her head already. Eric turning, his hands held in *Hod* position, and the expression he wore as the chains slipped through him. Blood covered the marble table, and the light above them dimmed.

Go! Get out of here! Eric's words grew louder and louder in her mind.

She could have—

"Leah!" Asmodeus shouted, slamming his fist on the table. It cracked beneath the force.

The light brightened, and the blood vanished as Leah blinked, finding focus on Asmodeus.

"You are not the only one who has lost against him."

Leah pushed herself up from the table. She was numb, and all she wanted was the darkness. She walked toward the dark, but the light above her followed. When she turned, the table stood right next to her, as if she hadn't moved at all.

"Let me go," she murmured.

"Succumbing to the dark will only postpone the inevitable. I can't let you. *I won't* let you. Not while I'm still here."

"It doesn't matter. Nothing does."

With one swift motion, Asmodeus reached out and curled his hand around her arm. The cold pierced her skin, and she shuddered as Asmodeus stood, a rage emanating off him.

"Legion destroyed everything. My loyal Xigat and Litars are his puppets, their minds enthralled as they carry his every order. Worse than that, he destroyed the ones who weren't useful. Drymmas, even the young Ky, all taken into the void, body and mind consumed. And worst of all, he made me watch. I watched it all happen, powerless to stop."

"I'm sorry. I can't. He—"

"He took your uncle and made me take your parents and teacher. Do you think he'll stop there? He took my entire people. Legion will stop at nothing to—"

Images surfaced from the surrounding darkness.

Images of her parents, Alma, and her uncle swirled around them. An artificial warmth spread across Leah's skin as the images took shape and depth.

Asmodeus let go of Leah, eyeing the storm of images. "Wake up. Someone is watching."

A callused hand pulled away from Leah's arm as her eyes fluttered open. White ceiling tiles looked down at her as she lay sunken in a bed.

"Well, this is a first," a voice from her left, with a thick Spanish accent, said.

A brown-eyed man with a perfectly trimmed beard and a sharp jawline peered at her. His brunette hair was perfectly shaped into a pompadour.

Leah's cheeks grew hot as she pulled her arm back. "Who are you? Where . . . where am I?"

The man stood up straight and smiled, a set of perfectly white teeth gleaming down at Leah. "The name's Nicolas de Cordoba, but you can call me Nick."

"Okay, Nick, but why are you hovering over me?"

Nick gestured around the room. "Because you're in the infirmary and I'm your caretaker."

Leah peered past Nick and found several other beds lining the walls. Studying them, she noticed ones occupied by Isaac, Gabe, and Sarah. She pushed herself up on her elbows, straining to sit up. "My friends, are they okay?"

Nick rested a hand on her shoulder, guiding her back down. "Take a minute before you try that. You've been asleep for a few days."

"Days?" Leah shouted, straining against his hand.

"You all collapsed, understandably, after what

happened." He grabbed an electronic thermometer and checked Leah's temperature. "You and your friends were placed in a chemically induced coma in order to properly monitor your . . . uh, unforeseen separation."

Leah pulled his hand off her. "What about—" she gasped as a sharp pain pierced through her upper chest.

"Careful, señorita, your wounds are still healing."

Before Leah had a chance to respond, Nick softly touched her shoulder and shut his eyes. Warmth washed over her, spreading down to her toes, followed by a calmness and serenity that weren't her own. A tension inside her chest relaxed, a tightness she didn't even know she had, and she finally felt at peace.

Nick lifted his hand, and peace retreated, leaving behind an emptiness for sorrow to fill. The fact that he could use *Chesed* so deftly, and without a sweat, without even knowing Leah, surprised her. The pain in her chest dissipated.

Leah eyed the other beds again and frowned. "Queen Helen? Nykima? Where are they?"

"Awake. Helen is already in her office. White Knight Amana, however, is in physical therapy. The incident left behind some irreparable damage."

Leah exhaled a breath and let her shoulders relax. They made it. Nykima was alive. And the queen was alive. Their squad's sacrifice wasn't in vain. Eric's sacrifice wasn't in vain.

The thought of Eric sent her mind into a spiral. Instinctively, she reached out, expecting to sense him in her bond, to still feel that ping of emotion and confirm that he was still there. Instead, as she reached out, she felt the frayed ends of something torn and a darkness waiting just beyond that.

"Queen Helen actually ordered me to bring you out,"

Nick said, pulling Leah back to reality. He set down a full syringe of something clear. "But you woke before I had a chance. How?"

Careful, Asmodeus said.

"I don't know."

"Pity," Nick said, smiling as helped her sit up. "In all my years as a Sage, that was a first. Even Knights give in to the coma after a bond break, but you fought it."

Leah frowned. "You're a Sage?"

Nick stepped back and placed his hands on his hips. "The one and only Sage of *Chesed*. But I prefer if everyone calls me The Lover if they don't call me Nick. It's more . . . suiting."

"I thought sages would be—"

"Older?" Nick cut her off. He held up his hands, inspecting them as he spoke. "Some are, but most Sages are so intrinsically connected to their chosen well early on that they gain Sage status before they finish being a Pawn. Promoted right up to White Rook status overnight." He pulled a pile of clothes from her bedside and handed them to her and turned his back. "Shout if you need anything."

Leah looked around at the open hospital room, at her friends lying unconscious. "You want me to change here?"

Nick waved his hand. "No one else is going to wake up. At least, they shouldn't. And no one comes into my infirmary without my permission."

Grabbing her clothes, Leah swung her legs over the side of the bed and carefully tested her weight before shakily pulling off her hospital gown and dressing in a loose pair of white sweatpants and a white undershirt. She cleared her throat and Nick turned around just as her knees gave out.

"Woah, take it easy, señorita," he said, catching her. After righting her, he reached into his pocket and retrieved a bar of unwrapped chocolate. "Here, you need this more than me."

Leah unwrapped the yellow and blue bar, eyeing the words, *Chocolate con Leche*. She nibbled on a corner, and it melted in her mouth, her tastebuds firing as the sweet silky chocolate coated her tongue.

She took another, larger bite, muttering, "This is amazing," between chews.

Nick laughed. "It's fresh from Venezuela. Got myself a big box before leaving my last post."

"In Venezuela?"

Nick nodded, holding out his arm for her to take, which she reluctantly did. "Shifter problem. They're not holding back, and our casualties are getting worse. At least I could stop a few of them from dying."

As they reached the door, Leah turned back and looked at her friends.

Nick grabbed onto her hand and squeezed. "They're in excellent hands. Promise."

His eyes peeled away and focused on the hallway ahead. Unlike the infirmary, which had no clear windows to the outside, one wall of the hall was pure glass. Beyond the wall, a dense forest of deep greens, with a hint of yellow and red as fall settled in, stretched out into the horizon.

"Beautiful, isn't it?" Nick asked.

"Where are we?" Leah asked again.

"We are at the Infinity Board headquarters, just outside D.C.," Nick said, gently pulling her from the windows. "Come on, our Queen is waiting."

CHAPTER 2

SECRETS

As they reached the elevator lobby, Nick brushed past Leah and pulled out a white card, tapping it on a tablet in the middle of the room. It lit up, and Leah noted that half the numbers listed were negative.

Nick tapped on floor three and the screen changed, notifying them that an elevator was being called to them on the sixth floor. The elevator to their left dinged, and they stepped inside.

Before Nick had the opportunity to ask her any additional questions, Leah chimed in, "So, negative floors?"

"We have to keep our secrets somehow. Most people outside the Infinity Board think this place is some kind of wellness retreat."

The elevator stopped on the fifth floor, and the doors slid open. An older woman, squat, wearing a royal blue knit cap and a white cardigan that matched her hair, stared back at her with milky white eyes. Leah moved back as the woman, who Leah suspected was somewhere in her sixties, stepped in, using a white cane to gently sweep the floor in front of her.

"Evening, Nona," Nick said, rocking on his heels.

"Nick. Hope your travels went well. Did you bring back anything good?" Nona stretched out vowels and rolled her Rs like the Polish accents Leah had heard growing up.

"Chocolate with your name on it," Nick said as the doors slid shut.

Nona smiled and tilted her head. "And who is this with you?"

"Leah Ackerman. One of the individuals who survived the Queen's Gambit."

Nona dropped her head. "Such a shame what happened. So many lost, but the Queen was saved in the end." She smiled and held out a hand. "I'm Nona Timashova."

Leah accepted the woman's hand and squeezed gently. "Uh, nice to meet you."

In an instant, the woman's already warm hand blazed hot, and a fiery serpent slithered up Leah's arm. It happened so fast, the serpent wriggling up her arm, down her spine, and breaching something deep within her. Before she had the opportunity to let go, the pain vanished and a faint yellow glow emanated from the woman's milky white eyes.

"What they hell was that?" Leah said, yanking her hand away.

Asmodeus spoke inside her. *Did she? Did she see us?*

I—I don't know, Leah answered back, rubbing her arm and eying the woman.

"You don't waste a second, I see," Nick said, leaning against the elevator wall.

Nona shrugged, looking like some innocent grandmother. "You know me; I always look. But no corruption. How strange, even with that thing inside you."

"Level three," the automated voice announced over the speaker.

As Nick and Leah stepped out, Nona gave a small bow. "I'll be seeing you two later. Don't be giving away my chocolate."

"I'd never," Nick said, grinning.

"Who was that?" Leah asked after the doors closed. "Why did she use *Tiferet* like that?"

"She's our Seer, the Sage of *Tiferet*." Nick placed his hands on his hips and shook his head. "And she's not too keen on personal space. Needs to see anything herself, even when my reports were very clear. Don't let her granny façade deceive you. Come on."

Leah followed him through a corridor filled with potted plants intermixed with carvings and sculptures made from wood and gold. They reached a set of double doors with a large Queen chess piece carved in the middle. Gold inlay drew branches and roots from the piece, stretching out beyond the frame. Nick gave a few soft raps on the door, and a familiar voice spoke from within.

"Come in."

Leah's heart skipped a beat as she heard that voice. She knew they were coming to see Queen Helen, but to hear her voice again, after she'd nearly died, brought a surge of emotion Leah wasn't prepared for.

Tears silently slipped down her cheeks as Nick guided her into the room. Queen Helen stood from behind an oak desk, her crystalline blue eyes locked on Leah.

Leah resisted every urge to rush to Helen's side. Instead, she stood at attention and waited for her Queen.

Helen stepped out from behind her desk. Her walk was slower and more calculated, but she still carried with her an aura of regality.

"At ease, Pawn. It's good to see you are well."

"Likewise," Leah whispered, her voice catching in her throat.

Helen gestured to the cushion chair beside her desk. "Please, sit."

Leah's gaze left Helen, and she took in the surrounding office. Bookshelves lined the walls on either side of the desk, with a solid glass wall overlooking the other side of the forest. In the left corner, there was a spiral wooden staircase that led into a small mezzanine above.

Nick pulled the chair out for Leah. "As you said, Queen: no corruption."

"Terrific news, Nicolas," Queen Helen said, slightly wincing as she settled back into her chair. "Please keep this between us for now."

Nick bowed his head and said, "Of course. I'll get working on the others." He glanced down at Leah and smiled. "Pleasure to meet you, señorita Ackerman."

The moment Nick left, Leah found it harder to breathe. She frowned and clutched her chest.

"He can be quite soothing," Queen Helen said.

"Why do I feel so—"

"Empty?" Helen asked. Her face softened, and she leaned close. "You lost your bond, a pain I wished you'd never have to face. The Sage of *Chesed* might help ease it when you're around him, but this is a wound that even he can't heal by himself."

Images of Eric flashed through Leah's mind. His smile, his stern look as he waited for her to learn a lesson, the pain in his eyes as the chains tore through his skin.

Helen stretched her arms across the table, offering them for Leah to take. "Stay with me. Eric's loss will *not* go in vain. He was dedicated to the Infinity Board. Many couldn't do what he did. But above all, he was a protector, to the bitter end."

Leah ignored the hands, instead clutching her fists.

"How did we miss it?" She groaned. "How did we miss Joanna? And the kid?"

Helen leaned back, pursing her lips. "Legion found a way past *Tiferet*, something I'd never thought he could do."

Leah stared down at her hands, the pain in her chest building. He found a way past *Tiferet* and killed half of them. There had to be something she missed. Something that could have stopped him.

After a moment of silence, Helen shifted in her seat. "I know this is hard. And I know you need time to grieve, but I need to ask you something."

"What's that?" she muttered.

"Back at the academy, you used the Tree of Death. Beyond what any Mystic should. Using it like that, you should be corrupted. Yet, you aren't. Nick can't find even a trace. How?"

Careful, Asmodeus said.

"I don't know," Leah said, her voice weak. The battle was a hazy memory. A flash of a woman, possessed, dying in front of her as she siphoned off her life. She did that. Leah killed her.

Helen intertwined her fingers. "Leah, please. If you truly want Legion. After all he's done. Then I need you to trust me. Not even skilled Mystics can escape corruption. So, how did you?"

Don't, Asmodeus growled. *We can't trust anyone. They'll test us. We'll never see the light of day.*

A buzzing tingle spread up her left arm, and Leah instinctively clasped at it, squeezing it as if she were stopping Asmodeus from taking over.

Helen stood and came around her desk, pulling a chair up next to Leah and grabbing her hands. "This place is not like the academy, Leah. You need people you can trust, people with more standing than a Pawn. I once put all my trust in your mother. Please, let me help you like she did for me."

No! Asmodeus screamed. At the same time, her left hand pulled away from Helen's grasp of its own accord, while the right remained in Helen's grasp.

I'm sorry, Leah thought as she took a deep breath. "You deserve to know."

Goosebumps formed on Leah's arms as the room grew cold. Helen pulled back from Leah, a frown on her face as Asmodeus pulled on *Nehemoth.*

Stop it! Leah yelled.

This Mystic is the one who defeated me in the first place. Tell her, and I'm dead.

"*I said STOP!*" Leah screamed out loud, smashing her left fist on the table. The cold stopped, and Helen cocked her head, eyeing Leah's arm as her eyes glowed yellow.

"It's Asmodeus," Leah said. The words spilled out of her, one tumbling after the other. "His mark, he used it somehow after Alma died. In a dream. We connected before Legion took him. I didn't trust it at first. I mean, why would I? But he's been helping me. He saved Isaac back at the orphanage. And helped get that kid back to the druids. And if it wasn't for him, we wouldn't be here. He wants Legion just as bad as we do, for taking his Kyem."

Asmodeus riled inside her as she spoke the words, trying to claw his way out, but she held firm, muting him in her head as much as he could. As she stopped talking, his voice came to a halt, both of them waiting for Helen.

Helen stared at Leah for a long time, then frowned and cleared her throat. "What was that last word you used?"

"Kyem," Leah said. "It means people in their language."

Helen nodded and spoke slowly, as if carefully choosing her words. "Thank you for trusting me. And I'm sorry again you've gone through this. Who else knows?"

"Sarah and Isaac know about the Tree of Death. I hadn't told Isaac about Asmodeus yet. Oh, and Gabe found out. He was pretty mad. He was pressuring me to tell everyone just before things . . ." Leah trailed off, the memory of Legion's attack surfacing with images of blood and pain.

"Given Pawn Tate's past, there's no surprise he'd be upset."

Leah furrowed her brow. She knew Gabe blamed himself for his father's death, but was there more? "What does that—"

"That isn't my story to tell," Helen said. "But I need to know . . . do you trust him?"

Leah let the question sink in. She unreservedly trusted Sarah and Isaac, like they were long-lost friends. But Gabe? "I do."

"Good. And have you told anyone else?"

The question stung more than it should have, a pain echoing in Leah's chest as she muttered, "There's no one else to tell."

"You must keep this secret. Understand? Ask your friends to do the same." The Queen leaned back and frowned. "We'll need to notify the Sages, too. They'll be working with you, and I wouldn't want any surprises."

"We're working with the Sages?" Leah asked.

"Yes, but we'll worry about that later. You and your friends need some time to rest."

Asmodeus nagged at the back of her mind. *What about Legion?*

Helen rose from her seat next to Leah and walked back behind her desk. "By the time our Mystics got to the academy, they only found rubble and fire."

Blood pounded in her ears and her stomach quivered. "So, what is the Infinity Board going to do about it? Wait another year to do anything?"

"No," Helen said, pacing behind her desk. "I called an emergency meeting with the Outer Council. Black Rooks have been pulled from their posts and are on their way here as we speak. I'll enact a Fortress, which if approved will centralize the Infinity Board's power to me, making our prime directive focused solely on hunting down Legion."

"You still need approval? You almost died! He killed nearly everyone in the Queen's Gambit. How—"

Helen held up her hand, cutting Leah off. "The Infinity Board must maintain checks and balances. Until the attack on the academy, Legion was just another threat on our long list. Convincing everyone else will prove to be a challenge, but if we do this right, then I will have the full force of the Board behind me. I'll need your support in the coming days. Go, get some rest, and fill in your friends." Helen pressed down on a small intercom resting at the edge of her desk. "Mathew, could you escort Pawn Ackerman to her quarters?"

A voice spoke through the speakers a few seconds later, "Yes, my Queen."

Helen crossed her arms as she waited. "I have to ask . . . has Asmodeus been listening in?"

Before Leah was able to answer, a whisper escaped from her. "I have. You've made quite a name for yourself since our last meeting, Helen Nielsen."

Leah grabbed at her throat, her eyes wide. He hadn't done that before. Hadn't taken her voice from her. She wondered what else Asmodeus could do that he'd been hiding from her.

Helen's back straightened, and she glared at Leah like a hungry tiger ready to pounce. "If you dare harm Elizabeth Mizrahi's daughter, I will personally see to it you are extracted and torn apart molecule by molecule. Do you understand me?"

Leah grinned, and Asmodeus spoke through her. "You have nothing to worry about, Queen Helen. We have the same enemy."

There was a knock at the door, and the Queen looked up. "Come in."

"My Queen," a deep voice spoke behind Leah.

"Leah, Mathew is my White Pawn and head of logistics here at headquarters."

Leah stood up from her chair and turned to find a short man with curly brown hair, dressed in a full White Pawn uniform. She gave a slight nod as Helen turned to Mathew.

"Please escort Pawn Ackerman to her room and update her on her schedule," Helen said.

"Schedule?" Leah asked.

"We will talk more tomorrow," Helen said. "I'm sure Nick has already brought your friends out of their sleep, and they are waiting for you."

CHAPTER 3
SOMBER REUNION

That was so stupid, Asmodeus hissed as Leah and Mathew stepped onto the elevator. *You told the last living person who had a hand in my downfall.*

Leah rolled her eyes. *I trust her. She won't hurt me, and if I say you're helping, she won't hurt you either.*

Asmodeus fell silent, but Leah felt his frustration bubbling at the edges of her mind.

The doors to the elevator opened on level five, and Leah followed Mathew down the hall.

They stopped in front of a room marked 5C, and he handed Leah a plain white card.

"This card will get you everywhere you are scheduled to be. Don't lose it."

The way he said it made her feel like a child being lectured, even though they looked to be the same age. "Got it," she said, holding back what she wanted to say while pocketing the key.

"Your alarms have been set for zero six hundred. I'll be waiting at your door by six fifteen. You and the others should refrain from eating in the morning."

Leah narrowed her eyes. "Why?"

"Queen's orders." Mathew waved his key in front of the door and pulled it open when it beeped. "Inform the others; I don't want to turn on the sprinklers to get you all out of bed."

"Great. Got it," Leah mumbled, entering the room.

Inside, there was a full white marble and oak kitchen to her left. To her right was a set of doors, and ahead was an L-shaped black leather couch with an oak coffee table in the center.

A head full of curly hair popped up, and Sarah's eyes met Leah's.

"Leah's here!"

A door just beyond the kitchen swung open, and Isaac stepped out. Somehow, he was taller now. Not as tall as Gabe, but as he came closer to Leah and wrapped his arms around her, she noted he was now taller than her. He'd tied his blond hair back in a small bun too, which only accentuated the blackened scar he'd gotten from nearly dying from a failed possession. How could someone grow so fast in the span of a few days?

"The gang's okay," he said, his voice just a hint deeper.

She broke away from Isaac's grip and looked around. "Where's Gabe?"

As if on cue, the pair of sliding doors beyond the living room opened, and Gabe stepped in from a balcony over-looking the forest.

Leah's heart thudded in her chest as a million unspoken words passed between them. Was he mad at her? Did he still like her?

She noted a slight wince in his eyes before he crossed the room and wrapped his arms around her. He smelled like pine with a hint of smoke, and all Leah wanted was to stay in his arms.

"I'm glad you're okay," he whispered.

Leah sighed. "Same."

Gabe pulled away first, turning and joining the others on the couch. *No kiss?* Leah thought to herself before slowly following suit and sitting down on the couch.

Sarah let out a loud yawn, and the other two sat in silence.

When she couldn't handle it anymore, Leah spoke. "So, Nick woke you all, right?"

Isaac nodded. "Yeah. Interesting guy."

Sarah scoffed. "Really? That's all you have to say? That guy was fine as hell."

Laughter burst out of the group, shaking off the tension that lingered in the air. For a moment, Leah forgot about everything else. She was just a teenager with her friends, laughing over something dumb until the muscles in her abs ached. But when the laughter died down, the pain ebbed its way back in.

"We couldn't stop him," Leah whispered, the hole in her chest tearing into her lungs as she spoke about Legion.

"We weren't ready," Isaac said.

Sarah slammed her fist down on the coffee table. "Damn it! We should have been ready! We had a fucking Black Queen, but he still . . ." Her voice caught in her throat and tears fell from her face. "He still . . ."

She pounded on the table again. And again. An audible crack sounded, and Gabe grabbed her arm. "Stop," he said, his voice flat.

Sarah rose from the couch and stormed off into her room.

Gabe pursed his lips and stood up, starting for the kitchen. "I'm gonna make something to eat."

"She's not taking it well," Isaac said, clearing his throat. "I mean, none of us are, but I'm worried. I tried talking to her, but she just changed the subject."

"I'll try talking to her," Leah said, meeting his gaze. This close, she couldn't help but stare at the jet-black line that trailed down his face and over his eye.

Isaac nodded. "And I'll help Gabe with dinner."

Leah gently knocked on Sarah's door as she opened it. The room was dark, except for a beam of light coming in from what looked like a bathroom.

"Can I come in?" Leah asked.

The faucet turned on and off, and Sarah sniffled. "Just a minute."

Leah peered through the open door to find Sarah resting her arms on the sink. Sarah caught her gaze in the mirror, her eyes red and puffy. "Sorry. I don't know what got into me."

Tears welled up in Leah's eyes, and she crossed the room, pulling Sarah's arms from the sink as she hugged her friend. "You don't have to hold it all in."

Sarah sank into the embrace, shuddering as she sobbed. "How—how are we still alive?"

The same question rang through Leah. How could she still be alive while the others . . . Eric's face flashed by, followed by Miranda's and Ricardo's and Grace's and—

"What are even fucking doing?" Sarah asked between sobs. "We're just teenagers."

"I don't know," Leah whispered.

"I can't take it. This pain. It hurts. I can't breathe. I can't." Sarah's breath turned shallow and quick, and she shook in Leah's arms.

Leah pushed Sarah back and guided her to the edge of the bathtub. "Hey, look at me!" Leah shouted. "Listen to me. In and out. Through your nose. Like this." Leah demonstrated a slow and controlled breath. "One at a time."

Sarah struggled to mimic Leah, taking in one slow breath after another, tears rolling down her face.

"I'm here. *We're* here. That's what matters right now," Leah said.

Sarah's breathing slowed, and she stood, approaching the sink and wiping away her tears. "Thanks."

"We're in this together. Just remember that." Leah caught the faint scent of garlic in the air, and her mouth watered. "Gabe's making dinner. Wanna join us?"

Sarah nodded and quickly washed her face. "Sorry . . . about earlier . . . with the table."

Leah shrugged. "I'm not one to talk. Remember when I sent Paige to the infirmary?"

Sarah chuckled. "She was being a bitch, though. At least she got better."

"She did. I hope she's still out there . . . somewhere."

"You think the Board is still looking for her?"

Leah started for the door and paused. "Probably not. With everything else going on. But, maybe it's for the best. Maybe she's been safe from all this."

"Wait," Sarah said, grabbing on to Leah's arm. "Can we, like, promise we will do everything in our power to kill that asshole? Please? For them?"

Leah paused, the thought of how many they'd already lost surfacing to mind.

I will stop at no end to see Legion destroyed, Asmodeus said.

She nodded, slowly. "I promise, we'll find a way."

Sarah let go of Leah, and they both headed into the kitchen. The pungent scent of garlic, intermixed with sweet basil, filled their nostrils as Gabe plated up four servings of spaghetti with a thick tomato sauce.

"Holy shit, that smells amazing," Sarah said.

"Yeah," Gabe grinned. "Pantry's packed with all sorts of goodies. Oh, and they already had this sauce prepped and frozen. Literally a chef's dream in here." He gestured to the plates. "But enough blabbering. Eat."

The four of them positioned themselves around the table and dug in.

The spaghetti had just the right bite, and the sauce carried a robust tomato flavor complemented with the peppery sweet basil and the almost nutty garlic.

"Oh, my god," Leah said between mouthfuls.

"I know," Gabe said. "I added in the basil and garlic, but that base is to die for."

Moments passed as they ate in silence, devouring the food in front of them.

Leah broke the silence. "So, I spoke with the Queen before you all woke."

"And?" Isaac asked. "What's the plan?"

"She's calling an emergency meeting. Something about voting on a Fortress."

Gabe snorted and shook his head. "Good luck getting that approved."

Sarah frowned. "Why? What's a Fortress?"

Gabe looked up at the ceiling as if racking his brain. "If I remember right, it removes all the power from Rooks and turns all decision-making power over to the Queens. It's only supposed to be used when things get desperate, but the Outer Council is basically voting to give up their power."

"She sounded like she had the votes," Leah said.

"Has it happened before?" Isaac asked.

Gabe nodded. "They did it back in the war against Asmodeus."

Asmodeus chuckled in Leah's mind. *Now I feel special.*

Sarah looked up from her plate. "Well, Legion is worse than him, right? So, that should be good enough."

Gabe shook his head. "We know that, but can Helen convince the others?"

"What does she need to convince them on?" Sarah asked, balling her fists. "He took out nearly all the Queen's Gambit. Even Queen Helen herself couldn't stop him."

"Right, but the Board has threats like that all the time. She'd need to prove he is a large-scale threat, and right now he took out one squad. Asmodeus was systematically killing Rooks by the time they took the vote."

"But the sacrifices, those have to show he's up to something, right?" Isaac asked.

"Maybe." Gabe crossed his arms and leaned back in his chair. "But half were chimeras. I doubt the Board cares about them dying off."

"She'll find a way to convince them," Leah said. "I know she will."

"I just want to see Legion's beady eyes when the life drains out of him," Sarah said through gritted teeth.

I like where her head's at, Asmodeus said.

"We don't have our bonds. You really think they'd let us get close enough to see?" Gabe asked, resting his head in his hands. "We're dead weight to them."

"Then why go to the trouble of putting us on some kind of schedule?" Leah asked. "I mean, we're supposed to be up tomorrow at six for something."

Sarah eyed the clock and groaned. "Really? It's not like we were all just in a coma. You'd think they'd give us a day or two to recover."

"The Queen wouldn't just toss us aside," Leah said. "She has a plan for us."

"Yeah, whatever," Gabe said, pushing himself up off his chair and carrying his plate to the sink. "I think I need a shower to get my head on straight. All this talk's got me going."

"We got this," Isaac said, bringing his plate over to the sink and starting the water. "You do that. We'll clean up."

The three of them stood shoulder to shoulder, cleaning and drying off the plates and pans.

"He's not wrong to be worried," Sarah said. "I mean, they picked off Pawns at the academy during the trials, so why aren't we getting sent off just like them?"

Leah didn't answer. Partly because she knew Sarah was right, and partly because she worried about what the Queen had in store for the four of them.

CHAPTER 4
CLASH OF QUEENS

"Two minutes late," Mathew said, staring down at his watch.

"Sorry," Leah said, breathlessly. "Alarm didn't . . . go off. Woke up . . . when you called."

Leah, Sarah, Isaac, and Gabe had raced out of their rooms, hopping over each other to get ready before riding the elevator to sublevel eight.

Mathew pursed his lips. "Fine. I'll be sure to call earlier next time. Come on, we're already late." He turned on his heels and marched down the small corridor, sickly bright fluorescent lighting the way.

Whereas the halls to their rooms, or even the ornamental halls that led to Queen Helen's office, were full of floor-to-ceiling windows and earthy colors, down here the gray walls and bland white tiling caused the space to feel more like some creepy hospital or underground bunker.

Mathew stopped in front of a rather nondescript door and led them through as he said, "Stay here. They will be with you shortly."

Just as Leah was about to ask who "they" were, Mathew swiftly closed the door, leaving the group inside a conference room. A lengthy, dark table extended toward a sizable white presentation screen, accompanied by another door on the left side.

"Well, someone's in a mood," Sarah whispered.

"He's the same age as us. Why is he treating us like kids?" Leah asked.

"I mean, we *were* late," Isaac shrugged.

Gabe hopped into one of the seats on the side of the table and leaned back. As the others joined him, grabbing seats on either side, he muttered, "Late for what? No one's even here."

The door at the front of the conference room opened then, and Nykima rolled in, sitting in a simple black wheelchair, followed by Queen Helen and two other men Leah had never seen before.

Nykima glared at the four of them and shouted, "What? A few days in a coma and you forget your training? Stand at attention, Pawns!"

Leah and the others rushed up to their feet, nearly knocking their chairs over as they stood up straight, feet together.

"Good," Nykima said, wheeling to the table. "At ease."

Helen stood by the edge of the table. "Morning. First, I want to take a moment to remember those whom we have lost. Their commitment to our mission will not be forgotten." She paused, looking down at the table and closing her eyes.

Leah's throat tightened up. The emptiness inside her crept into her mind, threatening to take over.

"I know these are difficult times," Helen continued, "but we must push forward. We are not out of the dark yet, and we need all of you more than ever. I can't guarantee your safety, nor promise we won't lose any more, but I can give you the tools to fight back. To keep fighting."

"How?" Sarah blurted out.

Nykima cleared her throat as she glared at Sarah, but Helen only smiled at the interjection. "Knights and Bishops have lost their bonds before. It is always a risk, but those that push through can reconnect directly to the tree."

"But we're just Pawns," Gabe said. "They don't—"

"They do if I ask," Helen cut him off. She stepped back and gestured to the two men in the room. The first was a rather short pale man with dark hair, wearing a loose pair of black sweatpants, a white shirt, and a flowing black cardigan. "This is Eli Abrams the Bonded, or Sage of *Yesod*. And this," she gestured to the other man, whose deep tan skin and black bushy beard with gray streaks contrasted with his bright white lab coat, "Sandeep Raman the Pacifist, or Sage of *Hod*. You will also have Nykima, who has been promoted to an advisory role, having gone through this process as well."

Leah eyed Nykima, sitting tall in her wheelchair, eyes locked on the floor.

"Eli," Helen said. "Would you like to start?"

"Sure," he said, his voice flat as he stepped forward. "Like the Queen said, we help Mystics establish a connection to the Tree of Life here after they've broken their bond. Pawns like you would usually be sent to the Shadow Board but . . ." He eyed Queen Helen before looking back at the four. "Extraordinary times. Your path ahead will be difficult and even dangerous at times. Failed attempts to connect to the tree could result in—"

The door behind Leah burst open as a woman in a formfitting jet-black combat uniform with a bright gold embroidered dragon spiraling up her side entered the room. Her black hair was tied into a tight bun, except for well-placed curls hiding burns and a leather eye patch on her left side.

Gabe was the first to react, standing up from his seat, back straight. Leah and the others slowly followed after him.

"What are you playing at?" the woman hissed, her eyes locked on Helen.

Helen stepped in front of Eli. "Everyone, this is Black Queen Jan Xie Kwan."

"I asked you a question, Helen."

Queen Helen's face remained unreadable, aside from the slight twitch in her eyebrow. "These are the last of the Queen's Gambit. They'll be working with the Sages."

Jan Xie's eye flared a bright yellow as she scanned Leah and her friends. "These are bondless Pawns. Under what authority do you undermine me and the rules of the Infinity Board?"

"I'm not undermining anyone."

"Then what are these White Pawns doing? Our law is clear: any Pawn who loses their bond will be transferred to the Shadow Board."

Leah shivered. The Shadow Board?

"These Pawns saved my life. Their commitment and tenacity will be better served if they are bonded to the tree as quickly as possible and brought back into the Infinity Board's ranking." Helen's words were sharp and cold.

"This is outrageous! These Pawns do not deserve—What about Micah, has he—?"

"We are not leaving this fight!" Leah said, interrupting the Queen.

"You dare speak?" Jan Xie spat, her fists clenching as the room grew noticeably hot.

Leah stared at the floor, her heart racing.

"You will look at me, Pawn, when I am speaking to you," the Queen said.

Leah pulled her head up and stared at the woman,

restraining every muscle in her face as she did her best to hold her tongue.

"Perhaps some work in the Shadow will set that attitude right." Jan Xie stepped forward, her gaze shifting to Helen. "We have laws and traditions for a reason. Bonding to the tree at their age? Might as well be signing their death certificates. I can't believe you even dragged the Sages into your little game."

Eli leaned out from behind Helen and spoke in the same flat voice as before. "Actually, no one dragged us into this. After talking with our White Queen Micah, we agreed to assist the members who survived the Queen's Gambit and learn more about this Legion they have been tracking.

Jan Xie clenched her jaw and glared at Helen. "First, the Fortress move and now this? You are compromising our efforts with the shifters for your revenge against a demon."

Helen crossed her arms. "He has all the signs of a level five, Jan Xie. Every action I've made has been to mitigate the deaths of our Mystics and countless others."

"And yet, where is the rest of your gambit?" Jan Xie asked, chin up as the pressure in the room rose. "I think it best I speak with our White Queen." She left the room.

Helen dropped her arms and crossed the room. "I'll need to sort this out. Sages, prepare them for their first lessons in bonding to the tree."

"Wait," Gabe said, as he looked at Leah and then the Queen. "I just . . . connecting to the tree. Do you think we should? I mean, after all that happened."

Leah frowned. *What was that about?*

Asmodeus laughed in her mind. *He means me. Can't you see it? That little fear in his eye.*

Queen Helen rested a hand on the door before turning around.

"Pawn Tate. The four of you have witnessed and faced

things that many Mystics here could only imagine. We need you. All of you. At your full potential, and soon. I believe Legion to be a greater threat than Asmodeus at his peak. Learn from your Sages, and ready yourselves for what is coming."

CHAPTER 5
THE FIRST MEDITATION

They followed Eli, who Leah noted was walking around barefoot, out of the conference room and down the corridor.

As they took another turn, leading them farther away from the elevators, Isaac spoke up, "Uh, I have a question."

"Yes?" Sandeep asked, slowing to shoulder up to Isaac.

"What is the Shadow Board, exactly?"

"Remember the students who weren't selected to bond at the academy after the trials?"

Isaac nodded.

"They were taken to the Shadow Board. It's a branch of the Infinity Board focused more on covert operations. Our bondless who know of the Infinity Board but don't have the connections to a mentor or the tree, are drafted to the Shadow Board. And Black Queen Kwan is their leader."

"So, that's why she's so upset?" Leah asked. "Because she lost four potential members?"

Sandeep placed his hands behind his back. "This is likely, especially considering you have a lot more fighting experience than the average boundless Pawn. But . . ." He cleared his throat. "The Shadow Board also keeps the Infinity Board in check. Think of it like Internal Affairs, and you four have some valuable information they'd want."

"So, Mystics spying on Mystics?" Sarah blurted out.

"Haven't had a civil war since they formed back in 1837," Sandeep said.

Eli cut in, his voice the same flat tone. "Without checks and balances, absolute power would corrupt over time. We need them as much as the world needs us."

As Eli and Sandeep stopped in front of a door marked with the letter G. Leah shivered and turned away from them, eying a different door across the hall. It looked no different from any other door they passed, but something called to her, like it was watching her.

Eli opened the door to room G and pulled Leah's attention back to him. "This is the meditation lab."

Inside, it was nearly twice the height of the hallway and at least fifty yards long. The walls were a soothing beige, and the floor was a carpeted brown, lit by warm lights. Oval-shaped capsules sat along the sides of the room, cables snaking into the walls.

"This is a lot for a meditation room," Isaac said, his mouth agape as he walked over to one of the pods.

Eli joined him, leaning against the pod and smiling. He spoke, and the tired, flat tone he'd expressed in the hallway seemed to come to life here. "One of my best inventions to date. Took a few tries to get where we are now, but this blends ritual with science to give Mystics a better chance of reaching the Astral."

"And it works?" Gabe asked.

The Sage of *Hod* pulled a white cloth from his lab coat pocket and removed his glasses, cleaning them off as he spoke. "Since I have taken the role of Sage and brought our meditations into the modern age, one in three Mystics have been able to traverse into the Astral. And of those, one in ten accomplish connection to the tree."

"Well, that's good, right?" Isaac peered into the pod.

Eli nodded. "Especially when I started. We were at one in fifty crossing over into the Astral."

Sandeep cleared his throat. "Through those doors, you'll find a rack of swimwear tagged with your names and individual changing rooms. Please, change and come back out when you are ready."

Leah stood on a scale in a skintight swimsuit as Sandeep wrote the results and measured her height.

Heat bubbled up in her cheeks when she looked over at Gabe, who stood awkwardly alongside Isaac, both in speedos. She couldn't help but glance over, tracing his toned arms she wanted nothing more than to be wrapped around her.

"Wait. Syringes?" Sarah asked. Leah stepped off the scale and saw Eli drawing a clear liquid from a vial. "Why?"

"All part of the process," Eli said.

Sandeep looked up from his paperwork. "Is that going to be a problem?"

Sarah flushed and slowly shook her head. "No, it's fine."

Leah came up to Sarah's side and nudged her shoulder. "So, after all this time, it's the needles that get you?"

Sarah elbowed her and laughed. "Shut up."

A hiss came from one of the pods to their left, and Eli raced over to help as a blond woman, a foot taller than him, stepped out. Deep black scars trailed up her back and onto her face, like she had been attacked by some wild beast. She spoke softly to Eli, shaking her head before wrapping herself in a towel and racing off to the locker rooms.

"Who was that?" Sarah asked.

"A White Bishop from the front lines in Venezuela. The shifter war has been taking its toll, so we're doing our best to preserve those whose connections falter."

"How long has she been at it?" Leah asked.

"A couple months." Eli gestured to the four capsules on their left. "But we're here for you four, so stand next to one of these and wait for Sandeep to administer the serum before getting in."

Each of them lined up as Eli paced between the pods, checking the sensors and wires connecting to tablets beside each of them. "These are sensory deprivation chambers. You'll be in complete darkness, floating in water. The serum will help your transition into the Astral Realm." He stopped and eyed Leah. "This will take time, and you may feel nothing during the first session. But with repeated practice, we will get you ready for the tree's test."

"Test?" Sarah asked.

"Coming into the Astral Realm is just the first step," Eli said, slightly pausing as he gave a smile to Sarah. "After that, we need to prepare you to approach the Tree of Life. There, you will be tested, and we will see if you're worthy of a connection."

Leah stepped back from the capsule, assaulted by memories of horrible creatures chasing after her. Not only was she about to traverse back into that world, but her friends were too, pumped with some kind of drug. The demons always seemed to find her on that side. Could this be another trap? What if Legion was waiting on the other side?

You should do it, Asmodeus said.

I . . . I don't know if I can. What if he is there? We aren't ready.

This Mystic knows what he is doing.

Leah tilted her head. *How can you be certain of that?*

They call him a Sage of Yesod. A master of connections. He is your best chance of getting your bond back. Our best chance at facing Legion.

Leah understood he was right, but still. She cleared her throat. "Uh, Sage?"

He looked at Leah and frowned. "This isn't a class. You can call me Eli."

"Okay, Eli. What about the things on the other side? The demons?"

Eli raised an eyebrow. "The Astral does host many threats, but as your guide, I will show you many tools to ensure your safety." He nodded to Sandeep, who held a tray of four syringes.

He approached Leah first, asking for her arm.

"What is this?" She asked as he injected the serum.

Sandeep pulled the needle out and bandaged the gauze around Leah's arm. "A variation of dimethyltryptamine of my making. Should help ease you out of your body without some of the more extreme hallucinatory effects."

"Oh," Leah said, giving Sarah a side-eye as Sandeep carried his tray on over to her. "Uh, thanks, I guess?"

Once Sandeep finished, Eli found a small cushion and sat in front of the four capsules. "You may all enter now."

"What about you?" Isaac asked.

"I don't need a capsule. Perhaps one day you won't either."

"What if we can't do small spaces?" Gabe asked, slowly pulling open the lid.

"Try. And besides, the lids don't lock. Though, once

you're inside and the serum takes hold, I doubt you'll feel claustrophobic."

Leah slipped into the lukewarm water, finding herself floating with ease. Inside, she noted etchings and markings that trailed all alone in the capsule's interior. Lines varying in sizes, crafting ritual markings in Hebrew.

Before she could ask, the lid closed, and she heard Eli's voice softly say, "Hope to see you on the other side."

CHAPTER 6
TWO DOORS

Leah floated in the darkness, memories surfacing in her mind. She recalled the summer her parents took her to the Dead Sea, and she'd floated in water just like this before her dad plopped a heap of mud in her hair and her mom snapped a photo of them. Warmth spread from her chest, the memory fading and a peace filling her. That peace numbed her senses, and soon enough she couldn't tell where her body was in this vast, endless pool of water.

She slipped free from her body, drifting down into an unending darkness. It was familiar, a shift into a place she was all too familiar with ending up when she went to sleep.

Her back landed on something solid, and she felt her body once again. Leah opened her eyes, but it was still dark wherever she was. She lifted her hand and pushed, opening the now empty capsule, and sat up. The room was cast in a sickly yellowed light that emanated from strange moss and plants that sprouted through cracks in the floors and walls. Much like everywhere else in the Astral Realm, this place wasn't the clean and pristine room she'd been in moments before, but somewhere that looked devoid of human life for the past hundred years.

She stepped out from the capsule, noting the swimsuit she'd been wearing had been replaced by her uniform, something more comforting than a one piece.

Voices pulled her attention, echoes coming from a strange red door that sat in the middle of the room. Leah approached slowly, eying the sign hanging in the front that read: *Closed*.

"It's been too long. We haven't recruited anyone since Frank," a woman said from beyond the door.

"But are you sure they're in the border?" a man with a deep voice responded.

"I am. Would you question me?"

Leah walked closer to the door, pressing her ear against it.

"I didn't mean to question your abilities, Cora. Only that last time was a dead end. How can you be certain that this is different?"

"We lost one, but it wasn't a dead end," the woman growled back. "Call the others. We're due for a new one."

Leah shut her eyes, listening in as footsteps echoed away from the other side of the door. She reached for the handle, feeling the metal in her hand as she twisted it.

"Impossible," a voice whispered behind her.

Leah turned to find Eli behind her, eyes wide. "No Mystic travels here their first time. Good thing I came here when I did."

Leah shrugged. "It's not my first time."

Eli stepped forward, grabbing Leah's arm as his eyes locked on the door behind her. "Best keep away from that thing."

Leah tried to pull her arm away. "Hey, what the hell?"

Eli positioned himself between Leah and the door.

"That shouldn't be there." He looked behind Leah and relaxed. "That's the door you need to go through."

"What?" Leah asked, turning around and spotting a white door standing on the opposite end of the room. "Where did that—"

"That is your test. Your path to forming your true connection with the tree."

Leah approached the door, noting the silence as she pressed a hand against the wood.

"But why are there two doors?" Leah asked.

Eli shrugged. "I'm not sure, but the reports from the late White Bishop Berkenshire stated you were a dreamer. Could be something to do with that? Or . . ." His eyes trailed down to her left arm.

Leah noted the strange markings on her arm, the demon mark left over when Asmodeus first marked her, then took up residence within her. She pulled it behind her back, but Eli had already seen it.

"I know," he said. "Helen briefed me on it."

He would have seen it anyway, Leah thought, dropping her arm. Although it would have been nice for Helen to give her the heads up. "So, what now?" she asked.

"You start your test. On the other side."

Leah turned to the other capsules that lined the walls. "And my friends?"

"They must come here on their own."

She peered at Sarah's capsule. She couldn't do this alone. Not unless her friends had the ability to make it here as well. What would happen if they weren't able to?

Let's get this over with, Asmodeus said in her mind.

"No, not without them." Leah marched to Sarah's capsule.

"Stop!" Eli said. "They must come over on their own accord."

Leah pulled on the lid of the capsule, but it wouldn't budge.

Eli stepped beside her and shook his head. "Each Mystic will come in their own time."

"I won't leave them behind!" She strained against the lid and pulled with all her might until, finally, the capsule opened.

Inside was a pool of jet-black liquid, no Sarah in sight. "Wait. What—"

A force sent her flying back, and she collided with the wall, falling to the floor. She gasped, clutching her chest as Eli slammed the lid to Sarah's capsule closed.

"Go through the door, Pawn. That's your task," Eli said, his voice flat and calm.

"No." Leah said, clutching her side as she stood.

"Fine." Eli placed his hands in his pockets and shrugged. "Then our meditation is over."

Leah gasped as she lunged forward, coughing up water. She pushed the capsule lid open, taking in the air with raspy breaths. The other capsules were already open, and her friends were slowly stepping out. Yet Eli was nowhere to be seen, and instead, Sandeep stood in front of them, eyeing a tablet.

"That's all for today," Sandeep said. "Get dressed, and your escort will come and take you upstairs for lunch."

"But nothing happened," Sarah said, yawning. "That was such a waste."

Sandeep's eyes remained on the tablet. "You'll try again tomorrow. And the next day, until something happens."

"Great," Sarah mumbled, heading to the dressing rooms.

Shortly after they changed, Mathew appeared in the doorway, checking his watch.

"You're running late. Come on."

"What time is it?" Isaac asked as they followed Mathew out the door.

"Twenty minutes into your lunchtime," Mathew said curtly, spinning on his heel.

Leah's stomach growled as she trailed behind, stepping into the elevator and riding up to the ground floor, through a doorway, and into was looked like a main lobby.

Even with a voracious need to eat, she couldn't help but pause and take in the beauty. The lobby was massive, with a ceiling that spanned up at least three floors and inlaid gold geometric shapes in the otherwise white walls leading to the back wall, which was entirely made of glass and looking out into the woods. Beautiful leather couches sat at the heart of the otherwise empty white-tiled room.

"It's gorgeous," Gabe whispered.

"Well, we know where all the big bucks go. Is that gold?" Sarah asked.

"Come on, quit gawking," Mathew said, pushing through a set of double doors. Inside was a room three times larger than the lobby, with round tables scattered between them and a wall of food that led into the kitchens.

"Okay, grab whatever you want," Mathew said.

Isaac frowned, looking out at the array of empty tables and the massive clock. "It's a bit empty for noon. Where is everyone?"

"They've been asked to eat in the other wing as we welcome some guests. I need you four on the third floor, east elevator lobby, in thirty minutes. Think you can manage? Queen Nielsen will wait for you there."

"Sure," Gabe said.

"Perfect," Mathew said.

Before anyone else had the opportunity to speak, he turned and left.

"Well, I'm starving," Sarah said, rushing toward the assortment of food.

"Me too," Isaac said, chasing after her.

For a moment, Leah and Gabe stood in silence, then he held out his arm and asked, "Care to join me?"

Leah gave him a half smile and wrapped her arm around his, trekking off toward the buffet. "Don't mind if I do."

Sarah leaned back in her chair, plate empty and a smile on her face. "I needed that."

Isaac swallowed the last of his food and nodded. "Whatever they injected us with has me starving. I could eat a whole other plate."

"Yeah," Gabe laughed. "I might lose it if we have to lie there starving for hours on end every day."

Leah's thoughts drifted to the red door and the voices behind it. It was calling to her, and Eli hadn't wanted her going through it.

"Leah?" Isaac asked, pulling her back.

She blinked, eyeing the last bit of food on her plate. "Sorry. Yeah, hours floating in a silent pod is gonna suck."

Ah, so you're lying? Asmodeus whispered in her head.

I'm not lying, Leah replied. *I'm just waiting until I know more.*

Mathew rushed into the cafeteria at that moment, tapping his phone furiously as he came to their table.

"What, couldn't trust us to get to the lobby in time?" Sarah asked.

"Ha ha," Mathew said flatly. "Change of plans, you've all been assigned to prepare for the ball."

"Uh, ball?" Isaac asked.

"Yes, ball. Turns out our higher-ranking Mystics have told to expedite their travels here. Your duties have been updated."

"Duties?" Sarah asked.

Mathew pursed his lips. "You're all still Pawns, right? Doesn't matter where you are, Pawns are expected to wait on the Mystics above their rank. You four will be assigned Rooks once they arrive for the Outer Council meeting tomorrow. Until then, you're helping set up."

"Tomorrow?" Gabe blurted out. "Already?"

Mathew rolled his eyes. "Yes, tomorrow. After you're done with setup, head back to your rooms. You'll be serving the Rooks tonight, so I've asked for new clothes to be sent to your rooms. Please look presentable. Any questions? No? Good. Then come, I'll take you to the ballroom." He didn't wait for a response, and the four Pawns had to race to keep up.

They stepped out into the lobby, running into a line of Mystics dressed in all black, carrying in boxes. Leah stopped dead in her tracks before shouldering into Sarah.

"What the—"

"Buck?" Sarah asked, cutting her off. Leah followed Sarah's gaze, spotting their friend who'd lost the trials nearly a year ago and was now walking right past them.

CHAPTER 7
OLD FACES

"**B**uck!" Gabe said, rushing forward.

Buck turned, his eyes brightening and a smile stretching across his face. "You're all still alive?" He rushed forward, wrapping an arm around Gabe.

"Could say the same to you," Isaac said. "It's been over a year now, right?"

Buck scratched his head. "Yeah, sounds right."

Leah noted the new muscles and definition pressing against his T-shirt and how he stood differently now. More refined. "What are you doing here?"

"I'm part of Queen Jan Xie's personal guard. I mean, I'm still in training, but got here faster than anyone else in the Shadow," he said, puffing out his chest.

"What happened after the Trials?" Gabe asked.

"They shipped me off to get training. Somewhere secret. Like, if I even tell you, they'll no doubt kill me. All I can say is I'm on the Shadow Board now."

"Yeah, Queen Jan Xie was trying to recruit us. Made a whole scene when Queen Helen told her no," Sarah said.

Buck nodded, "Makes sense. We definitely need more recruits in the Shadow. My mentor, Anat, taught me a bunch of stuff. Things the Infinity Board doesn't even teach. And the places I've been. People I've met. It's wild."

The way he stood and talked surprised Leah. He was so much more mature and refined from his days at the academy. Whatever he'd been through, training he'd had, seemed to change him.

"Oy!" a voice shouted from behind Leah. A lanky ginger-haired man glared at the five of them and said, "You all gonna stand there and chat while we do all the work?"

"No, Fred. Sorry," Buck said, leaning in toward the others. "We'll catch up after. I've heard some wild rumors about you four."

"They're probably all true," Sarah said, following behind him.

"Oh," Buck said, turning around and whispering. "Have any of you heard from my sister? I've tried to find her, but no one's given me any answers."

A pit formed in Leah's stomach. After everything she'd sacrificed, Serena still hadn't made it to him?

Isaac frowned. "She left the academy to find you. You haven't seen her?"

"She failed her last trial," Leah said. "They took her too. She wanted to be with you."

Buck dropped his shoulders, as if shaking off a thought. "I'm sure she's fine. She has to be. I mean, that's how the Shadow Board operates. Cut ties, train hard, and dedicate to the cause. I'll see her again once training's done." He turned and started toward the doors. "Come on, we've got a gala to set up."

They all followed Buck into a side storage room packed with chairs, tables, tablecloths, and everything one might need for a massive event. Other Pawns slipped in and out, rushing to get things set up. Leah joined in, grabbing a set of centerpieces with violet flowers, and setting them on the tables that were ready for the finishing touches.

Leah finished the center pieces and carried out fine crystal glasses and sleek silverware. It all screamed wealth, and she wondered why this was so excessive. Her thoughts spiraled, and the thought that the Infinity Board might not have it out for the benefit of all humanity crossed her mind.

She dropped the silverware she was carrying, and it clattered to the floor.

"Do you need a chair?" a voice called from behind her.

Leah kneeled and collected the fallen cutlery as a girl, not much older than her, joined her by her side. She had straight pink hair with one side shaved and dark brown eyes. Her ripped skinny jeans and red jacket over a white crop top were also vastly different from the uniforms worn by the Pawns or the members of the Shadow.

"No, sorry." Leah stood and headed back to the storage room.

"Oh no, you don't get off that easy. What's your name?" the girl asked, skipping behind her.

"Uh, Leah. Leah Ackerman. You?"

The girl let in a gasp and slipped in front of Leah, walking backward. "The famous Leah Ackerman who helped Helen escape?"

Leah dropped her head and tried to pick up the pace. "Yeah, that's me."

The girl stopped, and Leah nearly ran into her. "That means you faced off against Legion! What was it like? The report wasn't really clear, and I'd love to hear a first-hand account."

Leah took a step back and attempted to walk around the girl. "I should get back to—"

"Yuki!" a voice boomed from across the room.

Leah looked over her shoulder and found a bald man

with a silvery mustache standing on the opposite side of the ballroom.

Yuki let out a huff. "Jeez Des, you don't have to yell!"

He waved a hand at her. "Come on. We need you upstairs."

Yuki sighed and rolled her eyes. "Fine." She focused on Leah and said, "We'll catch up later."

"Who was that?" Sarah asked, stopping at Leah's side.

"No clue," Leah said.

"Damn, she was cute."

Leah watched Yuki leave and raised an eyebrow. "Didn't know she was your type."

Sarah shrugged. "What can I say? I like having options."

They both laughed and went back to work until Mathew walked in.

"No!" he shouted, waving his tablet around. "This is all wrong. You're going to have to set it all up again. Did anyone even look at the floor plan?"

They spent the next hour reconfiguring the room to Mathew's liking before rushing back to their room to get for the evening.

Hot water ran down Leah's back as she washed off the conditioner. Her mind drifted, wondering what had happened to Buck all this time, when a voice slipped into her mind.

Go! Get out of here!

It was Eric's voice, and it was so clear in her mind that her knees buckled and she fell hard on the tiled floor. She saw him in her mind again. That look on his face as the chains—

Whispers filled at the edges of Leah's hearing, clawing their way into her mind. Foreign tongues spat and cursed at her, creating a pressure in her thoughts that made it feel like it would split in two at any moment. A serpent from inside her uncoiled, ready to strike.

Enough! Asmodeus screamed, his voice tearing through the whispers.

They ceased in an instant, and the snake recoiled, leaving behind an uncomfortable but bearable tightness in her throat. Leah caught her breath and pulled herself up.

Thank you, she thought.

Mourn your loss in peace. I'll hold them back.

A warmth spread down her chest, and his voice faded away from her mind as her tears washed away in the water.

CHAPTER 8
GALA

Leah adjusted the checkered bow tie on her button-down shirt and smoothed the similarly checkered pants. This uniform was definitely the worst she'd worn, restricting her from some of the broader movements she might need in a fight.

She entered the ballroom along with her friends, and her eyes immediately fell on the tables filled with cheeses of all kinds, breads of all shapes and colors, bruschetta glistening with fresh tomato and basil, flaky pastries, smoked salmon, and little bowls of caviar. Her mouth watered at the sight.

"Well," Gabe muttered. "Now I feel bad about the tuna sandwiches I made."

Isaac swallowed, looking away from the food. "I mean, do you really think they'd let us have any of that?"

Leah laughed. "He's right. And that aioli you made was spot on. Bet these all took hours and several chefs to make, and you just had twenty minutes. They could never."

"I wonder if they ever need help in the kitchens," Gabe said. "Maybe I can talk to Mathew and—"

"And leave the rest of us to wait tables?" Sarah asked. "Hell no, you're coming with us."

"No. No, that's all wrong. Set the table again," Mathew said to another Pawn as they approached. He snapped his fingers at another Pawn and said, "Go get another floral arrangement, this one looks awful."

Before Leah could even ask him what he wanted her to do, he brushed past her and picked up a round black tray filled with spiraled, thin breadsticks. He shoved it into her hands and said, "These are Venezuelan tequeños. They're filled with cheese if anyone asks."

Leah's mouth watered at the food in her hands, but she resisted the urge to try one as Mathew waved her off to her assigned position close by the doors.

Moments later, Rooks poured in. Many of them wore black suits and a rook pin on the left side of their chest, but a few broke up the monotony with a myriad of colors and styles. A short woman with olive skin wore a dark blue dress decorated with embroidered white flowers. She talked with another woman with long, flowing black hair in a black, red, and green embroidered and patchwork dress filled with repeating patterns and geometric shapes. She even recognized the telltale enormous fur hat on an older Hasidic Jewish man walking alongside a young man in a black suit and a tightly wrapped matching turban.

. . . where there is power, politics follow . . .

Helen's words resonated in Leah's mind as she walked around the room, hearing a mixture of languages as the Rooks took from her tray and promptly ignored her existence. She looked over at the bar and spotted Isaac, who was pouring out a shaken martini like he'd been at it for years.

This is excessive, Leah thought.

And dangerous, Asmodeus muttered in her ear.

He was right. So many Rooks in one place, off guard. What if someone like Joanna got in? They wouldn't know. How could they? She'd been possessed, and no one saw it.

"Oh no, are you already out of tequeños?" a soft voice asked from behind Leah. Behind her wasn't a woman in a black suit or dress, though. Instead, it was more like a breathing blob of thick clothes haphazardly worn together. They towered over Leah, wearing at least two sweaters and a ski jacket, patterned knit gloves, a white hat and red scarves that covered almost the entirety of their face. A fragrance of roses and something sweet wafted off the blob as a shuffle beneath the clothes revealed a woman's face. "They're so good and warm."

Leah looked down at her empty tray and wondered how long she'd been walking around with it empty. "Oh, sorry. I'll go see if there's more." She smiled nervously and backed away from the clothing blob.

As she returned to the floor with a new tray, a voice boomed, "There they are!"

An older man with long gray-streaked ginger hair and a thick manicured silvery beard limped toward her and grabbed a tequeño from her tray. His suit was dark gray, and instead of a tie, he wore a deep scarlet scarf around his neck and a Rook pin on the left side of his jacket.

"You look familiar," the man said, with a thick, rolling Scottish accent. "What's your name?"

"I'm Leah. Leah Ackerman."

"Of course you are!" he boomed, snapping his fingers as something clicked behind his eyes. "I heard a rumor Elizabeth's daughter was here. Name's James McMillan." He extended his hand.

Leah balanced the tray of food between her hand and hip and shook his hand, feeling the rough calluses scrape her hand. "Um, nice to meet you, Black Rook McMillan."

"Please. Call me Jaime. I understand that it may be a bit late to mention now, but I would like to offer my sympathies for the loss of your mother and uncle.

A knot formed in Leah's throat, and she struggled to swallow. "Oh, uh. Thank you."

Jaime stood there, staring for a moment before grabbing another tequeño and taking a bite. "I had the honor of fighting beside her back in the war. Formidable woman. Ready to race to the front lines faster than anyone I've ever known."

Leah pictured her mother, the image of a happy stay-at-home mom long gone from her memory, but now a piece of who she was solidified in her mind. A fighter, just like her. "Really?"

"Absolutely. Truly an expert in the strategy of war. I'm aware that we aren't supposed to talk much about her, stricken from the record and all, but I was disappointed to see her leave. But war takes its toll in many ways. I should know." He half chuckled and tapped his leg, which made a metal clank. "Lost this one in the last battle with Asmodeus."

"Do you have any stories about her? No one who knew her shared much. I mean, if you have the time."

Jaime shifted his weight. "I'll be stationed here for a bit, and I love talking old war stories. But be warned once you get me going, I might talk your ear off." He reached for the tray again. "Have you had one of these?"

Leah shook her head. "I don't think they want us Pawns eating them."

Jaime waved his hand. "Nonsense. You've got to try one. Here." He grabbed one off the tray and handed it to Leah.

When she took a bite, the cheese inside melted in her mouth, mixing with the flaky dough. The closest approximation she could make was a mozzarella stick, but even that didn't come close.

Leah smiled. "It's really good."

"One of the few luxuries in the front lines down south. True Venezuelan cuisine at our feet."

Leah frowned, putting the pieces together. "Down south? So, you're helping with the shifter problem?"

Jaime's smile wavered for a moment as he leaned in and lowered his voice. "Precisely why I'm here. We can barely fight them off as is, but someone wants our focus back here. Can you imagine what that would do? All the lives lost?"

"But, Legion—"

Jaime shook his head and patted her on the shoulder. "I think that's enough tequeños. I'll need another scotch before the speech. It was a pleasure meeting you, lass."

He turned and headed toward the bar, leaving Leah alone in a sea of Rooks.

Glass clinked behind her, pulling her attention to a tall Black man with short salt and pepper hair and beard. Unlike the black suits that surrounded him, he wore a pristine white pearlescent suit. Helen and Jan Xie stood on either side of him, pulled into conversations of various Rooks vying for their attention. Her heart skipped a beat, as she realized the man was no other than Micah Green, White Queen of the Infinity Board.

Micah clinked his glass again, and the room fell silent.

Leah moved out from the middle of the rooms and found a familiar face. Eli, wearing a wrinkled suit, no tie, and bare feet, leaned against the wall nursing a glass of what looked like whisky.

"I take it you don't like these kinds of events?" she asked cautiously.

He lifted his glass to her and said, "Wielding power

should be a responsibility, not a luxury. Eventually, it will catch up to us."

The Queen's words resonated in her head once more.

Headquarters might look beautiful . . . But it is a snake lair.

Leah looked around as everyone stared at Micah, and whispered, "Couldn't agree with you more."

Micah's voice carried throughout the room as he spoke. "Thank you for coming here on such short notice. Before we begin, join me in following tradition and raising a glass for those Mystics that have given their life for humanity's sake." The room fell silent as everyone raised their glasses. "To the brave."

"To the brave," Eli slurred along with everyone else before downing the rest of his drink.

To the brave? That's it? Leah thought.

"I know an emergency Outer Council meeting is the last thing you'd all like to be attending, but there have been too many rumors causing a rift. I'm asking that everyone put these rumors aside and return focus to our core purpose. Queen Helen Nielsen called this motion and will present her case."

Helen smiled in her sleek formfitting black dress with a black onyx queen pin and earrings that glinted in the light.

Micah raised his champagne glass one more time. "Long stand the Infinity Board."

"Long stand the Infinity Board," the others repeated before drinking as well.

Chatter resumed, and Helen locked her sights on Leah, walking straight toward her.

"Well," Eli muttered. "That's my cue to leave."

As he left, Helen and Black Rook Reginald Platt, the former administrator of the Maimonides Academy, approached. He looked almost exactly as Leah remembered with a spotless black cane adorned with a golden crow head topper. Leah eyed the crow that hid a sword within the cane. The one Reginald had used when he fought against the White Knight William Wright.

"Glad I caught you. Black Rook Platt and I were just speaking, and he reminded me you and your friends have authorization to attend the Outer Council Meeting tomorrow."

"Oh," Leah frowned. "But I thought only Rooks and above could attend those?"

Reginald grinned, resting his hands on his cane. "Not if your Queen authorizes it."

Leah stared down at the ground, straightening her stance. "Yes, Black Rook Platt and Queen Helen."

"Be at sublevel seven by seven forty-five tomorrow morning," Helen said.

Reginald looked around the room before staring at Leah. "You are our witnesses if need be. You four have seen Legion's capacity for destruction, and the roles and responsibilities of your Queen don't weigh you down."

"If need be?" Leah asked. "Wasn't the academy burning down and our squad getting killed enough?"

Reginald nodded slowly and sighed. "It should be, but resources in the Infinity Board are pulled tight, and others wish we'd focus elsewhere."

"Like Jaime? I mean . . . Black Rook McMillan?"

Helen's lips pursed. "No surprise there. I'm guessing he approached you?"

"He talked to me about my mother. Then mentioned that he was down in the front lines with the shifters."

"Of course he did," Helen scoffed.

Reginald checked his pocket watch. "We need to meet with the Seer before it's too late."

"Wait," Leah said as the two turned. "Before you go. I was thinking . . ." She eyed the Black Rook.

"You can speak freely," Helen said. "Reginald was one of my mentors that saw my potential to Queen early on."

Leah nodded. "Okay, well, how do we know there aren't others like Joanna? Possessed, but we can't tell. They could have already infiltrated the Outer Council."

Reginald spoke first. "I don't doubt your suspicions, Leah. However, I will say that possessing a Black Rook is significantly harder than possessing a Black Pawn at an academy."

"And," Helen said, "Reginald and I will speak with Nona, the Sage of *Tiferet,* for her assistance before the Outer Council tomorrow. We believe her insight will be of use for any wolves in sheep's clothing."

Leah disagreed. *Tiferet* hadn't picked up Joanna. It was like the demons had learned to somehow use something like *Thagirion,* from the Tree of Death, to trick *Tiferet* into not working. "But—"

"I understand your concern," Helen cut in. "We'll take care of it. Now, I have a Seer to talk to. See you tomorrow."

Helen turned and left, leaving Leah behind with Reginald as the Queen weaved into the crowd.

"There is a lot dependent on this vote," Reginald said.

"How so?"

"Jaime and Queen Helen have a rocky past. After the defeat of Asmodeus, Helen took his place as forerunner to be promoted to Black Queen. And now that he's the face of the war in the south, he's not going to make it easy for her. But we'll sort it out. I'm sure you have other things on your mind. Still dating that other Pawn—O'Connor, I think it was?"

Leah's knees buckled, and she stumbled to find the words. "What? No. We were never. I mean, Isaac and I are just friends."

Reginald laughed and started toward the crowd of

Rooks. "Ahh, sure you are. Don't forget I remember you two sneaking around in the library stacks."

"Wait," Leah called after him. "No, that's not what happened."

By the time Leah realized, it was too late, and Reginald was already joining in another conversation as she was left alone with another empty tray.

CHAPTER 9
OUTER COUNCIL

The elevator door dinged, and Leah and her friends stepped out into sub level 7. This far down, the walls were no longer the pristine architecture they were used to, but solid rock, like some kind of cave.

Near the end of the hall, two hooded figures with long gray robes stood in front of a large wooden door. A warm sensation passed over Leah as both hoods glowed with yellow light. One guard raised their hands and said, "Stop. Full names and rank."

"Leah Ackerman, White Pawn."

The others followed suit, one by one, as the guards stood completely still.

"Follow me," the second guard said after a moment.

The large old doors opened, creaking loudly. Inside was a massive amphitheater carved out from the rock and lit by sconces, casting warm light like torches along the walls. Hundreds of leather seats arched around a small stage lined with chairs, three of which were raised higher than the rest.

They were guided down the steps and to the front stage, where a small area with wooden benches rested in the corner. As they settled onto the benches, doors opened behind them and Nykima wheeled in.

The four of them stood at attention as she approached, locking her chair beside the benches.

"At ease," she whispered. "How are you four holding up?"

Sarah shrugged as she sat back down. "They're keeping us busy."

A slight smile shone on Nykima's face. "Probably for the best."

"And you?" Leah asked.

Nykima looked down at her wheelchair. "Oh, you know, getting back on my feet."

Leah sat up straight, her hands turning clammy as she tried to find the words. "I mean . . you know . . . I . . . I'm sorry."

Nykima laughed. "I'm just messing with you. Nick suggested I use more humor. Probably not self-deprecating, but in all his Sage wisdom, he never clarified."

"So, you're a witness too?" Gabe asked.

"Yep. I thought I was going to be the only one, but Queen Helen pulled through."

Isaac leaned forward. "Do you think she has the votes for the Fortress?"

Nykima grinned and shook her head. "She really held nothing back. But this Rook business—it's above my rank."

The doors to the amphitheater all opened at once, and hundreds of black-hooded figures poured in.

"Uh, guys," Leah said, standing and eying the nearest exit, now flooded with figures.

Nykima grabbed at her side, "Quiet. The rest of you, stand."

Leah breathed in as her friends stood beside her, and in

a matter of seconds, the theater was flooded with people, though none of them talked as they stood in front of their seats, all facing toward the center stage.

Doors at the other end of the center stage opened, and six white-robed figures came in, pausing in front of the row of seats facing out into the amphitheater.

The doors closed, and they all took their seats. However, one seat among the Sages remained empty.

Seconds after realizing that, one set of doors creaked open, and Sarah whispered, "No way."

"What?" Leah and Isaac asked, looking toward the doors and seeing a bright head of pink hair and a white robe.

"That's the girl that talked to you yesterday," Sarah said.

"Yuki," Leah muttered.

One of the seated Sages cleared their throat, and Yuki huffed, yanking the hood over her head as she raced down the steps and found a place next to the others.

"But how is she a Sage?" Isaac asked. "She's got to be our age."

The doors opened for a third time, and the Sages joined the others on their feet as the guards in gray robes escorted the three Queens inside the courthouse. Both Helen and Jan Xie wore black robes, while Micah wore white. All three Queens had their hoods down.

They took their position at the center of the stage and sat, the rest of the amphitheater joining them. Micah struck a small wooden gavel three times, each of them resonating off the stone walls louder than Leah expected.

"By the right given by this counsel, I, Micah Greene, White Queen of the Infinity Board, officially open this meeting of the Outer Council."

No one else spoke or made a sound as his voice died down.

After a moment of silence, he continued, "Black Queen Helen has called for an emergency meeting, so I grant her the opportunity to present her statement."

Helen leaned forward in her seat, her back straight as she looked at Micah. "Thank you, White Queen Green." She focused on the others, one by one, as she said, "And thank you Black Queen Jan Xie, the Inner Council, and the Outer Council for coming together on such short notice. First, I would like to set the record straight and ease any rumors that some of you may have heard. About five months ago, I formed the Queen's Gambit, a collection of top Knights, Bishops and White Pawns, to investigate a string of sacrifices that had been going on around the United States."

Images of the bodies they came across flashed through Leah's mind. There were so many, burned and tortured. She'd seen nothing like it before. And if it wasn't for Eric, and the bond—she shifted in her seat, pushing the images away.

"These sacrifices were carried out by demons, not humans. And they were abducting children, successfully possessing in a way we hadn't seen before. Along with all this, they were experimenting on chimeras, creatures we only recently discovered were not extinct. We were close to finding an answer when Legion struck us." She paused and looked around the room, her voice becoming louder. "Legion is no ordinary demon, and I suspect him to be of level five on our rankings of strength—above that of even Asmodeus in his prime."

Murmurs echoed through the chamber, whispers as black hooded figures leaned in toward each other and spoke.

Helen cut them off. "I know what this means, and that a level five demon is something from the Great Eagle's time. But Legion's command over other demons, and the sheer power he wields, is beyond anything I've encountered before. He disposed of my squad like we were flies, and if it weren't for the brave surviving Knight and Pawns, I wouldn't be standing here before you all today. We are on the brink of a catastrophe if we don't act swiftly. That is why I have called this meeting. That is why I want to invoke the Fortress."

Commotion swept through the room as some hooded figures stood and shouted while others applauded. It was an indiscernible roar of noise echoing through the chamber. Leah held her breath, her stomach twisting in knots. She'd figured some people would argue, but this was not what she'd expected. There's no way they'd have the vote. No way that they'd be able to stop Legion in time. Three loud clanks sounded as Micah slammed his gavel.

Micah glared out into the amphitheater. "Sit!" he commanded, and everyone rushed to find their seats. "Thank you, Black Queen Nielsen. We will proceed as tradition calls and have civility as questions and counterarguments are brought to the podium by the council."

Small blue indicators lit up in front of several chairs, and Micah eyed something at his desk before pressing a button. One small light flashed, and the Rook stood.

A soft, feminine voice spoke from behind the hood. "My Queens, I understand the losses you've suffered. Our lost Black Bishop Gunn was a friend of mine, but activating a Fortress will only leave our other fronts open. Just this week, my team, along with the Mystics over in Japan, confirmed a Tengu in Nagasaki. The veils between us and the Astral Plane are weakening, and if we don't act now, there is no telling what else might come through."

"I'm aware of the situation in Tokyo," Helen responded.

"Prior to this meeting, I had a team perform a risk assessment on all the active cases, and I'll ensure the teams behind the ones that represent a high risk will keep their current resources."

The robed woman scoffed. "But we're stretched thin as it is. If you do this, then the rest of this council has no say in what you three decide until we neutralize Legion. How can we trust our voices will be heard?"

"Let me be very clear," Helen started. "I've faced Tengus and other creatures in the past and stopped them. Legion was up against some of our best warriors, and I couldn't even get a scratch on him."

The Rook hesitated for a moment, then took her seat, her blue light turning off. Others stood one by one, with similar concerns, teasing out how long the Fortress move would be in effect, how to present the Queens with requests during this time, and the line of succession if the Queens perished with the Fortress still intact.

"I can't tell," Sarah whispered in Leah's ear after the fifth person spoke. "Are we winning?"

Leah shifted in her seat, eying Queen Helen. As emotionless as Helen was trying to be, Leah could see a frustration in her eyes. "I don't know. Maybe?"

Helen continued to take each question with the same calm and regal tone, deftly facing off against each one until they sat back down and turned off their light. That was until one Black Rook seated in the front row facing the stage stood up and pulled off his hood.

Reddish hair with gray streaks shone in the dim light as Jaime McMillan spoke. "How many died in your Queen's Gambit?"

The Queen's lips tightened. "Seven Mystics. Two White Bishops, a Black Bishop, a Black Knight, and three White Pawns."

"And your report states four White Pawns, a White Knight, and yourself survived, yes? Nearly half your squad."

"And are you neglecting to account for the innocent civilians who've been sacrificed or the dozens of child abductions we've linked back to Legion?"

"Linked is such a strong word when you don't have the evidence to back it up. You don't have proof these sacrifices are linked, nor concrete evidence that the rise in child abductions is led by some demonic mastermind of the likes of which we've never seen before. Much of your reports come from hearsay of your own White Pawns. These hunches of yours are nothing compared to the lives we are losing in the south."

Leah's nails dug into her palms as she squeezed her fists. Was he saying that what she saw didn't matter? That it wasn't proof enough?

Helen remained calm, only raising an eyebrow at Jaime. "I can assure you, Black Rook McMillan, I wouldn't evoke an Outer Council meeting on a hunch."

"Of course not, my Queen," Jaime said. "But tangible numbers tell the actual story." He stepped forward and turned around, addressing the crowd. "We've lost over six-hundred Mystics in the war against the shifters. Intel suggests they've infiltrated the government and are rising in ranks that risk exposing us. My team has been reporting this for months, and this council has done nothing."

"This council has approved every request for aid it has received from our front against the shifters," Helen spat back.

Jaime raised a finger. "And yet, after four years of your 'aid,' we are still losing this war. I've asked for more troops, on more than one occasion, but the threat continues to be downplayed by this council."

Helen stood, her voice sharp. "The Infinity Board does

not have an unlimited supply of Mystics to throw at your war. I have urged you before to negotiate a peace treaty with the shifters, but your continued thirst for blood blinds you, Black Rook McMillan."

Jaime's laughter tore through the room. "You think they want peace? Shifters want control, and they won't stop until they have it. They were only a few dozen when we started tracking them, but now we've lost count in the thousands. If we don't stop them, they'll continue until every remaining human is culled and turned. Are you willing to let millions of innocent humans join their ranks in exchange for that peace?"

Micah banged on his gavel. "Watch your step, Rook McMillan. We are here to discuss the Fortress proposed by Black Queen Nielsen. If you do not have any further questions or counterarguments on this proposal, then please sit and allow other council members to speak."

Jaime gave a slight bow to Micah. "Of course, my Queen. Since we are talking counterarguments on this proposal, allow me to put into motion my proposal. I call for a Brinkmate."

A collective gasp rushed through the amphitheater, followed by a rush of voices shouting as little blue lights filled the room.

Leah frowned. "What's a Brinkmate?"

Nykima leaned over in her chair and spoke. "It puts all other missions on hold and transfers all the Infinity Board's attention to the specified threat until it is eliminated."

"And that's different from this Fortress?" Sarah asked.

"The Fortress gives all the voting power to the Queens. They can make major executive decisions without Outer Council's approval. A Brinkmate would freeze Infinity Board institutions entirely and redirect all the Infinity Board's attention and power to the specified threat."

Leah nodded, the pieces falling together in her mind. "So, we couldn't fight against Legion at all." She eyed Rook McMillan, who was shouting at two other Rooks. "Why would he do that?"

Humans and demons are so alike, Asmodeus whispered in her mind. *Power blinds, no matter which realm you are in.*

Micah banged his gavel three times, and the room silenced. "Enough! In your seats now or be removed from this meeting."

The White Queen waited a moment as everyone complied, then said, "A Brinkmate requires a second vote in order to be proposed. Does anyone—"

"I second it," Black Queen Jan Xie said, the first words to come out of her mouth this entire council meeting.

Helen's regal stature faltered for a moment as she glanced over at Jan Xie.

"Very well," Micah said. "We now have two proposals. Both are endgame moves. As such, they require a two-thirds vote in order to pass. Given these two moves can't happen simultaneously, only one vote will be allowed per Rook. We've had enough debate; I motion we move to voting."

"Seconded," Black Queen Jan Xie said, nodding at Black Rook McMillan.

Jan Xie is in on it too, Leah thought.

We can't let this happen, Asmodeus said. *If Legion is left to his own devices, there is no telling what he will do.*

Leah was on her feet before she knew it, her voice mixed with hers and Asmodeus's. "Are all of you blind?"

The chamber fell uncomfortably silent as every hooded Rook turned their gaze toward her. Her heart pounded, but she couldn't back down now. "One move would wipe out every other effort while the other brings our focus on

Legion without compromising anything else. How are they even the same? How—"

Leah's throat tightened, and her voice cut off, along with her airway. She struggled to catch a breath, her hand raising to her throat.

Micah stood, his eyes locked on Leah. "You, Pawn, are here as a witness. Only welcome to speak if asked."

Both Sarah and Isaac pulled Leah back down into her seat, and as soon as she sat, her neck loosened, and she gasped for air.

"Another outburst, from any of the witnesses, and I will have you escorted out," the White Queen added. "Let's proceed with the voting, and I demand no more inter-ruptions."

A projector turned on behind the Queens with three options: Fortress, Brinkmate, and Abstain, all with a zero next to them.

"Voting is open," Micah said.

The room filled with the sound of clicking as everyone pressed down on one of the buttons at their seat, ticking away in waves. Leah's heart beat heavy in her chest as she watched. This was it. This would decide if Legion was a big enough threat to the Infinity Board.

"Ten seconds." Micah said.

Leah squeezed her eyes shut. The thought of Eric surfaced in her mind as her chest tightened and the image of those chains tearing through him filled her mind. They could lose everything right now. Lose their chance to fight him. To get her revenge.

"Votes are in," Micah announced.

Leah opened her eyes as Micah eyed the tablet in his hands.

"With an Outer Council attendance of five-hundred and

fifty-two Black Rooks, equal to ninety-two percent of all Black Rooks, and a full Inner Council attendance of seven, we have the following results: Abstentions, fifty-seven. Decline of both proposals, fifty-one. The Fortress, two-hundred and fifty. The Brinkmate, two-hundred and one. As neither proposal reached the required two-thirds vote, we officially have a stalemate. Per the bylaws, we will reconvene for another Outer Council meeting in thirty days and have a second vote."

CHAPTER 10
INNER COUNCIL

After the council was dismissed, and the other Queens waited on the Black and White Rooks to leave, Queen Helen stood and waved for Leah and the others to follow her out the side exit. Helen barely spoke a word as her heels clicked down the empty hallway.

"They can't really expect to wait thirty days," Sarah said after they were out of earshot of everyone still in the amphitheater.

"What are we supposed to do now?" Leah asked. "We can't wait another month while Legion—"

"We act swiftly," Queen Helen said, turning around and keeping her voice low as they approached the elevator lobby. "We must sway the votes before someone else does. Before they undermine me, and our cause."

She pressed the button and waited for the doors to ding open before turning to Nykima. "Take them to the meeting room on sublevel 2. The others should be there any minute."

An elevator ride later, they entered a large meeting room with Sandeep and Nick seated at a long table.

"Hello, hello!" Nick said with a smile that showed off his perfectly white teeth.

Leah smiled back, a warmth budding in her chest.

"Hell—" Sandeep suddenly stopped talking, covering his mouth as he yawned, "—o everyone."

"What are you all doing?" Nykima shouted, swatting Leah's back. "Stand at attention!"

Leah composed herself, standing straight, arms behind her back, as did her friends, as they shifted to stand beside the wall.

Eli walked in behind them with a mound of clothes concealing a young woman. Both didn't even glance at the Pawns as they took their seats.

"At ease, Pawns. Please, take a seat." Nick gestured to the chairs beside him.

Shouts came from outside as they sat, and everyone looked to the doors as the voices grew louder.

". . . authority! You can't just wander off when you're called to a meeting with the Queen," a deep voice boomed.

The door opened and Yuki stepped in, hands in her pockets, escorted by a bald man with a gray mustache. Leah had seen him before when prepping the ballroom, but now —up close—she noticed deep fissured scars that marred his otherwise aged and handsome face.

"Sorry for being hungry," Yuki mocked, yanking a chair out and plopping into it. "I wanted a snack. Is that a crime?"

The scarred man sat next to her and sighed, resting his head in hands filled with burn scars. "My gravestone is going to read 'stressed to death by Yuki Nakamura.'"

"You know you love it, old man." Yuki said, pulling out her phone.

The man glared at Leah and her friends. "What are Pawns doing here?"

Training kicked in, and Leah jumped to her feet, along with Isaac, Sarah, and Gabe.

Nick shook his head and sighed. "Seriously, stop standing at attention and relax."

"Says who?" the bald man asked, eyeing him.

Nick raised his hands, looked at Yuki, then at the man. "Sorry. Didn't realize your ego needed all the saluting."

Yuki giggled and slouched into her chair.

Before the bald man could protest, Nykima spoke, "Queen Helen sent us. I'm White Knight Nykima Amana, and these are White Pawns Leah Ackerman, Isaac O'Conner, Sarah Turner, and Gabe Tate. We are the few survivors from the Queen's Gambit."

"And do you all already know who we are?" the old man asked.

"Well," Gabe said, still standing at attention. "You're the Sages."

The old man nodded and rested a hand on his chest. "I'm Desmond Hawthorne, Sage of *Netzach*, The Invulnerable."

"We already met," said Nick with a wave of his hand.

"Same here," said Eli, staring at them with a blank expression.

Sandeep yawned. "Yeah, yeah. Next."

The woman wrapped in layers of clothes revealed her face, which was long with dark eyebrows. She spoke with a soft, melodic accent. "Name is Zafirah Nasser, Sage of *Gevurah*. The Elemental."

Yuki glanced up from her phone for a second and waved. "Yuki Nakamura, Sage of *Malchut*. The badass Warrior."

"Yuki!" Desmond spat.

"What?" she said, focused on her phone. "I *am* badass."

The doors opened again, and Helen entered with Nona.

All the Sages quickly stood at attention to the Queen as she guided Nona to the table.

"At ease," Helen said, helping Nona into her seat. The Queen stood at the end of the table, resting her hands on it as the rest sat. "I assume introductions are over?" Everyone nodded, and Helen extended a hand toward Nona and added, "Nona Timashova, Sage of *Tiferet*. The Seer."

"Pleasure to meet you again," Nona said in a kind, grandmotherly voice.

"Perfect," Queen Helen said. "Thank you for all gathering on such short notice after the stalemate was called. My urgency hasn't changed, and a month could be detrimental to our cause. I ask that you lend your ears and consider helping us moving forward."

"The Outer Council has already spoken, my Queen," Desmond said. "What do you expect us to do?"

"Join my cause. The Inner Council can sway votes. With a unified front, we won't run into another stalemate in thirty days' time."

Zafirah pushed herself away from the table and pulled off layers of clothing as the conversation carried on. Leah looked around the table, frowning at the fact that the Queen, nor the other Sages, seemed to take notice or care.

Desmond leaned forward in his seat. "Forgive me, my Queen, but the Rooks have a point. I've seen the situation in the south. Nick too. And it is as dire as Rook McMillan presented it."

More clothes came tumbling off Zafirah, revealing long brown hair and a sharp nose that became more and more defined. She was absolutely gorgeous, and Leah wondered why no one else seemed to take notice.

"I understand, Desmond," Helen said. "But we had a demon appear in the middle of an academy with a horde of demons. They tore through our barriers like they were nothing. Moreover, his ability to materialize chains and consume anything he wants tells me he is a level five. Even at the height of his power, Asmodeus wasn't able to do anything like that."

Because I am not a monster who uses my Kyem's lives for power, Asmodeus hissed in Leah's mind.

Sarah cleared her throat, and Leah saw her friend's gaze on Zafirah, who was now unbuttoning a pair of ski pants. Another moment later, and the woman was standing in a bikini that barely covered her. She fanned herself as sweat beaded up on her forehead, then sat in her chair, crossing long, bronzed legs. Leah and Sarah weren't the only ones staring now, as both Gabe and Isaac looked like they needed to pick their jaws up off the floor.

Leah cleared her throat as she shot a look at Gabe and Isaac, who both immediately straightened their backs and looked away from Zafirah.

"Well, let's hope you are mistaken. Two threats at this magnitude would mean the end of the Infinity Board," Desmond said.

"No, we have to fight!" Leah interrupted, her hands balling into fists.

"And how do you suggest we do that?" Zafirah asked, her eyebrow arched high.

"I . . ." Leah started failed to find the words. "I don't know. But we can't just sit here and give up while Legion builds an army."

Desmond laughed. "Who said anything about giving up? I'll fight tooth and nail until the bitter end alongside my fellow Mystics."

Leah sat up in her seat. "And what if Legion's army is already among us? What if they sabotaged the vote?"

"I personally checked all the attendees," Nona said, her gray eyes peering at Leah. "I saw nothing out of the ordinary."

"But that doesn't work on these demons." Leah shook her head. "They were able to conceal from *Tiferet* somehow."

"Watch how you talk to the Seer," Zafirah growled, steam somehow forming off her skin. "If she says she checked them all and saw nothing, then they were not possessed."

Helen cleared her throat. "This was actually something I wanted to discuss with all of you. I checked one of these possessed, but even I couldn't see traces."

"What if they are using *Thagirion*?" Leah asked. "That could conceal them, right?"

"This girl knows her shit." Yuki grinned from behind her phone.

"Not quite," Nona said with a slight smile. "Demons can't access the Trees unless they possess a Mystic who succumbs to the commands. Even if they were to use *Thagirion,* which can conceal from the average *Tiferet* user, someone adept in *Tiferet* will always see through the concealment. But as you see, such use of *Tiferet* comes at a cost." She waved at her clouded eyes. "However, a possession the Queen was unable to even detect is troubling, and something I would personally like to witness."

Desmond shook his head. "Even then, Rooks aren't easy to possess. The waste of energy to conceal and resist a rook would be damn near impossible for Nona not to see."

"We've fallen into the weeds and lost sight of the bigger picture." Eli leaned back in his chair and crossed his arms. "We've all read the report, and yet we still haven't discussed how Legion is using chimeras for rituals. These creatures were thought extinct, then they return and Legion starts sacrificing them? That's too much of a coincidence."

After a moment of silence, Nykima spoke, "They used a chimera we captured to teleport Legion past the blockades and right into the Academy."

"And don't forget, he was immune to my attacks. It was like something was shielding him," Helen added.

A memory surfaced in Leah's mind, something that had been long forgotten in the haze that came after losing Eric. "There was a kid! The one we saved. He was protecting Legion with some kind of spell. I saw it when I used *Tiferet*."

Helen raised an eyebrow. "You didn't mention this before."

"I'm sorry. I didn't even remember it until now."

Sandeep took off his glasses and cleaned them as he spoke. "Losing a bond effects the memory. I know what you're thinking, my Queen, but this wouldn't have swayed the votes. White Queen Micah didn't even call your witnesses up to testify. But perhaps we can use this to our advantage."

"How?" Zafirah asked.

"Possessed children aren't common." Sandeep placed his glasses back on his face. "Yet, it is clear that they can do things beyond what we thought possible. Our best approach is to understand what else these children are capable of. Present everything all at once as a final say in it all."

Nick cleared his throat. "Okay, then let's do that. We're Sages of the Infinity Board. I think if there is any information hiding about child possessions, we'll find it."

"I'd like to help," Nona said. "I will investigate ways to fool my *Tiferet*."

Sandeep nodded. "I'll help too, although it would be easier if we had a specimen to study."

Desmond scoffed. "And are we all forgetting about the meeting with Black Queen Kwan later today? Or that Queen Helen rushed to put this meeting together before? Before chasing these little fairy tales, why don't we hear out the Shadow Board before Queen Kwan makes things more difficult for everyone?"

Helen raised an eyebrow. "So, what is it you are proposing, then? To completely delay until one of us complains louder?"

Desmond pushed himself out of his chair and stood behind it. "We have two options, both presented with a substantial risk. We Sages should split and cover each, giving both ample resources and access. Zafirah, you seem to lean with me toward the shifters, yes?"

"Yes," she said, a small flicker of fire dancing on her fingertips.

"And Nick," Desmond continued. "Your help with healing would be appreciated down on the front lines. They could use all the support they can get."

Nick nodded. "I had planned on returning there next week, before all this."

"What about me?" Yuki asked, curious enough to look up from her phone. "You're not leaving me up here, are you? I want to fight some shifters."

"I can't force you to stay," Desmond said, glaring at her. "But need I remind you of the fuckup you had in Iowa? Perhaps it would be best if you stayed here and worked with Eli a little more."

Yuki sighed and dropped back into her phone. "Fine, whatever."

Helen eyed Leah, then Yuki. "You could help train our Pawns. Perhaps incorporating some physical training on top of their meditations to reconnect with the tree might benefit them.”

“Sounds better than doing nothing,” Yuki mumbled.

Queen Helen nodded and stood beside Desmond. “Then we have a plan.”

CHAPTER II

TENSION

"How can I be so sore my bones hurt?" Sarah asked, collapsing onto the couch. "I mean, look at this." She lifted her arms, and they shook.

Leah stifled a yawn as she leaned up against the kitchen island in their shared apartment. "I can barely feel my legs."

Isaac stretched and cracked his back. "How are we supposed to keep going like this? Lie in a vat for hours on end, then get the crap beaten out of us by Yuki, then get swept up by Mathew to work until eleven. Every day this week. I mean, come on."

Gabe pulled open the pantry and sighed. "Sandwiches again? I think that's all I can make at this point."

"As long as you're willing to make it, I'm not complaining," Sarah said, staring up at the ceiling.

Leah worked alongside Gabe, slathering on crunchy peanut butter for four and carrying out places for everyone before collapsing in the couch alongside Sarah.

"I don't get it. We aren't getting anywhere," Isaac said, untying his bun and letting his shoulder length hair drop to one side.

78

"Says you. I think I might finally beat Yuki the next time we train," Sarah grunted. "If I can just dodge her right hook."

Isaac bit into his sandwich and shook his head. "I mean with the stalemate. It's been a hell of a week, and all they have us do is meditate, fight, and chores. Couldn't they be using us for something?"

"I doubt they'll find anything to do with the concealed possessions," Leah said. "I mean, they barely believed anything I had to say."

"I'm fine with all this mindless work," Sarah said. "I mean, it keeps me from thinking about all that happened. Hell, I don't even know if I'm ready to go back to the Astral Plane. Not after last time."

Gabe choked on his glass of water. "What? You were in the Astral Realm? When?"

"Back at the Academy," Sarah shrugged. "Leah's invisible thing brings you into the Astral. I think. Either way, she did it to me and Isaac."

"That was when we suspected Sid kidnapped Paige," Isaac said, his voice catching on the mention of Sid. "Leah did something to make us all invisible and we snuck into his truck. Whatever she did brought us into the Astral Plane, I think. I mean, it had to be. There was that creepy monster that chased us."

Gabe turned to Leah and asked, "Is that what you did at the warehouse? When we rescued that druid kid?"

"Yeah." Leah stared down at the last bit of her sandwich. "It's *Thagirion*, one of the Tree of Death wells. Opposite to *Tiferet*."

Gabe frowned, eyeing Sarah and Isaac. "Is the Queen aware you use it? Does she know about the demon possessing you too?"

"She's not possessed," Sarah said, rolling her eyes.

Gabe threw the rest of his food down on his plate. "And you kept it a secret too? You let your friend just—"

"The Queen knows!" Leah yelled, her heart pounding. "She knows. She saw me using the Tree of Death when we fought Legion. Nick tested me and everything. No signs of corruption. So, get off my fucking case!"

Gabe pushed himself up off the couch, his face red. "Then she's using you, Leah! Don't you see?"

Leah stood up and met him face to face. "So what? If I can help bring down Legion, who cares? You've done nothing but judge me or give me the silent treatment since the warehouse. Why don't you just say what you want to say?"

"I'm just trying to protect you!" Gabe turned away and stomped into the kitchen. He rested his hands on the countertop. "They'll use you. Use all of us until we're husks. We can't let them."

Leah took a step forward, but Sarah grabbed her arm. "Guys, cut it out. Yell any louder and Mathew will—"

"The Queen has done nothing but help us," Leah said, yanking her arm free from Sarah. "You think Pawns like us get the chance to bond to the Tree without going to the Shadow Board? We're lucky we're still on the Infinity Board."

"You really think the rest of us matter?" Gabe asked, nodding to Isaac and Sarah. "It's *you* they want, Leah. I bet you had to say something to keep us. Am I wrong?"

Leah stepped back. He wasn't wrong. Anger still flowed through her, and she clenched her fists. "If you hate it so much, then why don't you just leave?"

"If I had somewhere else to go, I would," Gabe said, his nostrils flaring. "I'm done with this. Good fucking night." He turned and stomped off to his room, slamming the door behind him.

Leah let out a groan and crossed her arms. "Good fucking night."

"You didn't tell me about the demon," Isaac said, eyebrow raised. He looked at Sarah. "You knew?"

"I'm sorry," Leah said, turning back to her friend. "I wanted to tell you, but everything just happened so fast."

"But you told Sarah?" Isaac asked, his head dropping.

"I wanted to, but—"

"But you didn't think telling me you had a demon inside you was important? Really? Are you even you anymore?"

If she wasn't, do you think she'd be having this conversation? Idiot, Asmodeus whispered.

"It's not like that," Sarah said.

Isaac stood up, looking at Sarah and Leah. "It's not? Then why didn't you tell me? We're a team!" His face reddened, and the blackened scar on his face seemed to pulse.

"Because I was more worried about saving you. Asmodeus is helping us," Leah said.

"Asmodeus?" Isaac's eyes widened. "The same Asmodeus who killed Alma? Who killed your parents?"

"It's not like that, he—"

"You're telling me we've been working with Asmodeus this whole time? What if he and Legion are in this together? Leah, you can't be serious."

If he keeps making accusations, I may regret helping him, Asmodeus mused.

"No, please," Leah said. "I can explain."

Isaac looked down at the floor and shook his head. "I can't—I can't work with a demon."

"He helped save you," Leah said, sitting up and chasing after him. "He didn't have to, but if he didn't, you wouldn't be here."

Isaac turned around. "Demons don't show mercy."

And yet, here we are, Asmodeus said.

"He did. Please, I'll tell you everything right now if you want," Leah said.

"Fine." He plopped back onto the couch and stared expectantly at Leah.

She told him everything, from the mark to her dream, with Legion nearly consuming Asmodeus, to their conversations. He knew she used the Tree of Death, but not as much as she admitted now. As she spoke, Leah realized how many times Asmodeus had stepped in when he didn't need to. When he called Eric through the *Yesod* bond, protected her from Joanna, or pulled Isaac away before he was fully possessed.

Isaac took it all in and sat in silence. After some time, all he managed was, "They're monsters, Leah. That's not normal demon behavior."

Leah nodded. "I'm aware, but I think something happened when I helped him in the train station. It wasn't all of him, just a sliver that latched on. I can see into him the same way he can see into me, and I know we want the same thing, to save our people by destroying Legion."

"People?" Sarah asked. "You didn't say that before. You mean his horde of demons?"

"I do. I can't say that what demons have done is good, but I can see why. Just like that monster that chased us out of the library. That's just a scared ghost kid turning into something terrifying and dangerous to protect himself. He—" A thought suddenly dawned on Leah as the memory of a young boy came back into focus. "Holy shit."

"What?" Sarah asked.

"He warned us." Leah sat up straight, the conversation ringing in her ears. "Holy shit, it was right there!"

"What?" Both Isaac and Sarah asked in unison.

"The ghost warned me about the possessed kid!" Leah stood up, her heart beating heavy in her chest. "We have a way to detect the hidden possessions."

CHAPTER 12
DEVISING A PLAN

Leah's hands trembled as she replayed the ghost's voice in her head. "He said he didn't like the thing in the infirmary. He meant the kid we saved from the orphanage. He knew. He knew he was possessed with something, and I ignored him."

A wave of grief washed over her, a pain threatening to pull her back into the dark. "I could—I could have . . ."

Sarah grabbed Leah's shoulders. "Leah, what is it?"

"I could have saved them." Tears streamed down her face. "The ghost warned me, and I didn't listen. I didn't know." Sarah helped her back onto the couch as she continued, "I was so mad about Gabe, I just yelled at him. If I would've listened . . ."

Her chest tightened, and her breath was shallow. Darkness swelled into the edges of her vision as the image of Eric, chains tearing through him, burned into her mind.

"Hey! Focus on your breathing. Stay with us," Isaac said.

"You didn't know," Sarah said, leaning in and squeezing Leah's arm.

Isaac nodded and caught Leah's gaze. "Legion was always one step ahead of us. That ghost warned you right before you came to the infirmary, right? So, we would have only had a few minutes before Legion attacked."

"It was more than a few minutes," Leah said. "I'd stepped outside with Sarah. I wasn't thinking. If I wasn't so mad, then things could have been different. Sid . . . Grace . . . they could have made it. We could have prepared better."

"Leah, listen," Isaac said. "Hypotheticals won't get us anywhere. Legion was going to get to us one way or another."

Sarah stood up and headed to the kitchen, pouring a glass of water. "Even if we got out of the Academy, those waves of demons would have been on us."

Sarah returned and handed the glass to Leah, who took a drink, finding her breath once again. She stayed silent, her rushing thoughts slowing and bring a weight down on her shoulders.

Isaac leaned forward and rubbed his hands together. "We have something to work with now. Think we could get this ghost kid to help us find these demons?"

Those things aren't demons, Asmodeus hissed in Leah's mind.

Sarah frowned. "But the ghost didn't say anything about Joanna, right?"

"Yeah, he didn't," Leah said. "She was in the library a lot, too."

"I mean, she acted like herself most of the time. Maybe it was dormant?" Isaac suggested.

That's not it. Let me talk, Asmodeus said.

Talk? Leah asked. *What does that mean?*

Let me take over. Just for a moment. It'll be easier that having you relay everything.

No! Leah said.

A sharp pain shot through Leah's head, and she winced.

"Everything okay?" Sarah asked.

"No." Leah rubbed her temples. "Asmodeus has something to say."

Isaac tensed up. "Like, now? To us?"

"Yeah. He'd rather speak on his own than have me repeat what he's saying."

"I don't know," Isaac said, rubbing his neck.

Leah winced again, a sharp pain forming in the back of her mind.

Sarah crossed her arms. "Fine, let him speak. But if he steps out of line, I'm exorcising his ass."

Leah frowned. "I don't think you can."

Isaac eyed Sarah. "Are you sure? We don't know what he's capable of."

"If he wanted to hurt us, he would have already. And I want to make a couple of things clear," Sarah said while cracking her knuckles.

Leah smirked and closed her eyes. "Just don't beat me up."

Something inside her changed, and she suddenly sensed her control over her body vanish. Her legs moved beyond her control, and Asmodeus stood, turning around to face Sarah and Isaac.

"Legion is no normal demon. Even our best Xigats couldn't explain how he can control so many of us." Leah's voice was nearly the same but accented slightly. Her vowels were rounder, and her tone was more authoritarian. She raised a finger toward Isaac. "Before I saved you in the Orphanage, I saw that possessed woman with the child. It was profane. No face or essence of its own. It was as if someone had stripped one of my people of everything and put a mindless puppet in that human. Around the child, I felt nothing, same with the one you call Joanna."

"So, there are different types of demons under Legion's

command? Ones that can hide from you," Sarah said, grimacing at Leah.

"Demons have always been able to detect each other when in a vessel, but—"

"You mean in an unwilling human's body?" Sarah interrupted him.

Asmodeus eyed her, and Leah felt the sudden urge to rip out Sarah's throat, which was quickly quelled as she breathed in. "Sure. As I was saying, these demons are different. They aren't normal, and they appear to have some kind of dormancy stage I've never seen before. Something that lets them be unseen, even by demons."

"Wait," Leah said, pushing her mind forward as she sensed herself slide back into her body. "Don't forget that demon at the orphanage could see and hear you, Asmodeus. She sensed you. It is possible that she concealed herself because she knew you were there?"

"So, less of a dormant thing and more of them hiding while they control the person they are in?" Sarah asked.

"Or Asmodeus could be working with them, and this is all a ploy," Isaac said, his voice trembling as he eyed Leah.

Asmodeus burned through Leah's throat. "Saving you nearly killed me. Why would I stop one of Legion's possessions if I was on his side?"

"To make Leah trust you." Sarah shrugged. "That's what I'd do."

Asmodeus sighed and sat on the coffee table. "I came forward to tell you these demons aren't normal and that even Legion himself is something more than an ordinary demon. Do with that what you will."

"So, we are back to square one then," Sarah said.

Isaac clasped his hands together. "But that's where the ghost comes into play. They're hiding from Asmodeus, just like they can hide from *Tiferet*, but that just reinforces that we need this ghost's help."

Sarah let out a sigh. "Too bad the Academy burned down. Probably took the ghost with it."

"Maybe," Isaac said, standing and pacing the room. "Or maybe not. Ghosts are sometimes attached to objects, like their remains. We wouldn't know if he was gone unless we went there, or if there was something they brought back. I mean, he stayed in the library most of the time, right? So, it was probably something in there."

"How do you know so much about ghosts?" Sarah asked.

Isaac shrugged. "Side project with Sid. We were studying if we could get a ghost from one of the sacrifices to talk."

"I doubt he's here," Sarah said. "I mean, last time he was a monster trying to eat us. It might be a little obvious if that thing was lurking around."

"True," Leah nodded. "But I have spoken to him before. It would be worth it to try, even if he just confirms that none of the Rooks are compromised." Leah shivered at the thought. What if they were already too late, and the council was taken over by Legion's army?

Asmodeus spoke through her again. "We must act now. Every second that passes gives Legion more time."

Sarah stretched and let out a yawn. "We should ask the Queen or one of the Sages if they can help—"

"No, that's not a good idea," Isaac interrupted. We don't know who's possessed. Queen's Gambit members only from here on out."

Leah leaned back and rested her arms on the table behind her. "Then we ask Queen Helen."

Isaac shook his head. "No, she's a big target for Legion.

If she isn't already possessed, then bringing her in on this would only make her a bigger threat."

"I doubt she's possessed. She's voting to fight Legion," Sarah said.

"For now," Isaac replied. "But she could be compromised any minute, and Legion would know what we were doing."

Leah sighed and looked up at the ceiling. "So, we're on our own, then?"

"Or we bring in Nykima," Isaac suggested. "A White Knight would have better access than us, and I doubt Legion sees her as a threat now."

Smart, Asmodeus whispered in Leah's mind.

Sarah clapped her hands together. "Great, we've got a plan then. Let's get Nykima and find that ghost." She stifled another yawn. "Tomorrow then. Sometime between all the bullshit."

"Perfect," Asmodeus said to the group.

In the blink of an eye, Sarah turned and grabbed Leah by her T-shirt, raising her from the coffee table.

"What the—" Leah started.

"Listen to me, you demonic shit. If this is all just some bullshit ploy, and you're using Leah as a doll, I'll kill you. You hear me?"

Leah blinked and raised her hands. "He's gone already. It's just me."

Sarah let her go and straightened Leah's shirt. "Fine. Whatever, just tell him I said that. Alright?"

Leah laughed. "Got it, message sent."

CHAPTER 13
ASTRAL TRAP

Leah propped the capsule open, her eyes adjusting to the yellowish orange light emanating from her. She pulled herself up and out of the pod, carefully avoiding the patches of strange moss that wound its way up the side of the metal enclosure.

The two doors were still there, completely unblemished by the moss or decay around them, positioned on either side of the room, one white and the other red.

She couldn't keep her eyes off the red one, muffled voices tickling at her ears as if calling to her to step through.

Someone cleared their throat, and Leah turned, spotting Eli as he stepped out from behind the white door and folded his arms behind his back.

"We're going to do things a little different today, thanks to your stubbornness." He raised a finger. "I'll give you one last chance. Go through the white door or face the consequences of your decisions."

"No," she said, her hands clenching into fists. "I told you I won't go through there until my friends are here with me and ready to go as well."

"What a pity," Eli uttered, gazing at the ground. "Very well. Let's hope you don't go mad."

She stepped back. "Mad? Instead of wasting your time threatening me, why don't you help me figure out a way to bring them over?"

"Mystics can't force each other to come into the Astral. And we don't have time to wait for your friends." Eli tilted his head and shifted his weight to one foot. "I guess you'll have to learn the hard way." His face stretched and melted before her eyes, dripping down to the ground as if he were made of wax. The rest of him followed, and in an instant, he transformed into a puddle, absorbing into the cracks on the ground.

"What the . . ." Leah backed up, raising her fists and pooling *Malchut* into them.

Before she could react, the ground beneath her gave out. Her stomach twisted in knots as she stared at Eli's materialized body inches from her face. "See you on the other side," he said.

She fell through the hole and landed hard on her back, a sharp pain spreading up from her arm. Her breath caught in her chest, and she struggled to breathe as the hole of light above her closed. She moved to one side, examining the gravel and red sand that broke her fall, holding her ribs as she struggled to catch her breath. Something glinted and caught her eye, and as she looked up, she caught her own reflection staring back at her.

Leah frowned, feeling her eyebrows move and the crease in her forehead, but the reflection smiled back at her. She pushed herself away and quickly got to her feet, eyes locked on this smiling Leah that mimicked her moves.

"What the hell?" she muttered, backing away.

She pressed up against a flat wall and turned to look, only to find a little girl staring back at her inside a mirror. It was Leah, but she was younger, much younger, with a toothy smile, hair up in a ponytail, and a pastel flowery dress.

Leah stepped back and spun around. Mirrors appeared all around her like rectangular shards of glass jutting up from the ground in a vast and otherwise dark red desert.

She focused back on the little girl, tilting her head from one side, then the other, and the little girl did the same as she held at the sides of her dress.

"Where am I? What the hell is this?" Leah shouted up into the darkness.

"I told you there would be consequences." Eli's voice boomed from all directions.

Leah turned around, and more reflections of her sprouted from the ground. Versions of herself, at different points in her life, wearing clothes both familiar and not, all staring back at her as if waiting for her to move.

"Let me out!"

"Let yourself out," Eli mused. "Or be consumed by all the versions of yourself."

All the mirrors shifted, sliding a few inches in the red sand toward her, closing in. Leah's chest tightened, and *Malchut* pushed against her skin. Would they all just keep closing in until she had no room to escape? Would they squeeze her to death?

It happened again, the mirrors sliding toward her. She let out a wave of *Malchut*, a force that would shatter the mirrors and let her free from this impending prison. Instead, the energy washed past the mirrors as if it were a weak gust of wind, and Leah became more translucent, the effect of using the Tree in the Astral plane.

"*Malchut* won't work here," Eli's voice boomed. "There is only one way out, unless you want to be lost in your reflections forever."

The mirrors shifted and spun in the sand, crafting long corridors and paths. As it did, there was one thing that caught Leah's eye, far off in the distance, just beyond the maze of mirrors. A door, standing pristine and unblemished, waiting for her to step through.

"Not without my friends. How hard is that to get through your skull? I'll just sit here and wait to wake up!" Leah yelled, turning around and spotting a version of herself standing tall. This time, she was much older, with black and white paints marking her otherwise naked body.

Eli laughed. "I don't think you understand what this place is. Time in the Astral is not always so clear, and a place like this, a trap of my own making? Well, time here has the ability to feel like a millennium before a minute passes by in the real world. You wanted the hard way; you'll break, sooner or later."

The mirrors moved once again, and Leah's breath caught in her throat. She looked up into the dark sky, her heart racing. "Bullshit! The Queen wouldn't allow this!"

"This is my realm," Eli boomed. "The Queens don't get a say here. Go through the door or stay and let your reflections crush you one by one. I'll leave you be. Perhaps I'll check back in a month or so."

CHAPTER 14

OLD STORIES

"**N**o, wait!" Leah ran forward, but as she did, a new mirror appeared in front of her. She collided with it, bouncing back onto the ground. "Fuck!" she yelled, rubbing the small of her back as she got to her feet.

Reflections doubled every time she turned her head. Faces, all her own, stared back at her. There was no way out, and the more she tried, the more mirrors that appeared.

Collectively, the mirrors shifted toward her again, closing in.

A voice echoed in her mind. Not Asmodeus, but someone who carried a weight that ached her heart. *Go! Get out of here!*

"Eric?"

Eric's words echoed, and the image of him staring at her, chains tearing through flesh, seared through her mind.

Leah took in a deep breath and looked at the ground, resting her hands on her knees. "No, stop. Keep it together. He can't win," she whispered.

She looked down at her arm, seeing the dark lines that traced it, the demon mark she could only see in the Astral.

"Asmodeus?" she asked. "You there?"

The reflections all stared at her expectantly, but no one responded. She stepped forward, and one particular mirror caught her eye. The woman looked older, with her hair up in a tight ponytail, in a clean uniform. She looked exactly like . . .

"Mom?"

Leah stepped closer to the mirror, tilting her head as the woman in the mirror did the same.

The reflection matched a photo she'd seen of her mother back in the academy. Leah rested a hand on the mirror, and the reflection did the same.

"Is that really you?" she asked, but the lips in the reflection just mimicked her words.

Her shoulders dropped; it was only a reflection. Still, being so close to her, even if she wasn't really Leah's mother, was enough to push her forward. She slid her hand past the mirror, onto the next one, which looked exactly like Leah did at the moment, even wearing her same Pawn uniform. Leah frowned until she noticed, shining on the reflection's chest, rested the Star of David necklace she had stopped wearing years ago and later had lost the night she destroyed her home. Leah instinctively reached for it, but of course, she didn't actually have it.

"Leah." The whisper made her jump and turn.

Seven reflections stared back at her, all younger versions of Leah.

"Leah, are you there?"

The whisper came from her left, where the door stood. She approached it slowly, ignoring the surrounding mirrors.

"Leah, over here!"

Two knocks made her look right. Asmodeus stood with his fist against the mirror. He was taller than Leah, wearing a crisp black suit, with his hair combed backwards and his beard trimmed, just like he would look in their small meeting room. Except here, she could see his black eyes more closely and notice what seemed to be stars inside, as if looking into a clear starry night.

"Asmodeus! Thank goodness I've found you!" Leah placed both hands on the mirror.

"That bastard trapped us here," Asmodeus grunted. "You *have* to go through the door, Leah. It's the only way out."

Leah shook her head. "No, there must be another way. I won't give in to his demands. Eli can't force me to do this. Maybe we can use the Tree of Death to get out?"

"Leah, listen, his power here surpasses yours and mine combined. If I could do something, I wouldn't be trapped in this mirror meta bullshit he's created."

"There's got to be a way out," she said, turning and intending to walk away.

Asmodeus rushed to the closest side of the mirror within his reach to get to Leah. "Wait! Wait! If you leave, I don't know if I will be able to see you again. Please Leah, I'm begging you, we need to get out of here."

Leah stomped her foot. "I said no! He won't beat me like this. If I go through that door and get bonded, it could be over for my friends."

She turned away from Asmodeus and found a reflection staring back at her, an odd smirk on her face. Leah frowned and got closer.

"Leah, stop, please!" He hit the glass between them repeatedly. "We need to get out! We need to get out!"

But Leah ignored the demon, instead approaching this reflection, her eyes on its left arm. The arm wasn't her normal demon marked one. Instead, it was longer, thicker, and seemed to be made of obsidian stone intertwining with her flesh. She opened and closed her hand, and the reflection did the same, displaying large sharp claws made of the stone. Leah raised her own, still translucent, hand and stared at the demon mark, which seemed to have grown since she had last seen it.

Something caught her eye, and she stepped back, fear rumbling up inside her as *Malchut* pressed against her skin. A figure stood only a few feet from her, nearly seven feet tall, made of some kind of cracked and fissured glassy black stone. It looked almost like some kind of obsidian statue, with black eyes peering down at her. It mimicked the way Leah approached, and she spotted the edges of another mirror that contained this thing within.

"I've seen you before," Leah said. She turned back to the reflection of Asmodeus standing in a suit. "This was you. What you normally look like."

The Asmodeus in a suit turned his back against the mirror and slid down until he sat in the dirt. "Yes. That was me."

"Was?" Leah asked, eyeing the glass demon.

"Before Legion took everything."

"What happened?" Leah asked.

Asmodeus paused, then said, "Legion's army surrounded my palace. He'd took many of my people, my Kyem, and consumed them, leaving only dust behind. Phenex, my council, my Xigat, begged me to escape. But I'm Kyjak; I can't leave my Kyem. I faced him, but he was too strong. Stronger than all the Kyjaks combined. He didn't consume me like the others, though. He bound me to him and sapped my strength for his own. The next thing I knew, I was here, being commanded to kill Elizabeth Mizrahi and her family."

Hearing her mother's name sent a pain through her chest as she made her way back over to his mirror. But the pain no longer came with anger. Asmodeus was a prisoner who'd lost everything. "I'm sorry," was all she could muster.

Leah rested her back against his glass and slid down, sitting back-to-back with this version of Asmodeus as she stared at his stony form.

"Your mother didn't deserve what I did to her," Asmodeus said.

Leah swallowed hard, a tear slipping down her cheek, but she remained silent.

"I was angry," the demon continued. "Angry about what happened to my Kyem. Angry with our failed attempt at seeking refuge here. You all were just energy for us. Energy we could use, but we lost against your people. I lost against your mother, and I wanted revenge for my Kyem."

"Your defeat here left you weak when Legion attacked," Leah said, her voice flat.

"It did, but there was more to it. The Valley—my home—is dying. Our energy is drying up, and I was too focused on saving us all to see Legion rise to power. When I was sent back, weakened by your mother, Legion took the opportunity to attack." Asmodeus paused and sighed. "I don't know why I'm telling you all this. Maybe part of me regrets some things I've done."

Leah wiped away her tears and looked around at the standing mirrors, all with a reflection of her standing and waiting. She needed a way out of here, out of this trap.

Violet light flickered in the corner of her vision. She pushed herself up off the mirror and turned toward the light, squinting in the dark.

"What is it?" Asmodeus asked.

"I don't know," she said, stepping away. "I think I saw something."

"No, wait!" Asmodeus said. "The door. Go through the door and take me with you."

Another flicker of purple light caught her eye, and she continued forward, ignoring the shouts from Asmodeus. Moments later, she stood in front of a nude version of herself. This version of her looked older, and her skin seemed to radiate in a glow that was almost too perfect. The reflection stopped mimicking her every move and grinned before turning to show off two large tattoos on her back. They were simple large black swirls, spiraling in opposite directions, mirroring each other on her shoulder blades. Leah leaned in closer, and the black ink glowed with a deep violet light.

Her reflection turned back and placed a hand on the mirror, pressing hard against the glass.

Leah raised her own hand to do the same but stopped inches away from touching the mirror. "Can you get me out of here?"

The reflection only nodded, and Leah drew a deep breath and placed her hand against the mirror. Violet light filled the mirror, shining out, and Leah's hand pressed against flesh, her reflection interlacing fingers between hers.

The reflection pulled her forward, hard. Leah shut her eyes and winced, expecting to ram headfirst into the mirror. Instead, she heard glass shattering as the violet light burned one last flash of bright light, and Leah fell into pure darkness.

CHAPTER 15

TWO SWIRLS

Leah landed on solid ground, her vision slowly returning as the familiar moss-covered floor and pods from the lab in the Astral realm materialized around her. She found Eli standing beside Gabe's pod with a clipboard in hand, gaping at her.

"That's not possible," he whispered. "You . . . you can't do that."

Leah straightened her back, a rage vibrating inside her as she gestured toward the pods with her friends inside. "I said I'm not going through that door without my friends."

Something took over, a force that felt familiar and foreign all at once. She let it take over, and she opened her palms and raised her arms, extending them out from her waist. The reflection of her with the spiral tattoos was still with her, inside her, and moved her body, guiding her on what to do next.

An energy pulsed through her, violet and warm, and not something that came from her wells of energy. As it pulsed through the air, it connected with the three capsule pods, forcing them open.

"What are you doing?" Eli asked, dropping the clipboard and stepping forward.

Leah's fingers twitched. She could feel them, her friends, like little pinpricks of light beneath the black liquid, yearning to break free. She raised her hands up, and the light slipped out of the water, her friend's bodies materializing and hovering above the liquid. The energy released, and Leah landed on her knees, pain jolting up her body as her friends landed on the ground in front of her.

Eli raced toward her, helping her up. "That's not. You. You're not supposed to do that."

Leah looked up at her friends. Isaac was hunched over, clutching his stomach, while the other two leaned against their pods, blinking and looking around the room with dazed expressions.

Eli eyed Leah for a moment longer before clearing his throat and turning around. "Congratulations, White Pawns. You have passed the first test. Welcome to the Astral Plane. Coming through by pod is always difficult the first time. Try to acclimate to your surroundings and get used to this place. We'll end this session soon."

Leah toweled her hair off as she stepped out of the changing room, finding both Isaac and Sarah smiling in their uniforms.

"One step closer to making our bonds to the Tree!" Sarah said, doing a little dance.

"Finally, something after a week. Feels surreal to break through," Isaac said, adjusting his uniform.

Gabe stepped out of his changing room and huffed, shaking his head.

"Something wrong?" Leah asked.

"No. Just—"

Eli stepped into the doorframe and cut Gabe off. "There will be no session tomorrow."

"What?" Isaac asked. "Why? We just got through finally!"

"You did, which takes much energy to do. Your spirits need to rest, and your minds need time to acclimate to the idea of separation. I know some of you have improperly traversed into the Astral before, but we will go by the book here. We'll resume the day after. Rest up, as we need you sharp of mind and ready to train. The trial to connect with the tree is not easy." He locked eyes with Leah and tilted his head. "A word, before you leave?"

"That's our cue," Sarah said, grabbing Isaac's arm. "We'll meet you in the cafeteria."

Gabe trudged behind Sarah and Isaac, passing by Eli without a word.

The Sage crossed his arms, his eyes still locked on her. "No Mystic has ever escaped that trap. I might have toned it down for you, saved you from some of the more dangerous bits, but that trap is inescapable. How did you do it?"

Leah nearly gave in, but she frowned and shook her head. "You were going to leave me there for a month. Why should I tell you?"

"You were supposed to go through the door."

"And if I did, my friends would end up in the Shadow Board. I told you: I won't leave them."

Eli ignored her, instead leaning forward. "You did something I've never seen anyone do, and I've interacted with my fair share of beings. Your friends don't have an iota of what you have. Someone like you, with that immunity to the Tree of Death, you'll climb high in the Infinity Board if you're willing."

"And if I'm not, locking me up in a prison until I go insane is a bit much," Leah said.

"If moving you along gives us leverage against Legion, then I will do my part."

"And have any of you found anything?" Leah asked.

Eli pursed his lips. "If you stop working against me, maybe I'll tell you."

Tell him what you did. It's better he knows and is willing to help, Asmodeus whispered.

Leah looked into Eli's dark eyes and said, "Fine. There was a reflection. She had these swirls on her back. Tattoos. And they glowed."

She explained everything from the moment she saw this version of herself to how she felt the energy that pulled her friends free from their pods. Eli simply waited, his arms crossed as he listened.

"Well, the report makes sense now."

Leah scrunched her brow. "Report?"

"Constance had a file on you. Noted a unique affinity with dreaming. I don't think she really knew what you were."

Leah frowned. "What I am?"

"They call themselves witches. Immortal witches, to be exact. I've never seen one in person. They connect to the tree like Mystics, but differently. This energy you describe sounds similar to theirs, but I'll need to study it more before I can be sure. We don't have much time, though. Not if my suspicions are correct."

"Suspicions?"

"Better you know now." He let out a sigh. "I suspect Legion is planning to attack during the Winter Solstice."

"Why? Isn't that only a couple of months away? Right when the vote is happening. We're not ready."

"Two and a half months, to be exact. The solstices are a

time when the veil between the Astral and the material world is at its thinnest. It makes sense for Legion to make his move then, since he could pull off more possessions then."

"What can we do?" Leah asked.

Eli uncrossed his arms and nodded back toward the pods. "We focus on getting your bond back. Brace yourself. The next few weeks will be difficult."

CHAPTER 16

MYSTIC'S CORNER

"Wait so, you yanked us into the Astral Plane and now he thinks you're some kind of witch?" Sarah asked as she cleaned out pint glasses behind the bar. They'd been given cleaning duties for the rest of the afternoon, thanks to Mathew, and while Gabe ran off to the kitchen, the three of them were left prepping one of the bars for the Rooks.

"Yep, that pretty much sums it up," Leah said, wiping down the counter.

Isaac flipped chairs down onto the ground. "Guess that's another thing you can add to the list." He smirked. "Mystic, demon-taxi, witch."

"Ha. Ha," Leah said, rolling her eyes.

The bar wasn't particularly big, ten small round tables with a long checkered counter, dark red walls, and a black ceiling.

Isaac put the last chair down and rested his hands on his hips. "Could be related to . . . you know?" he nodded to her arm.

Leah shook her head. "Eli already knows about him.

This was something different he'd planned to investigate. Something his trap revealed."

"The trap he was going to leave you in for a month?" Sarah said, tossing the cleaning towel over her shoulder. "That's so fucked up."

Isaac looked up at the clock and groaned. "We open in five minutes. Ready?"

"Guess so," Sarah said. "Never thought I'd be working a bar, but here we are."

"No one else I'd rather do it with," Leah said as Isaac pressed play on the music system.

Frank Sinatra played over the old speakers, his smooth voice bringing back memories of Leah's dad dancing in the kitchen and belting out songs.

"Classy," Leah said.

Sarah leaned her back against the bar and eyed the wall of liquor. "Hope they don't want us making anything fancy, like a long island. They're gonna get beer, wine, and shots from me."

"Long islands aren't that bad," Isaac shrugged. "A little vodka, gin, tequila, rum, and a splash of soda."

"Wait, what? How do you know that?" Sarah asked.

"My dad taught me so he and his buddies could have a personal bartender when he was too drunk to make them himself. Was making all sorts of drinks from the time I started walking."

"Oh, geez," Leah said, looking down at the ground. "That sounds terrible. I'm sorry."

"Is what it is," Isaac said. "At least I can make a killer martini now."

Sarah held up a bottle of beer from the small fridge. "Think we can sneak a couple back to our room when the night's done?"

"I," Isaac started, "I'd rather not."

"Oh, right," Sarah said, looking down at the bottles. "Sorry, I was just thinking out loud."

The door opened and two women, one with curly ginger hair and the other blond, walked in brandishing dark uniforms with the Rook insignia on the left side of their chests.

"Two Coronas with lime," one of them said as they found a table.

"Coming right up," Leah said, grabbing the beers out of Sarah's hands and popping off the lids before grabbing two lime wedges.

Others poured in after them, and soon the tables were full and conversations around them picked up. Booming laughter echoed from the corridor leading to the bar.

Shortly after, Jaime McMillan entered, followed by a woman with short black hair and sharp features with a White Bishop insignia on her chest. Behind her, two Black Rooks made up the rest of their party.

Leah overheard Jaime speak as she approached, ". . . right across the face. He was so dumbstruck he just stood up and left."

The Rooks laughed as they approached a filled table. In seconds, the people at the table cleared it off and pulled out the chair for Jaimie. He simply smiled and sat down, stretching out his bad leg.

Leah approached and smiled. "What can I get you?"

"If it isn't Elizabeth Mizrahi's daughter!" Jaime shouted. "Working her way up the ranks. We'll take four scotch on the rocks. Top shelf." He held up a hand, raising three fingers and a thumb. His pinky finger was curled, but Leah noted he was missing most of it.

When Leah returned, with drinks in hand, she overheard Jaime speaking in a low voice, "Whitney, you're wise. You know the numbers don't add up."

"I get that, but if both you and the Queen are right, there's no good resolution to this stalemate." She eyed Leah and leaned back, folding her arms.

"Thank you, dear," Jaime said, grabbing his drink and taking a long sip.

The woman, Whitney, glared at her, and Leah understood this conversation was not one she was welcome to eavesdrop on, so she backed away, finding Sarah behind the counter.

Sarah leaned in and whispered, "Isn't he opposing Helen? Didn't know he was so buddy-buddy with you."

"We're not. I don't think. We met at the gala. He fought alongside my mom in the war." She looked out toward the table, watching as Jaime leaned in close to Whitney. "I wish I knew what they were talking about."

"Too bad the place is so small," Sarah said.

"Too bad I can't use *Thagirion.*"

"Probably for the best. Could you imagine if one of these Mystics bumped into something invisible? They'd probably burn the whole place down."

Leah fell into a routine of serving drinks and bussing tables, never quite getting the chance to eavesdrop, as Jaime and the others always quieted as she slipped by.

As Leah eyed the table for what seemed like the hundredth time, Isaac nudged her, pulling her out of a daze. "What?"

"Look who's here." Isaac nodded toward one of the far tables where Nykima was positioning her wheelchair. "We're closing in a bit. Maybe we can ask her to stay so we can tell her about our plan?"

Leah shook her head. "Too risky. Even after hours. Someone might see her staying behind and eavesdrop."

"Then when? We need her on our side," Isaac said.

"Tomorrow morning, before we go to meditation with Eli, we can meet in the apartment."

Isaac nodded and rushed to make a drink before weaving through to Nykima's table.

As the night went on and the bar emptied, Leah noted Nykima had left without speaking even a word to her. Even Jaime's table was empty, and only a handful of Rooks she'd never met before remained.

"Fuck," she whispered, resting her arms on the counter.

"Don't be too disappointed. Eavesdropping on a Rook isn't easy." Jaime leaned against the counter next to her.

Leah jolted upright. "I . . . I wasn't."

He smiled and lifted his glass of scotch to her. "I do commend you for trying, though. Why don't you just ask me what you want to know?"

She thought for a moment, then said, "You're recruiting Rooks to your side. I want to know what you're saying to them."

"Straight to the point. Just like your mother." Jaime eyed his glass, slowly turning it between his fingers.

"What if you're wrong?" Leah asked. "What if Legion attacks while you're turning everyone toward the shifters?"

Jaime chuckled and met Leah's eyes. "And I'd ask the same to you. How can you be certain that Legion poses a greater threat?"

"But the Queen's proposal doesn't abandon our front in the south. Yours will pull us away from everything *but* the south."

"We can only fend them off with the full force of the Infinity Board. Without that, we are fighting a losing battle." Jaime repositioned himself, adjusting the scarf around his neck.

Leah noticed something behind it, something that marked his skin. She leaned in close, glaring. "Care to tell me what's under that scarf of yours? You're not hiding something, are you?"

Jaime frowned and threw back his drink in one large gulp. "Here I was, hoping to have an intelligent conversation with Elizabeth Mizrahi's daughter, and instead, I'm talking to someone who'd rather pry into things they shouldn't be asking." He placed the glass on the bar and turned. "Perhaps one of these nights I'll let you sit at our table, if you can manage restraint."

CHAPTER 17

DARK MAGIC

"Are you sure you told her the time?" Leah asked, pacing the kitchen.

Isaac slumped into the couch in the living room. "I did. She's not coming."

"Or she didn't hear you," Sarah suggested, lying on the other couch and staring up at the ceiling. "It was loud in there last night."

"What if—" Leah started but stopped as the door to Gabe's room creaked open.

He stepped out, nodded to Sarah and Isaac, then paused as he saw Leah in the kitchen.

"See you there," he said, rushing past them and out the door.

"You two need to talk it out," Sarah said.

Leah rested against the counter. "I don't need to talk anything out. He needs to get over himself."

A loud knock sounded, and the three of them jumped. Leah rushed to the door to find Nykima on the other side, her eyes piercing through Leah. "Mind telling me what I'm doing here?"

"Please," Leah whispered, looking up and down the hall. "Come in."

As Nykima rolled inside, Isaac and Sarah jumped to their feet and stood at attention.

"Pawn Ackerman, get me a water." She nodded toward the other Pawns. "At ease."

Leah complied, filling a glass while Nykima wheeled herself up to the kitchen table. The others joined her at the table.

"Saw Pawn Tate in the hallway. I take it he's not joining us?" Nykima asked, taking a sip from the water.

Heat filled Leah's cheeks, and she sat down in the chair next to Nykima. "We aren't exactly on talking terms at the moment."

A half smiled appeared on her face. "Can't say I'm shocked. Dating fellow Mystics can be frustrating."

Nykima let out a sigh, and Leah smelled the alcohol on her breath. "Is everything okay?"

"Yes," Nykima said. "Why?"

"It's nothing," Leah said, looking down at the table.

"What she means to say," Sarah said, leaning her elbows on the table, "is that it smells like you had a fun night."

"I lost my legs, not my liver. Why don't you worry about your own problems? Starting with why you asked me to come here so damn early."

Leah bit her lip, wondering if a hungover Nykima was the best person to be talking to right now. "We believe that the vote on the Outer Council was rigged."

Nykima eyed the three of them, her lips pursed. "Yeah, I'm aware. You made that pretty clear with the Sages, and they're looking into it."

"But that's not enough," Leah said. "We think we know

something that will help. Back at the academy, there was a ghost."

"The one in the stacks?" Nykima asked.

Leah nodded. "He knew about the possession before anyone else. He'd said it, but I didn't understand what he meant until now. I think he can see these different possessions. The ones that aren't quite demons."

Nykima took another drink. "That's what you think Joanna and the boy were? 'Not quite demons?'"

Isaac nodded. "It's like they have some kind of switch where the demons lie dormant, and *Tiferet* doesn't work on them."

Nykima lightly tapped her index finger on her lips. "And you think this ghost of the kid can see through that?"

"Yes," they all said in unison.

"That's why we need to get back to the Academy," Leah said. "Or find whatever object the ghost is attached to. We wanted to ask the Queen, but if we're right, then anyone voting is at risk of being possessed. That includes Queen Helen."

"Assuming the object survived the flames," Nykima said. "You think you can talk to the ghost and get it to work with us?"

Leah dropped her shoulders. "I don't know, He's talked to me before, but who knows if the object he's attached to made it out of the fire?"

Nykima rested her elbows on the table. "That depends on the ghost's attachment to the object. Seeing as this is the library ghost, it's likely that their object was a book. Lucky for you, many books survived." She paused and frowned. "I do, however, think it would be extremely difficult for a Rook to be possessed. But if you had told me two months ago the academy would be destroyed, I wouldn't have believed you. So, why come to me with all this?"

Leah looked at her friends. "You're part of the Queen's Gambit and the least likely to be possessed. And if we plan on sneaking out of here to get to the academy, then we're going to need help."

Nykima gave a slight smile and then took another drink from her glass. "Lucky for you, almost everything that survived the fire was brought back here. They're still reviewing it all, assessing damage and any risk. The books are all down on sublevel eight in the forensic lab, but good luck getting anything from there. I tried getting some of my own belongings from them. It's all tied up until the investigation is complete."

"So, we need the Queen then," Isaac whispered.

"No, not quite," Nykima said. "The items from the academy are being reviewed for potential demonic residue or rituals that might have aided Legion or Joanna during the attack."

Leah fell back into her chair. "This is the key we need."

Nykima eyed the three of them for a moment before leaning forward. "It won't be easy to sneak in undetected. It's full of Bishops all day, so we'll have a better chance at night. We'll need two teams. One who can break into the camera room when security is out patrolling, and the other to guide them safely to the lab."

Isaac scratched his head. "And how do you think we'll be able to pull this off? I mean, we're bondless. And who knows if we'll get that back before the vote?"

"And I'm in a wheelchair," Nykima said. "Not quite the star team for a heist, but it's the team we've got."

Sarah cleared her throat. "Couldn't the Queen teleport us in or something? I mean, why not ask?"

"If we're caught, and she had any involvement in this, then there's a possibility they might vote to abandon her request for a vote and opt for Jaime's proposal for a Brink-mate," Nykima said.

"Even if she could, we can't ignore the possibility of possession, which is the whole reason we brought Nykima in on this," Isaac said.

Sarah rolled her eyes. "Okay, then give us a better plan, Einstein."

Nykima sat back and eyed the three of them. "There *is* another way. But first, Leah, are you sure you can recognize the object this ghost is bound to? Otherwise, this whole plan is pointless."

"Yes," Leah lied. She was not fully aware, but a feeling in her gut warned her against confessing. Not now.

"Fine," Nykima said. "I know some rootwork that can help."

"Rootwork?" Sarah asked.

Nykima bit her lip. "It's a kind of magic some voodoo people use. I can make a powder that will divert others from out path. I just need a few ingredients that might be hard to find."

"Wait, how do you know voodoo magic?" Isaac asked.

"Rootwork," Nykima corrected. "And that's not your concern, Pawn."

"Hold on." Sarah held up her hands. "You said you need ingredients for this. You mean you want us to get those ingredients, don't you? If this is another ritual, I'm out. We've only had bad experiences with rituals."

"You've had bad experiences because the three of you are children playing with things you don't understand. Dark Magic begets Dark Magic, and in the wrong hands, bad things happen. I know exactly what needs to be done, and this is our best shot at getting this little heist of ours to work."

A memory surfaced in Leah's mind. An old woman,

dressed in white with gold and yellowed teeth and a face that looked oddly familiar now.

Dark Magic begets Dark Magic...

"You're Madeline's granddaughter," Leah whispered, the face in her memory overlaying on top of Nykima's.

Nykima sat upright, her eyes piercing Leah. "How would you know that? Explain. Now."

Leah swallowed. "Back at the Outpost. Alma took me to this town, and we went inside a jazz bar. In the basement there was this woman, Madeline, and she asked Alma about her granddaughter. She said she was moving up in the ranks. That's you, isn't it?"

"It is," Nykima said through gritted teeth. "And it would be best to keep that between the four of us. Understand? Now, if you want my help, I'm going to need those ingredients."

"Well, I'm in," Isaac said, breaking the silence.

"Me too," Sarah said after a nudge from Isaac.

"Same." Leah stood and grabbed a notepad and pencil, handing it over to Nykima.

"Contact me when you've fetched these," Nykima said. "Understood?"

Leah pulled the paper close to her and looked at her friends. "Yes."

Nykima rolled out from the table and headed toward the door. Before she opened it, she paused. "I left that life years ago. Few know, and I'd like to keep it that way."

CHAPTER 18
THE WARRIOR

"How does she expect us to get all that?" Isaac asked, resting his elbows on the cafeteria table, pushing away his half-eaten pastrami sandwich.

Sarah tossed the last bit of her sandwich into her mouth and chewed as she talked. "I mean, half the ingredients we can steal from the kitchens. Salt, black pepper, sage, and red pepper should be easy."

Isaac looked up from the table. "Sure, but what about the live snake? Or the snails? How the hell are we going to get those?"

"Shh," Leah hissed. "Keep your voice down. I know it's not ideal, but if we want her help, we need to play by her rules. The snake doesn't have to be big. I'm sure we can find one out in the woods."

Sarah nodded toward the kitchens as Gabe stepped out, carrying a tray of salad. "He'd be perfect right now."

"Save it," Leah grumbled.

"What?" Sarah asked, leaning back in her chair. "He would be."

"He chose to ignore us." Leah folded her arms.

Isaac moved his head back and forth. "Well, you did sort of make that easy for him. I mean, if you just talked to him, he'd probably come back. He doesn't have anyone else."

Leah rolled her eyes. "He isolated himself. If he wants to come back, he can talk to us."

"Right, because that's always worked well for the three of us," Sarah said. "Even so, who else does he have to talk to? He knows Isaac and I are your friends. I would have done the same, to be honest."

Leah's face grew hot. *How is it that Sarah might be siding with him?* "Fine," she spat. "Maybe he's right, and I should just get rid of Asmodeus and make everyone happy."

"That's not what we mean," Isaac interjected. "Both you and Gabe just need to talk and agree to disagree."

Leah pushed her chair back. "Agree to disagree?" she shouted, then paused to control her voice. "Why do I have to agree to disagree when he's the one who disagrees with what is happening to me? He could just stay out of it."

Isaac leaned in. "I'm just telling you, as a friend, whatever animosity you have toward Gabe won't help you in the long run. You might need to just be the bigger person and swallow your pride."

"This has nothing to do with pride." Leah said, standing up. "Come on, we've got training with Yuki."

The three of them stepped outside onto a small sand pit a few moments later. Leah spotted Gabe on the other end of the field, talking with Yuki, who twirled her bright pink hair.

Something in Leah's gut twinged at the sight, and she clenched her fists.

Jealous? Asmodeus asked.

No. Shut up, Leah thought back, gritting her teeth.

Could have fooled me.

Yuki turned and spotted them, hopping up and down as she ran toward them in black leggings and a white sports bra. "Finally. Let's get this party started."

Gabe followed behind her as she stood dead center in the middle of the volleyball court sized sand pit. Gabe joined beside Isaac, and they all stood at attention as Yuki hopped between her left and right foot.

"Congrats on your recent development in the Astral Plane. Eli let me know. Now, we get to focus on *Malchut* training here on out." She kneeled and grabbed a handful of sand and let it slide through her fingers. "Find a corner on this field and use your *Malchut* to dig a hole six feet down. Whoever gets there the fastest will have a private lesson while the rest put the pit back together. We need your Malchut back up to par now that Eli will have you going through the door. Got it?"

"Yes, White Rook!" they all said in unison before finding a spot on the pit.

Leah uncoiled the energy within her, allowing *Malchut* to slither down her arms and fill her hands. She'd already used it in the Astral, during their practices with Eli, but here, in the material plane, the sensations were stronger, and she felt more powerful.

"Begin!" Yuki commanded.

Malchut burst through Leah's hands, unleashed on the sand below, tossing it up in the air. Moments later, she saw a small hole, most of it already collapsed in from the dry sand. She looked over toward her friends, spotting the same small impact of sand.

Yuki gracefully walked by each of them, stopping in front of Sarah and saying, "Not bad. Again."

The Pawns unleased *Malchut* pushes, one after another, toward the ground. The more they dug in, the more the sand around them collapsed. Leah's mind drifted to Gabe, and her pushes became more rapid. Even if they stayed friends, that would be better than right now, right? They'd have someone else to help them, too.

Sweat poured down Leah's brow, and her *Malchut* became weaker as the energy in her well dried up.

"If your well is emptying, return to basic posture." Yuki turned and pushed her chest up, her hands forming an upside-down triangle. "This will allow you to push your well to the limit. Use your feet to direct the blow if needed."

Leah took the form, and more energy flowed out of her, as if she had unkinked a hose. However, it wasn't long before that faltered too. She slumped to her knees, sand sticking to her as she eyed the hole in front of her, which was barely two feet deep.

She clenched her jaw. In what way would she be able to defeat Legion if she couldn't even dig a hole?

She threw another fist toward the ground, but the sand barely moved.

Go! Get out of here! Eric's voice shouted in her head.

Another punch, and no *Malchut*.

Go! Get out of here!

Another punch. This time, a gust of cold wind rushed toward her, rustling the trees as the buzz of whispers tickled at her ears.

"Hey!" Yuki grabbed Leah's shoulder, her eyes flashing yellow. "Calm your mind. Don't give in to your anger, especially with your well empty. *Nehemoth* has a way of spreading, and even if you're safe, your friends aren't."

Leah blinked a few times, the Sage's words pulling her back. "You still have a little left in you. Keep going. Focus."

Yuki nodded and walked over to inspect Sarah, who'd dug herself deeper than Leah.

"I . . . can't . . . do it," Isaac huffed, holding his side.

Gabe plopped down on the ground, sweat pouring from his face as he slammed a *Malchut*-infused fist into the sand next to him.

"I never told you to stop!" Yuki shouted, rushing over to Gabe. "I want that *Malchut* well dry as a bone."

Sarah was the only one standing up straight, in their first position, stomping her feet down into the ground, throwing up heaps of sand as sweat soaked through her uniform. She let out one final push, which launched her backward and onto the sand.

"Am I dead?" she groaned, her arms flopping on either side.

Yuki chuckled. "Is that everything you've got?"

Leah looked down at her pitiful hole of sand. Even Sarah's pit was barely four feet down at this point, and it was already caving in. "You do it then if you're so powerful." The words slipped out of Leah's mouth before she could even think.

Yuki tilted her head, her smile widening. "*Malchut* turns potential energy into kinetic. Most Mystics are taught that this energy is stored up inside them for them to push out." She took a knee and placed her hand on the sand. "However, if you push sand one direction without considering where you want it to go, it will only collapse. When you control *Malchut*, you control movement."

The ground trembled, dropping Leah to her knees as an explosion of sand filled the air. Grit blew in Leah's face, and she could all but turn away to avoid the sand from getting into her nose and mouth. As the gust of sand settled, and Leah turned and opened her eyes, she saw Yuki standing in a massive crater no less than ten feet deep.

Yuki brushed off her hands and smiled. "Well, of you four, Sarah wins. The rest of you can get shovels out of the shed over there. Remember, back to the way it was."

CHAPTER 19

THE LOVER

"That was awesome!" Isaac exclaimed as he used his shovel to collect the scattered sand and bring it back to the pit. "Guess we know now why they call her the Warrior."

Leah rested against the end of her shovel, staring at Gabe, who was alone at the other end of the field. It wasn't right, none of this. He shouldn't be shut out from the rest of them. It wasn't right.

A knot formed in her throat, and she looked away.

"You could just go talk to him," Isaac said.

"No, I . . ." Leah hesitated. "How could I, especially after all this time?"

Isaac tossed in a shovel full of sand and drew a deep breath. "Then maybe it's my time to be brave. Follow my lead."

"What? No, Isaac don't—"

"Hey, Gabe!" Isaac shouted as he crossed the field. "I need to check in with Mathew. He's got me down for a session with Sandeep later about some textbooks. Can you come help Leah? It'll keep things moving fast over here."

"Isaac!" Leah hissed.

Gabe rubbed the back of his neck. "Sure. That makes sense."

Isaac hefted his shovel onto his shoulder and winked at Leah with his scarred eye. "There you go. Now you just need to do the rest."

Leah glared at him, then looked over at Gabe, who was fast approaching. She hissed, "Thanks," before Gabe was in earshot.

Finally, time to make amends, Asmodeus whispered.

Leah paused, holding a shovel of sand. *What? Since when do you care?*

He's useful. We have fewer barriers to getting those ingredients. Which brings us closer to the ghost, and closer to finding Legion, Asmodeus said calmly.

Leah tossed the sand in the hole. *But how can I make amends when he won't accept us?*

Great leaders seek common ground. You don't need him to accept us. Focus on what you two want and go from there.

"A common goal," Leah whispered.

Exactly.

Leah stood up straight and faced Gabe. His ashen hair was a mess, and his face was full of dirt. On top of that, his shirt was damp with sweat, sticking to his muscular chest. He didn't stop to talk, but instead went right to work, scooping up sand right next to her.

"Uh, can we talk?" Leah asked.

Gabe paused for a moment, then stopped his shovel in the sand and stood up. "Sure. What do you want to talk about?"

"You. I never asked what happened? How did you end up in the outpost?"

Gabe shook his head and laughed. "What is this? Trying to get on my good side again?"

Leah closed the gap between them and reached for his

arm. "No. I want to know why you don't trust me. Every-thing you're willing to share with me. I'll listen. And you don't need to sugarcoat it. You already told me you lost your dad, and how you lived with your nan. I just want to understand your side."

Gabe's shoulders dropped. "How do I know I'm talking to the real you?"

Leah squeezed his arm. "Remember the chimeras? And how you'd called me strong-willed for saving one? Asmodeus was already with me then, but you said that after everything we went through, I was still me. So, what does your gut tell you?"

Gabe looked down, his face paling as his eyes shifted from left to right. "My parents were Knights. They didn't make it easy for me growing up. I trained. A lot. They wanted me to be strong. Stronger than them. They knew having me made them vulnerable." He paused, his voice softening. "I was five when I met Mr. K. He was nice. Nice enough that I didn't question when he came out from the shadows as a tall man in with a black derby hat and gold buttons for eyes. He played games with me when no one else would. He was a friend."

"I don't think anyone could blame you for that. You were a kid," Leah said, stepping closer to him.

He smirked and shook his head. "My entire childhood was a constant grind. Study every aspect of the Infinity Board and train like a full-fledged Mystic. I barely knew my multiplication table when I would be outside practicing *Malchut* stances until the sun went down. They treated me as if I possessed the ability, despite knowing how uncommon it was for a child to channel. Mr. K treated me like a kid when I needed it most."

"That sound's horrible," Leah said. "How could they treat you like that?"

"They were protecting me. But through all that, they didn't once teach me about demons or rituals. So, one night, when Mr. K woke me up to play a game, I didn't know. It was just a little salt and rosemary on the floor. A mess my parents would need to clean in the morning. It didn't even cross my mind to question him when he wanted me to pick one of my scabs and drop some blood on the lines of salt. It was a harmless prank."

Leah wrapped an arm around his shoulder. "You didn't know."

"Dad must have heard me moving around. Either way, he came into the kitchen and stepped right into the middle of the salt." Gabe's voice cracked. "He froze, and Mr. K started laughing. It was so loud. Before I knew it, Mr. K was in the circle with him, then it was like his shadow had just disappeared. I remember seeing those gold button eyes where my dad's eyes used to be as he picked up the knife. He laughed, the same laugh as Mr. K, then just stabbed himself, over and over, while he laughed. My mom came running in, however, it was already too late. All he did was smile at her before his arm fell."

Rain sprinkled around them, masking the tears that slipped from Leah's face. "That's horrible"

"Mom sent me to my nan's right after that." Gabe took in a deep breath. "I spent too long believing I was a mistake. Guess it doesn't matter now. Not like it will bring him back. But what I know now is you can't trust demons."

Leah looked down at her left arm, picturing the demon mark that hid beneath her skin. "Asmodeus marked me the night he murdered my mom. He used my dad's body to do it, and I had so many dreams of watching my father's body being toyed around with like a puppet as he rotted." Leah shivered, her stomach turning. "After Alma tried to kill Asmodeus, Legion took him. He threw him into a frail body and tortured him. I found them in a dream, and Legion let me watch. He could have taken him then, destroyed Asmodeus in front of me. Maybe that would have given me peace. But I couldn't sit by and watch. As much as I hated him, I couldn't watch. I helped, and a part of him came into me."

In an instant, Gabe wrapped his arms around her and squeezed. He pulled her into his chest, and for a split second, it was the only place she wanted to be. Tears streamed down her face, and he held on for a long while.

His breath caught in his throat, and he pushed away. "I'm sorry. I . . ."

Leah wiped away her tears. "I haven't told anyone else that. I know you don't trust Asmodeus, but he and Legion are enemies. He's caught up in this just as much as we are, and if he's willing to take him down, then I want him on our side. Do you think you can join us again? As a friend?"

Gabe smirked and looked at the ground. "I missed you guys. The other chefs don't compare. Even so, I don't know if I can trust a demon."

"You don't have to trust him. Not yet. But just know Legion is his enemy too, and we all want to take him down."

"I can agree with that. A truce, maybe?" Gabe said, eyeing the gray sky.

Leah smiled. "Truce."

CHAPTER 20
SURVIVAL ETHICS

"Where is she?" Leah asked, lying down on the sofa and staring up at the ceiling. It had been nearly five hours since they'd left the training field. And since then, the three of them were forced to clean up the cafeteria after dragging in sand.

"I don't know," Isaac said. "But she deserves a good punch from you when she gets back."

Gabe rubbed his shoulder, wincing as he asked, "You don't think something happened to her, right?"

"Ha," Leah said. "Doubt it. She probably snuck off somewhere and took a nap. I'd do the same, especially after training with someone like Yuki."

The doorknob of the apartment clicked, and Sarah tiptoed in. She paused when she saw all of them on the couch and smiled. "Oh, uh. Hi."

Her hair was a mess, and she was in a new uniform that looked to be a size smaller than she normally wore.

Leah sat up. "And where were you?"

"Studying with Yuki." Sarah said, turning into the kitchen and grabbing a glass of water.

Gabe let out a laugh, grinning at Isaac. "Studying? It's eleven."

Sarah grinned and plopped down on the sofa next to Leah. "Yeah, and?"

"And," Isaac started, "you can't keep that smile off your face. While you were 'studying,' the rest of us were stuck cleaning the cafeteria."

"Pretty sure you were doing more than 'studying,'" Gabe joined in, smirking.

Sarah looked between him and Leah and sat up. "Oh look. You two are talking again?"

Leah pushed herself up. "Yep, we made peace. Yada yada, are you going to tell us about this study session, or are we going to have to beat it out of you?"

"Ugh, come on," Sarah groaned, her cheeks turning red. "You're going to make me kiss and tell?"

Isaac let out a laugh as he stood up and walked into the kitchen, leaning against the counter. "That is exactly what we're doing. Especially after you ghosted us."

Sarah rolled her eyes. "Okay, fine! We hooked up! Happy?"

Leah jumped up, nearly falling out of the couch. "Hold on. What? You and Yuki hooked up? Details. Now!"

"Really? Can't it wait? I'm tired," Sarah asked, finishing her glass of water.

"Tired? We're tired. While you two were off canoodling, we were cleaning tables for the past three hours," Isaac said.

"And the floors." Gabe added.

"And the trays." Leah said.

Sarah raised an eyebrow. "Canoodling? Really?"

Isaac cracked his knuckles. "I might not win in a fair fight, but it'll be worth trying."

"Okay. Fine, fine!" She paused and cleared her throat. "We went back to her place. She went over a couple of old texts on *Malchut* concepts. Did you know she's our age and already a Sage? Apparently, she could use *Malchut* as a baby. They shipped her off to Desmond, that Sage of *Netzach*, before she could even walk. They say her ability with *Malchut* outranks even the Queens, and no one knows why."

Leah crossed her arms. "Quit tiptoeing around it."

"Fine. Okay. So, she started showing me some of the more advanced stances for *Malchut.* She wanted me to get the stance just right. I can't remember if it was her or me who started, but one thing led to another. Anyway, we went over a few more . . . uh . . . stances after that."

"Damn," Gabe said. "I mean, good on you."

"So, are you two a thing now?" Isaac asked.

"Maybe? Maybe not. I don't know. Does it matter?" She shrugged.

"Well, do you want to see her again?" Leah asked.

Sarah bit her lip and looked down. "I mean, obviously."

"The rest of us can run off tomorrow," Isaac said. "If you're looking for another one-on-one session."

"Okay, okay," Gabe said, raising both his hands. "Let's give her some space before she tries one of those moves on us."

Leah met Sarah's gaze, and the two of them laughed.

"I didn't mean one of *those* moves!" Gabe said, his cheeks reddening.

They all fell into a fit of laughter as they readied for bed. As Leah walked back to her room, she elbowed Sarah and said, "Hey, I'm happy for you. Seriously."

"Can I ask something?" Leah said as she sat down at the marble table in the black abyss.

Asmodeus turned around, an eyebrow raised, as he inspected the room. He sat in the chair across from her and waved his arm. A large teapot and two teacups appeared in front of him, filled with a steaming tea. "Didn't know you could manifest this room. What is it?"

"Mr. K. The demon that used Gabe. Why did he do that?"

He sipped his tea and stared off into the abyss. "Do you know how humans treat cattle?"

Leah frowned but remained quiet, waiting for him to go on.

"They treat them poorly. Sure, they tell everyone how well they are cared after, but at the end of the day, they slit their throats and use their flesh for food. They are your energy, and no one bats an eye."

"But demons toy with humans. They haunt them and torture them."

"Most demons don't. They siphon off the energy they need, deliver it to their Kyem, and no one knows better. But the energy you give can be so addictive, and some of us defected, seeking energy for themselves instead."

"How many people did you hurt? How many children did you trick into killing their parents?"

Asmodeus frowned, and his nostrils flared. "Our people were dying, and I did what it took to get them the energy they needed."

"You're a monster."

Asmodeus pushed his chair back and stood. "What would you have done? Let everyone you know die slow deaths while your kind live in abundance?"

"I would have found a different way," Leah said,

jumping to her feet to meet him eye to eye. "One where we worked together."

Asmodeus scoffed. "The famine made us desperate. You've never seen your world coming to an end, but you are going to sit here and lecture me about working together? Your kind is even worse than us when it comes to working amongst each other, let alone with a whole other species. You continue to destroy your planet with no regard to its life, for the sake of resources. Soon enough, you'll be just like us. No, you'll be worse." He rested his hands against the table, calming his breath before sitting back down and folding his arms.

Leah joined him, staring at him across the table as they sat there in silence for a long while.

"So," Leah finally spoke. "What's gonna happen after? When we defeat Legion, I mean. What then?"

Asmodeus looked at her with his dark, starry eyes. "I don't know. My Kyem might all be dead for all I know. It's been too long since I've been to the Valley."

"If we win, you'll be their leader again, right?" Leah asked.

Asmodeus looked down at his hands. "I don't know."

"Well, I need your word. I need you to promise you'll get them to stop using us like cattle."

He inspected his hands, running a thumb along his smooth skin. "I am becoming something different. No longer the demon I was. I am a tool of vengeance, somehow entwined with you. I will do everything in my power to stop Legion. But when that is all done, I don't know if anything will be left of me."

Leah sat up, leaning in to stare at him in the eyes. "That's not an answer. If you live, will you seek peace with us?"

Asmodeus picked up a teacup and sipped from it. "I

can't give you the answer you want. I no longer speak for my Kyem."

"Fine," Leah said, clenching her jaw. "We'll cross that bridge after we kill Legion." She stood, and as she did, the table fell away, and she slipped into darkness.

CHAPTER 21

SPECIAL MISSION

"Ready for another day with Eli?" Sarah asked as they walked down the long hall to the meditation lab.

"Now that we're in the Astral, it should be better," Isaac said. "Then we need to find a way into the woods."

"Anything is better than lying in that thing for hours doing nothing," Gabe said.

Leah looked at Gabe. "And you're sure you can get those ingredients from the kitchens while we get the rest?"

"Yeah, shouldn't be a problem."

When they stepped inside, the four of them were not only greeted by Eli and Sandeep but two burly Black Bishops dressed in full black tactical gear and dark sunglasses. They both locked on to Leah and approached before she could even speak.

"Leah Ackerman?" the taller of the two, with a full head of black hair and a deep voice, said.

"Yes?"

"Change of plans, you're coming with us," the other one, who was bald with an orangish beard and thicker frame, said.

134

"Where?" Leah asked, looking back at her friends.

"Confidential," the tall one said. "Orders from the Queen. Let's go."

Eli approached them and smiled. "The rest of you are with us today. We've got to get you ready to get through that door." He eyed Leah and gave her a slight nod.

"Fine," Leah said, eyeing her friends. "Don't wait up for me tonight. I don't want you to miss out on any plans because I'm not there."

Sarah got the hint first and nodded, followed by the others.

Leah joined the two Bishops as they headed out of the lab and rode the elevator up to the top floor. The doors opened to a massive penthouse off on the left with large glass windows looking out at the floors below. There was no doubt in her mind that was Queen Micah's quarters.

They went right out a set of glass doors and onto the roof, where a helicopter was starting up. Wind picked up before she could shout out her question, and the Bishops pushed her along as they crouched and hopped inside the helicopter. They strapped her in and put headphones over her ears, which drowned out the sound.

They flew for what felt like a half hour before landing in a small airport in the middle of nowhere. Aside from the SUV and a small jet on the runway, the place looked completely abandoned.

The two Bishops escorted her out of the helicopter and up the stairs of the jet without a word. Inside, it was beyond luxurious, with large white leather seats and gold inlays, as well as a white table with an inlet tray filled with pastries and fruits. There were about eight seats altogether, each with the ability to swivel, allowing complete privacy or turning to face everyone else.

"Grab something if you want," the larger Bishop said,

grabbing several pastries himself. "Then buckle up. We've got a four-hour flight ahead of us."

Leah joined him at the table, grabbing a chocolate croissant before asking, "Where are we going?"

The tall Bishop closed the door to the plane, locking it in place, then said, "El Paso, Texas. The Queen is waiting for you there."

Leah buckled in without another word and waited for takeoff. After they were in the air, the Bishops went up front to the cockpit, closing the door behind them. Every once in a while, Leah heard them laughing, but otherwise she felt like she was on the plane completely alone.

She unbuckled and paced the entirety of the plane, looking out the windows as they flew over mountains. Why did Queen Helen need her in Texas, of all places?

She grabbed another pastry and a mug of lukewarm coffee after a couple of hours of pacing, hoping her mind would stop wandering. They never said it was Queen Helen she was going to see. What if Queen Micah, or worse Queen Jan Xie, had called for her? She'd be hundreds of miles away from anyone she trusted.

Too late now to panic, Asmodeus said. *If things go sour, I'll be there to help.*

"Well, at least I have that going for me."

They landed an hour later, and they escorted Leah into the back of a black Lincoln SUV. As she slipped inside, her shoulders relaxed as her eyes landed on Queen Helen sitting inside. She sat across from Helen, with the bearded Bishop closing the door and pounding on the roof for the car to move.

"Good to see you made it in one piece," Helen said. She wore a long black trench coat on top of a satin black pantsuit. Next to her, her two katanas rested, ready for her to grab them at a moment's notice.

"My Queen." Leah said, trying to sit up straight.

Helen waved her off. "At ease. Apologies for the short notice, but I only had a small window to make your extraction go unnoticed."

Leah frowned. "Unnoticed? Isn't flying off in a helicopter going to be noticeable?"

"True, but there were several individuals who might question or stop my orders who were having a meeting when I made the call. The paperwork only showed me summoning my Bishops for a mission, which falls under standard protocol. You are conveniently scheduled all day with Eli and shouldn't be bothered."

"So, what's the mission?" Leah asked as the SUV turned onto the highway.

The Queen peered past Leah, toward the driver, then she pressed a button and the divider slid up. "I have a small group of Rooks willing to boost our support in the upcoming vote. I'd wished for more at this point, so I need to prepare for the worst-case scenario."

"You mean if we lose?" Leah asked.

"Jaime is proving to be very persuasive. He's also stayed at headquarters to spout off his concerns with the shifter front. I'd hoped he'd go back at least once before the vote."

Leah leaned back and crossed her arms. "Legion is just as bad as these shifters, if not worse. If he wins, we'll be open for who knows what from Legion."

"Just as bad? Seems his little speeches have reached you too. Which is why you're here—to help me prepare for the worst."

Leah stared out the window. "Why me? What can I do?"

Helen cocked her head and smiled. "Eli told me you escaped his Astral trap. He spoke of an energy and symbols that he hadn't seen before. Luckily, he came to me first, since this information in the wrong hands could be, well, terrible for us."

Leah frowned. "What information? What do you mean?"

"Constance noted it first. Your ability with dreaming. We have little on them, but Eli saw more than that. What you displayed with him put everything in place for me. Someone with that energy and ability only comes once or twice every century."

"But that wasn't me. That was a reflection. A different version," Leah said.

"And still, you wielded it," Helen replied. "Different version or not, Leah Ackerman, you are an Immortal Witch, and we are heading to their coven."

CHAPTER 22
IMMORTAL WITCHES

Leah picked at her fingernails, watching the desert pass by. They'd already driven out into the middle of nowhere, and the sun had set. "But what does that mean?" She finally asked, turning back to Helen. "Immortal Witch? What, like casting spells?"

Helen took a deep breath. "We have limited information about them, to be honest. They are a small number of individuals who keep to themselves. Other Queens have tried in the past to contact them, but even they get turned down. But with you, I might have a chance to bring them on our side."

"But I'm not one of them. I don't know what to say."

"I just need you to be you," Helen said, reaching forward and patting Leah's knee. "You have the tenacity to make people listen when others can't. They won't listen to me, but you have a better chance. They need to know Legion's threat, and if we can't stop this vote, we'll need all the help we can get."

Leah rubbed the back of her neck. "Right, okay. What should I expect?"

"Their leader is a high priestess named Cora. She's the one we need to get on our side. Treat her like you would Queen Micah."

The name Cora rang a bell in Leah's mind. She had heard it before, but she was unable to quite pinpoint where.

The SUV slowed, and they pulled into the parking lot of a two-story brick building. Leah frowned, looking out both windows, noting that there was nothing but desert in both directions.

"What is this place?" she asked.

"Old biker pit-stop," Helen said. "All in one place to refuel, eat, drink, and get tattoos."

The Bishop got up and held open the door for the pair.

As Helen stepped out, she nodded. "Thank you, Solomon. Wait here."

Leah stepped out into the dimly lit parking lot and looked up at the bright red neon sign, which said *Spiral Ink*. Below that were the words *Tattoo Parlor*, just above a familiar red door.

I don't like this, Asmodeus whispered.

Helen turned back to Leah. "Something wrong?"

"No," Leah said. "Just that I've seen this door before. In the Astral Realm with Eli."

"Ah. That's a good sign." Helen started toward the door, waving Leah along.

Leah paused for a moment before joining Helen, who opened the door.

As it opened, the voices inside stopped. They stepped into a bright shop with pictures of various Americana and brightly colored tattoos covering the brick walls.

The scent of booze hit Leah's nostrils the moment she stepped inside, and she immediately took her attention off the decor as several people stared back at her. She'd expected some kind of biker gang, all dressed in black leather with ink covering their arms. Instead, the assortment of people in various forms of dress, from suits to short shorts, looked more like a group of random individuals. Yet, they all had the same beauty emanating off them.

"Hey, can't you see we are closed?" A short Indian woman asked, glaring at them.

"Yeah, this place isn't for you," another shouted.

Others joined in, standing up and glaring at them.

Leah stepped back, everything in her urging them to leave, but Helen stood firm. Leah eyed the people in the room, starting with a teenager, no older than herself, straddling a chair with what looked to be a fresh shoulder tattoo. She looked like she was too perfect, with long rich brown hair and skin that seemed to glow. They all were too perfect, Leah noted as she looked at each of them, as if she'd walked into a room of models who'd spent hours with a team doing their makeup and hair.

A tall woman with brown eyes that almost looked black and long thick locks stood in the middle of the group. She raised her hand, and the rest of them stopped talking instantly.

"Apologies for showing up unannounced, High Priestess Cora," Helen said, giving Cora a slight bow as she lifted her hand to her chest. "But it's an urgent matter."

Cora eyed her up and down, her lips pursed as if she were a parent scolding a child. "Helen Nielsen. You're interrupting our ritual." She waved her hand. "We want nothing with you."

Leah firmly clenched her jaw and squeezed her hands. How could they talk to Helen like this? How was Helen not correcting her for the disrespect? She was a Black Queen, not some Pawn to be waved off. The others in the room puffed their chests and sharpened their faces. A palpable density filled the air as everyone else in the room flanked behind Cora.

But Helen stood her ground. "Please, Cora, I wouldn't show up like this if it wasn't important."

Cora stepped forward, and she somehow seemed to grow taller with each step. "You showed up unannounced because you know I would have rejected your request otherwise."

A man in a long tattered trench coat stepped out from the back room, peering from behind Cora with bright green eyes. "Well, well, well, will I be damned." He spoke in a thick Irish accent as he joined the rest of them, his bright ginger hair and ageless face matching the others. "It's good to see you again."

He looked familiar, but she struggled to place him, his features hazy in her mind. "Have I met you before?"

The man stepped around another one of the witches, a tall, broad-shouldered man, and said, "Not formally. We've crossed paths before, but it was too late."

Too late? Leah frowned. She looked at Helen, noting a small smile appear on her lips before vanishing.

"What's your name, young lady?" Cora asked as the feeling of her looming presence vanished.

"Leah Ackerman."

Cora looked back at the man in the tattered trench coat and nodded. "Very well. We will move into the back office for a private meeting. She turned her head to the muscular man. "Omari?"

"Yes?" the man asked, stepping forward.

"Please proceed with the ritual. There is more here than meets the eye."

Omari rolled up his sleeve, revealing a thick single-line

tattoo that coiled around his arm. It reminded Leah of the Tefillin her dad would sometimes wear when praying in the mornings. Cora stepped up to him and placed her hand over it. The density in the air thickened for a moment, then vanished altogether, as if Cora was willing it into Omari. A few seconds later, he nodded and headed to the back door. The others joined him. All but the young woman straddling the seat.

The Irishman appeared back in the doorway and snapped his fingers at her. "Oi! You're coming with us."

She frowned, looking at Leah and Helen, then Cora, before pushing herself up and joining the rest of the group in the back room.

"Follow me," Cora said, turning and walking through the same back door.

Cold air and a strong earthy smell hit Leah the moment they stepped into the tight hallway with dark gray walls and black doors on either side.

They entered one of the black doors into a small office filled with old books, deep red leather chairs, and a large mahogany desk.

"Sit," Cora said, gesturing toward the chairs as she took her place behind the desk. As they did, she asked. "What is it you want?"

Helen looked at Leah, her eyebrow arched.

Leah took the hint and leaned forward. "We need your help. There is a demon, and he—"

"I did not ask for your Pawn to speak for you, Helen," Cora said, glaring at the Queen. "If you wish to ask me something, then I want to hear it from your tongue."

Helen nodded and cleared her throat. "Listen, Cora, I know the Infinity Board and the Immortal Witches haven't had the best relationship, but it's imperative that we join forces, if only for this one fight. Legion is the strongest demon humanity has ever faced." There was a plea in Helen's voice that Leah had never heard before.

"You know," Cora said, leaning back in her chair, smiling. "You Mystics have come crying to this coven ever since you were founded. You approached me for assistance last time with your little demon problem, and I didn't help you then, so why would I help now? Your Great Eagle would be ashamed of how little you seem to be able to take care of yourselves. Why would we care about earthly affairs? Our duty is to the Astral Plane, and the Astral Plane alone."

Leah dug her nails into her palms. Cora didn't care. She was just as bad as the other Mystics who couldn't see what Legion really was. He'd been the hand that killed so many that she loved, and her disinterest was just another stab in the gut.

Helen shook her head and placed a hand on the desk. "Demons have to cross through the Astral Plane to get to our dimension."

"Aye," Cora said. "And we have killed the ones we've caught trying. Our main purpose is maintaining balance in every dimension of the Astral Plane, while yours is ensuring demons and other things that slip through don't wreak havoc here. Our watchful eye can't be everywhere all the time, but you and your numbers can. So, you do your job, and we'll do ours."

She paused as if expecting some remark from Helen. When none came, she continued, "The Immortal Witch coven has lasted as much as humanity itself, mainly because we know our duty, we focus on our tasks, and we let the others be."

Leah glared at Cora, and the words escaped her mouth before she could think. "Why did you allow this meeting if you aren't willing to help us?"

Cora turned toward Leah, her smile widening as her eyes glowed a brilliant violet. Pressure built in Leah's chest. Pressure that wasn't the serpents of *Malchut* or any of the other wells, it was something else, something more volatile.

"Because of you, little lost witch."

<h1 style="text-align:center">CHAPTER 23
PRIVATE MEETING</h1>

Leah jumped out of her chair as the surrounding room shifted and changed. Books rippled, replaced with rotten replicas covered in yellowed moss. The ceiling opened up, a fissure that looked decades old peering out into a barren desert behind Cora. The seat that held Helen tumbled to the floor, no Black Queen to be seen.

"You took me to the Astral Plane," Leah whispered.

"So, Frank was right," Cora said, steepling her fingers in her moss-covered chair. Her eyes slipped down to Leah's arm for a moment, the markings clear now.

Leah backed up against the door, placing her arm behind her back. "But how did you . . . how am I here?"

"You're in a circle, dear. One I carved decades ago. Do you think we witches aren't prepared?"

"Take me back," Leah protested.

"Not until we chat."

Leah looked over at the crumbled chair where Queen Helen should've been. What was she seeing right now? Did the two of them vanish, or were they both passed out in their chairs?

"Don't worry," Cora said. "I've made time slower in this

layer. We'll be back before she even notices we're gone. I just have a few things to ask. Please, sit."

Now that the Queen wasn't present, Cora's tone was much softer as she gestured to the chair. Leah hesitated for a moment before sitting down in the aged chair.

"You have the potential. I can practically smell it off you. You see entities who cross into the material realm, yes? Ghosts? Monsters?"

The image of the boy peeking out from behind the bookshelves surfaced in her mind. "I have."

"And you clearly know about the Astral Realm. Do you come here in dreams? See things and places you haven't been to? Listen in on conversations you later find out are real?"

Leah shifted in her seat, recalling all the conversations, chasing after Paige as she was kidnapped, and Legion consuming Asmodeus. "Is that what you Immortal Witches do?"

Cora nodded. "Frank reported seeing you on one of his Astral walks. Unfortunately, you were already a Square. We don't meddle with Mystic affairs often, lest we get people like Helen showing up uninvited." She paused and leaned forward on her desk. "But now for the real question: when you are in these dream states, are you physically present, or more of an amorphous watcher?"

"Physically present. I think? But like, I wake back up in bed."

"Good. And my last question. Have you ever successfully interacted with these visions? Changed something or talked to someone?"

Cora peered at her with violet eyes, which felt nearly the same as when someone looked at her with *Tiferet*. She felt small and naked in her chair. "Yes," she said, the image of her gripping on to Asmodeus as he was being consumed by Legion flashing in her mind.

"Show me," Cora said.

I don't like this, Asmodeus said.

"Show you? Show you what?" Leah asked.

Cora held out a hand, palm up. "Grab my hand and recall one of these times. I would like to see it for myself."

Don't, Asmodeus said.

Leah bit her lip. Something gave her the impression that she could trust this woman. That if she was who Cora thought she would be, then she would be on Leah's side. She would fight with them. Leah's hand wrapped around Cora's, and she thought back to the train station, lit by candles, and the man floating in the air.

The room melted away, and Cora stood from her chair as yelps of pain echoed off the walls. They stood against the wall as an echo of Leah appeared and started talking to the voice from the shadows. Cora's hand tightened around Leah's as Legion pulled himself from the dark and transformed into the thing that would try to eat Asmodeus.

She pulled her hand away as the echo of Leah reached for Asmodeus, and the room transformed back into the office. Cora dropped into her chair, panting as she eyed the markings on Leah's arm.

"He's still there?" she asked. "Inside you?"

Leah looked down at the floor and nodded. She felt the glow of Cora's eyes on her, peering through her.

"You possess the skills to become an Immortal Witch. Maybe with enough training, a witch who could even best me."

"So what? You're saying I'm immortal?"

"Gods no," Cora laughed. "You simply have the potential. Your connection to the Astral Realm is higher than most witches. Some still can't interact with beings in the

Astral Realm while in their body. But here you are. A one-in-a-millennia prodigy, even before the initiation ritual."

"Initiation ritual?" Leah asked.

"You actually walked in on one," Cora said. "We don't get many new recruits. Funny that you seem to find us on the one day in decades that we bring one into the fold."

"The girl getting the tattoo—that's the initiation ritual?"

"It's the start of one," Cora said, extending her arm forward and rolling up her sleeve. A pair of tattooed eyes with swirls in place of irises stared back at Leah. "This was mine."

Leah's eyes widened as she traced the spirals with her eyes. It was the same two spirals, rotating in opposite directions, as the ones tattooed on the back of her reflection in Eli's astral trap.

"The spirals catch your eye?" Cora asked, leaning forward. "You've seen them before? Haven't you?"

Leah nodded, but words failed to come.

Cora leaned back in her seat, eyeing the place where Helen would be, back in the material plane. "I won't lie to you, Leah Ackerman. Our coven needs someone like you. Your potential could lift this coven a hundredfold. You'd learn and see so much more than what those Mystics know."

Leah glanced at her hands and at the marking that signified Asmodeus. "But why me? Why am I like this?"

A small smile spread across Cora's face. "If only we knew. The Tree chooses its guardians. But here you are, dual paths given from the Tree and a soul intertwined with a being from worlds away. You are an enigma, child. Something I haven't seen in my centuries on this earth." Cora stood up and frowned, pausing for a long moment before adding, "An enigma I can't overlook. I will give you a choice.

Join us. Become an Immortal Witch and learn secrets you couldn't even fathom. Or stay as a Mystic, among your friends until the day you die."

Leah's heart pounded in her chest. With a simple nod to High Priestess, her whole life could change again.

But she'd leave everything she knew and everyone she knew. Could she leave her friends?

"Huh," Cora said, cutting the silence. "Nearly every other witch I've asked that to has jumped on the offer. But you."

Asmodeus murmured in her mind. *Don't take her offer. Something feels—*

"You will be silent, demon," Cora hissed.

Leah furrowed her brow. "You can hear him?"

Cora's eyes flashed violet, and she waved her arm. Tiny tendrils of purple light streamed out from Leah's arm, and in seconds Asmodeus, in his human form and bound to a metal chair, appeared beside her.

Leah jumped out of her chair as Asmodeus fought against his restraints.

"I could make this permanent, you know. Keep him bound to this chair for all eternity. This plane bends to our will," Cora said.

"You can't keep me here forever, witch," Asmodeus growled. "Your tricks wane, even now."

"I said silence." Cora waved her hands again, and little purple serpents wrapped around his neck and mouth. She looked back at Leah and gestured toward her chair. "Please, sit. Let us talk."

Leah slowly sat back down and eyed Asmodeus as he fought against the restraints. "We came here to talk about Legion. The one you saw in my memory. Helen is trying to band the Mystics together to face him, but the others don't see it that way. There's a vote, one that could force us to give up preparing our fight against him to face a threat of shifters."

Cora rolled her eyes and laughed. "Petty politics."

"I think it's more than that," Leah said. "I think Legion has already infiltrated the Infinity Board and is using his demons to sway the vote."

"And does your Queen know?" Cora asked.

"Queen Helen? I think so, but I have a small group of people I trust. People whom Legion would be less likely to corrupt. We can't detect these demons."

Cora cocked her head. "Not even with your gold eyes? What do you call it? Tifara?"

"*Tiferet*," Leah said. "And no, we can't seem to detect them. It's like they go dormant. They already attacked us once, killing half the team investigating him. Including my uncle."

"I see."

"So, will you help us?"

Cora's eyes fell, and she rested her hands in her lap. "When my coven tangles in Mystic affairs, things never turn out well. We aren't foot soldiers. Nor do our abilities fare well on the material plane. There are so few of us and so many places and beings beyond this world that need us."

Leah's shoulders dropped. "So, you won't."

There was a moment of silence, then Cora said, "If you were to join us, then your strength would allow us to make room to investigate this Legion, and his impact to the Astral Realm. If he poses a risk, especially to the Tree, we will destroy him."

Asmodeus struggled in his seat, groaning beneath the serpent restrained. He stared at Leah, his eyes wide.

"Can you let him talk?" Leah asked.

Cora snapped her fingers, and the bindings slithered back, holding him in place but releasing his mouth. He took a moment to breathe, looked at Cora and then Leah, and said, "Her offer is worth considering. You've lost your bond, and there's no certainty you'll get it back. This could get you the power we need."

"You've lost your connection?" Cora asked.

"I'm getting it back," Leah said. "No matter what." She looked at Asmodeus. "But what about you? Or the what if she doesn't think Legion is a threat to the Astral?"

"There will be," Asmodeus said. "Sooner or later, you Watchers will be dragged into this war."

Cora chuckled. "A demon fighting for us. Leah Ackerman, you truly are an enigma."

"Not for you. For my Kyem. For revenge," Asmodeus hissed.

"Too bad you won't be around to see it. If she joins, that is. You'd be useful."

"What do you mean?" Leah questioned.

Violet serpents appeared on Cora's arm, slithering to her hand as the woman inspected them. "The initiation ritual would purify you, burning away any bonds, pacts, or connections. This parasite of a demon wouldn't survive."

"I . . . I can't then," Leah said, looking at Asmodeus. "I saved him for a reason."

Asmodeus laughed, shaking his head. "Selfless Leah at it again."

"What is that supposed to mean?" Leah asked.

"It means you're losing a real opportunity. A chance for power beyond anything you could imagine. Power you could use to stand a chance against Legion."

"No," Leah said, turning from Asmodeus and catching Cora's eye. "Put him back. I decline your offer. He won't die. Not yet."

"Stubborn child," Asmodeus whispered.

"And my friends," she said, glancing over at Asmodeus. "If you prevent me from helping, they'll die."

"Hmm," Cora looked between Leah and Asmodeus, staring at something between them as her eyes unfocused. "How strange."

"What?" Leah asked.

"The bond you two have is not normal. Your souls are blending, can't you tell? He's becoming more human. And you? Something else." Cora turned her back to Leah, looking out through the crack in the wall. "So be it, but I will still urge you to learn to control your dreams. You don't need rituals or Trees to access the Astral Realm, and the sooner you learn to control it, the safer it will be for everyone."

Cora waved her hand once more, and the sickly yellow of the Astral Realm faded away.

CHAPTER 24

REGROUP

"Leah," Queen Helen said, reaching for her arm, "There's no need to get heated."

Leah blinked, her eyes adjusting to the light in the office. Leah was seated back in her chair, as was Cora, who turned to look at Queen Helen as if the conversation between her and Leah hadn't happened.

Helen let go of Leah and leaned forward. "Cora, there has to be something we can work out."

Cora interlaced her fingers and rested them on the table. "Unless you have proof that Legion is harming the Astral Plane, we will keep our affairs separate. That is my decision."

"What proof do you need?" Helen asked. "I could put my best Bishops to work. We could—"

"We will look for ourselves," Cora interrupted. "We don't need more of you venturing into places you shouldn't be. Or have the Mystics forgotten the last time that happened?"

Helen cleared her throat and stood from her seat. "Very well, High Priestess Cora. I see we will not come to an agreement tonight. I'd hope you see the truth before it is too late." She turned and walked out the door without another word.

"You're making a mistake," Leah said, glaring at Cora as she got to her feet. "I hope you know that." Leah turned and headed to the door.

"Things could have been different," Cora called behind her. "For you."

Helen didn't speak as they got back into the car, or for most of the way back to the airport. She'd even ordered both Bishops to sit up front while Leah and she rode in the back.

Leah watched as the dark desert slowly shifted back into city and illuminated highways until Helen finally broke the silence.

"Cora spoke to you. Didn't she?"

Leah looked away from the window and at Helen. "She did. How'd you know?"

Helen nodded and let out a slight laugh. "Thought so. There was a moment after she called you a witch. She tried hiding it, but there was a change in her attitude. I take it the conversation didn't go well?"

"She offered me to join them. To become a witch. She said I'd make their coven strong."

"Figures she'd try to recruit you. Did she ask about your dreams? Or about Asmodeus?"

"Yes, she did," Leah said, biting her lip as she recounted the conversation. "She did something, and we went back to the time I saved him."

"Did that bother her to see?"

"No. I don't think so," Leah said. "But she was clear that he'd die if I became a witch."

Helen raised an eyebrow. "Really. She told you that? How would he die?"

"The initiation would 'purify' me, whatever that means."

"I see. Surprising that she'd want you so bad but risk telling you that. Perhaps my suspicions are correct."

"Suspicions?"

"I suspect she knew you wouldn't take that offer. Not if Asmodeus would die. But she also didn't kill him on the spot. So, he's not a threat. Not like Legion."

Leah shifted her gaze toward her hands. "Is that why you brought me here? To see if I, or Asmodeus, am still a threat to you?"

The Queen nodded. "It was one reason, yes."

Leah paused, thinking through her next words carefully. "I could have joined them. I almost did."

"You wouldn't betray your friends like that." Helen smiled. "You are Elizabeth's daughter. That much I know."

Leah stared out the window, frustrated by how she was so easily used. Not that Queen Helen had lied to her, but the fact that she was always several steps ahead and Leah was racing to catch up. As the signs to the airport passed by, she asked. "So, what now?"

"We move forward. The vote is fast approaching."

"Leah!" Sarah's voice called as something shook her awake.

"Stop," she mumbled, attempting to roll over.

"You're gonna be late for training. And I want to hear all about where you've been."

Leah slowly opened one eye, then the other, dragging herself out of bed. She hadn't come back to headquarters until late, after all the travel back, which she'd done without the Queen. After getting dressed, Leah stepped out of her bedroom, finding Sarah, Gabe, and Isaac waiting by the living room.

"Dude, you're killing me here," Sarah said as she dramatically collapsed onto the couch.

"We're going to be late," Isaac said, eyeing the clock.

"Walk and talk people," Sarah said, hopping up and hooking arms with Leah.

She filled them in as much as she could as Sarah dragged her along. By the time they stepped out of the elevator, they'd gotten as much of the story as Leah could muster.

"Holly shit!" Sarah said, yanking her along.

"That's one hell of a story." Isaac said, nodding.

"At least we know why you have those dreams now," Gabe said.

"Yeah, I think that explains how I pulled all of you into the Astral too. I mean, she did the exact thing to me."

"Too bad they won't join us. We could really use them," Isaac said.

"We just need to keep pushing forward," Leah said. She paused and looked up and down the hall. "Speaking of, where are we with the ingredients for Nykima?"

"Well, now that we have Gabe on our side," she said, elbowing him. "We got everything we could from the kitchen."

Leah caught Gabe's eyes and smiled. "Awesome. And the rest?"

"Still need it," Isaac said.

"If I distract Yuki," Sarah said. "You three could slip off into the woods during training. I could be very persuasive."

"If we get everything today, we can do this tonight. We need that ghost now more than ever," Leah said.

CHAPTER 25
ANXIETY

"**A**gain!" Eli shouted, standing at the edge of a massive obstacle course filled with odd angles and shapes that could never exist outside the Astral Plane.

Leah and her friends had just raced through it, dodging and leaping through massive chasms as if their lives depended on it.

Leah held on to her side as Isaac doubled over. Both Sarah and Gabe had already collapsed on the ground, staring up at the sky, hyperventilating.

"Am I dead?" Sarah asked.

"No," Eli said. "You're just not used to training your spirit. Now, get up and go again. Entities here won't let you take a break. They'll kill you on the spot."

"Wait. I have a question," Isaac said, forcing himself upright.

"What?" Eli snapped.

"What kind of entities are we talking about?"

Eli glared at Isaac. "The Astral Realm is a place for spirits, ideas, nightmares, and things beyond your wildest imagination, all hungry for your energy. There are hundreds of layers and worlds to get lost in here, and if we use too much of our wells here, we'll vanish. It doesn't matter what entity you might encounter here, the only thing that matters is if you see one, you run. Now, get off your ass and go. Again!"

They didn't have a chance to ask another question as Eli thrust his hand forward and let out a burst of *Malchut* that crumbled the platform beneath the four of them.

Leah rushed forward, grabbing her friends and pulling them through a waterfall of sparkling light and onto a platform filled with strange yellowed plants. Eli chased after them, throwing out tiny blasts of *Malchut* that triggered the platform to either collapse or make the plants react and try to ensnare them.

After what felt like days, they pulled themselves out from the meditation chambers, stretching and rubbing stiff muscles.

Eli closed in on Leah as the others started toward the changing room and whispered, "I got the report back from the Queen. So, it is true, you've got talents very few have. The sooner we get you through that door, the better it will be for all of us."

"Then help me get my friends ready," she said back to him.

A genuine smile spread across his face, and he nodded.

"Got it," Isaac said, holding up a small wriggling snake. He and Leah had successfully snuck off into the woods near the end of practice as Sarah pulled Yuki aside. And now they kneeled in the wet, fallen leaves in the middle of a darkening forest.

"Perfect," Leah remarked, presenting a jar filled with three large snails. "Toss it in here and we'll head back. Gabe should have had enough time to grab the rest of the ingredients and find Nykima."

"Poor little guy," Isaac said, dropping the snake in the jar. "I can't imagine he's going to come out of this alive."

Leah closed the lid and pushed herself up. "When I was at the voodoo town, they rubbed a live chicken all over my body, then killed it in front of me. Who knows what this ritual will be, but if it helps, then I'll do it."

Isaac shivered. "I didn't need to know that."

Leah grinned and shrugged. "Well, now you do."

He laughed and looked down at the ground, his shoulders slumping.

"Everything alright?" Leah asked.

"Yeah. I think . . . I don't know."

"What is it? You can tell me." She gestured around them. "I mean, here is the best place, right?"

Isaac nodded. "It's been hard. I mean, I know it's been hard for everyone, but I feel like I'm getting nowhere compared to everyone else. Ever since Sid died, I've just felt lost."

The thought of Sid standing next to her uncle, chains tearing through them both, flashed through her mind. *Go! Get out of here!*

She knew his pain all too well. Leah jumped forward, dropping the jar to the soft ground and hugging him.

"I'm lost too," she said. "I feel like I'm simply going through the motions."

"You do? But you look like you have it all together," he said, his voice shaking as he hugged her back.

"Eric was everything I had left." The pain in her chest tightened, and tears fell from her cheeks. "Without him . . . I . . . I don't know what to do."

Isaac pulled away and looked her in the face. "We fight. Together. You're not in this alone. Not while I'm here."

Leah nodded. "You, Sarah, and Gabe, you all keep me from falling apart. I wouldn't leave you. I couldn't."

"But what now? If we all feel so lost, then are we doing the right thing?" Isaac asked.

"I don't know," Leah said. "But it's better than doing nothing right. We get our bonds back, and we help Helen with the vote. Those seem like the right things to do."

"Yeah," Isaac said, wiping away a tear and picking up the jar. "Guess the only thing to do is keep moving forward."

"Oh, my god." Sarah gagged. "What is she doing in there?"

Leah covered her nose as she stuffed the bottom of the door to their apartment with towels, careful not to irritate her freshly cut finger. She looked back to the bathroom, where Nykima had taken all the ingredients, including a few drops of her blood. "I don't know, but if she keeps it up, someone's going to come knocking."

"Smells like she burned those poor things alive," Isaac said.

The bathroom door opened and Nykima rolled out, carrying a couple of small plastic bags filled with a dark ashy powder. "Okay, carry a small bit of this in your hand. If anyone gives you trouble, blow it in their face and say, *oublie moi*. That should put them in a trance long enough for us to get what we need and leave."

"Sounds easy," Sarah said, grabbing a bag. "Leah and I will get the book while you three take care of security. Leah finds the thing the ghost is attached to, and we run."

"Don't forget my things," Nykima said. "Specifically, a little black book. The first page should say *Grimorium Aeternum* in brown ink."

Leah frowned. "That's the name of the book we used at the Outpost. The one Alma had."

"And the one Helen took and brought to the Academy," Nykima said. "I would like it back."

"Got it," Sarah said. "Get the creepy book, check."

"Don't take anything else," Nykima said. "The forensic lab holds many objects with entrapped entities. The worst thing you can do is to disrupt the rituals holding them."

"More entities? Great," Isaac said.

"They keep an evidence locker down there from all the cult and sacrifice investigations. Just look for the ones marked for the academy and get out of there," Nykima said.

Leah looked over at the oven, noting the time, ten minutes to midnight. "No time like the present. Let's get this over with."

The mop splashed onto the ground as Leah and Sarah mopped the second-floor lobby. They had planned this all out. Pretend to be the night cleaning crew and hope security didn't question why they were walking around this late at night.

For the next fifteen minutes, Leah kept looking over at Sarah. What if this didn't work? What if the book wasn't even there? What if they were caught by security? Four Pawns and a Knight pretending to be janitors at headquarters would be investigated heavily, and their chance at finding out if anyone was possessed would vanish.

Calm yourself. Breathe and stay focused, Asmodeus said.

Leah took a deep breath and let it out slowly, gripping her mop tight.

"Hey," Sarah said. "It'll be okay. We've done worse than this."

Leah smiled. "Yeah, you're right. It's just—"

"Got it!" Isaac said, rounding the corner holding up a small keycard. "Your turn. Good luck!"

Leah and Sarah took their mops and buckets with them as they called the elevator and descended to sublevel eight. Maybe they'd done it, and it would be smooth from here on out. Or maybe . . .

The doors opened, and on the other side stood Black Rook Jaime McMillan.

"Well, good evening, Pawns. What brings you two down here at this hour?"

CHAPTER 26

SHELVED GHOSTS

Leah gripped mop and stumbled over her words. "We're, uh . . . we're here to mop."

Jaime stepped aside and let the two of them exit the elevator as he said, "Interesting. You know, I saw two Pawns already down here a few hours ago cleaning."

"Uh, yeah, we're second shift," Sarah said. "We were told the lab level needed more work."

"Hm," Jaime said, eyeing both girls.

As he did, Leah caught Sarah slipping her hand into her pocket, no doubt readying herself with the powder.

"Who was it who sent you down here? Someone had to give you access."

Before having the chance to answer, a shout suddenly came from behind the Rook. "Jaime! How have you been?"

Reginald Platt walked toward them in a dark suit, carrying his cane with the golden crow head topper.

"Reginald? Huh, the lab seems to be rather busy this evening."

"Ha! Been looking for you, actually. Figured you'd be getting in some late-night treatments."

Jaime shifted, standing up straighter as Reginald approached. "You'd be right."

Reginald glanced at Leah's mop, then at her, and nodded. "Carry on, you two. We have some private business to discuss." He wrapped an arm around Jaime and veered him toward the elevator. "How about we head up to the Corner and grab a scotch?"

The pair vanished in the elevator, and Sarah let out a long sigh. "Holy shit, that was close."

"Come on," Leah said, heading down the hall. "Get that powder ready; I doubt we'll get lucky again."

They set the cleaning gear next to the entrance to the lab, and Leah grabbed a handful of the powder before swiping the card and opening the door.

Inside, the place was pristine, with one side lined with rows of storage racks containing hundreds of white boxes. The other side of the place was filled with benches, computers, and instruments Leah had only seen on TV.

"What are you doing here?" a shorter woman with bobbed black hair and large circular glasses asked. She stood behind one of the bench tops, next to a man with a short buzz cut inspecting a set of glass tubes.

Leah started toward them. "We're looking for Black Rook Platt. The Queen sent us."

"Pawns don't have access to the lab. How did you get down here?" the man asked, walking around the desk.

Leah raised the keycard. "I already said Queen Helen gave me this and told me to come get Rook Reginald Platt. Have you seen him?"

The man looked back at the woman, shaking his head. That was all Leah needed. She stepped forward and held out her other hand, blowing the powder into his face.

Sarah moved seconds after, opening her hand and blowing a cloud of powder at the woman.

"*Obulie moi*," they said in unison.

The man and woman's breathing slowed, and they swayed where they stood. The man blinked several times, as if he were trying to wake from a deep sleep, but then his shoulders slumped. The woman did the same, and both stared at Sarah and Leah, their eyes unfocused.

"I think it worked," Leah said.

Sarah snapped her fingers right in the woman's face, and she remained unflinching. "Damn!"

"Shh!" Leah said. "We don't want anyone else coming in."

"Right. Sorry." Sarah glanced down at the papers in front of the woman. "Think they might be able to help us?"

Leah shrugged and looked at the woman. "Hey, where is the evidence for the Maimonides Academy incident?"

"What?" the woman asked, grasping her stack of papers, her eyes blinking slowly as if she were half asleep. "It's in aisle thirty-seven."

Sarah backed up. "So, we just leave them, right?"

"I guess?" Leah said. "They'll probably be fine. I think."

The two of them turned and walked down the aisles, traveling deeper into the lab. Lights turned on above them, activated by their motion.

"Thirty-six and thirty-seven," Sarah said, dipping into the aisle.

It took only a minute for Leah to find the boxed marked "93-25-FH Maimonides Academy Incident."

"Here they are."

"That's it?" Sarah asked, pulled out one of five boxed marked from the academy. "That's all that survived?"

"Guess so."

"What do you think it is? The thing the ghost is attached to?"

"A red book. I don't remember the name, but they showed it to me once. That *has* to be it."

"Got it," Sarah said, popping open the top. "I'll hand you anything I find."

Something feels wrong. Keep alert, Asmodeus whispered.

Leah opened a box and found a set of burned books individually wrapped in plastic and a strung closed by a thin silver chain. Beside those were other artifacts, each burned nearly beyond recognition and wrapped in a similar fashion. All but one small corked bottle with a thick green liquid inside.

"I can't believe it," she said.

"Is that—"

"The flask the Druid Chief Cían gave me. It's a mandrake potion. Like the one we used to save Isaac." Leah pocketed it.

"What are you doing?" Sarah asked. "Nykima said—"

"Chief Cían gave it to me for a reason. It might come in handy," Leah said as she opened the next box.

Moments later, Sarah held up a small black book. "Found Nykima's book. Ugh, I was hoping I'd never see this again."

Leah looked up from her pile of sealed books and caught her finger on one of the small silver chains. She felt it give in her fingers, and then the light above them went out.

"Fuck!" Sarah yelled.

Something tapped on Leah's shoulder. She turned, peering out in the dark, making out the silhouette of the aisles. "Who's there?"

"What?" Sarah asked, then Leah heard a tumble from where Sarah was, followed by. "Fuck, I hate this. I wish I had *Tiferet* right about now."

Something groaned loudly to their left, a low guttural sound that put Leah's hair on end.

"You left me," a voice whispered in Leah's ear. The apparition of a small boy formed in front of her, a slight glow in his form.

"Sarah, you seeing this?" Leah asked.

"Seeing what?"

The boy suddenly burst into flames, his face distorting. "Everything burned, and you left me!"

"I'm sorry!" Leah shouted. "I should have listened to you! You were right about that boy."

The apparition grew taller, and the boy's face stretched and contorted. "I'm so hungry."

"Leah, what's happening?" Sarah asked.

"I'm sorry for what happened," Leah said to the boy. "But I understand now. Please, tell me, is it the book that keeps you here? The red one? I'll take it with me, and I can get you out of here."

The monster in front of her vanished, then reappeared, inches from her face. "They kept me sealed for so long. I hunger."

We need to run! Asmodeus yelled.

Leah backed up, her hand brushing up against a book. A book that was missing the silver chain. *This has to be it,* she thought as she squeezed her hand around the book. All she needed now was the chain.

The creature stepped closer, sniffing at her leg. A stream of drool fell from his mouth as he said, "You smell so good." The boy's mouth was full of teeth as it opened and latched onto her leg.

Pain seared through her body as needles tore into her. She let out a scream, and then, to her horror, the thing started sucking.

"Leah! What's happening?" Sarah shouted.

"He's got me," she said, flinging a fist at the boy monster, but her hand passed right through. She needed the silver, needed anything that would stop it. Her hands felt at the floor, fingers brushing along the tile for the small chain. Her fingers wrapped around something thin as the boy bit deeper.

She let out another scream as she flung the chain up and wrapped it around the book.

The boy shivered and let go, shifting back into his human shape. She secured the book in metal, and the boy whispered, "You left me to burn."

Then he vanished.

The lights above flickered on, and Leah sat up, peering down at her leg.

She'd expected it to be mangled, torn bits of flesh staring back at her. But there was nothing. No tear in her pants. No blood.

"Is that the book?" Sarah asked, eyeing the red book in Leah's hand.

"Yeah," she said. "We got him."

CHAPTER 27

PRESSURE

Leah tossed the red book back on her side table in her room. It had been days since they'd taken it out of the lab, and every time she removed the silver chains, nothing happened. The ghost apparently wanted nothing to do with her.

She collapsed onto her bed, sore from another day of training with Yuki. They'd been learning how to use *Malchut* while on a tightrope thirty feet in the air, and Leah had somehow only fallen four times onto the not-so-soft forest floor.

There was a light knock on the door, and Sarah peeked her head in. She eyed the book on Leah's nightstand. "Still nothing?"

"Nope," Leah exclaimed, gazing at the ceiling.

"Can I do anything to help?" Sarah asked. "Nykima cornered me earlier today to ask how it was going."

"Not unless you know some secret way to talk to ghosts that I don't." There was a certain spite in Leah's voice that she didn't intend.

"I'm just trying to help," Sarah said, dropping her gaze to the floor.

"Sorry," Leah said. "I just need a way to talk to him. Tell him we didn't leave him."

Cora's words echoed in her mind. *You don't need rituals or Trees to access the Astral Realm.*

Yet try as she might, she couldn't even get a ghost to talk to her. "I've tried everything I can think of. I've talked to the book, slept on the book, whispered to it, apologized, yelled, threatened to tear it in half. Still, nothing. He doesn't want to talk."

"Okay, but if he won't talk to you, then maybe someone else should try?" Sarah suggested.

Leah grabbed the book from her bedside and hopped up. "Sure, knock yourself out," she said, tossing the book at Sarah before passing by her. "I need some fresh air, anyway."

The sun settled on the horizon as Leah walked around the forest paths surrounding headquarters. She clutched her coat as the wind blew by her, rustling the dried leaves on the ground. She'd screwed it all up. Wasted their time chasing after a ghost that didn't even want to help them. And now they were closing in on the vote, and she had done nothing to help their cause.

Music sounded in the air, the soft melodic strums of a guitar just at the edge of her ears. She followed it, twisting through paths she'd never been down, following the source as it took her to an old, mossy tree.

Sitting just beyond it was Nick, the Sage of *Chesed*, playing with his eyes closed and his fingers deftly plucking the strings, humming to himself.

She stood there, listening for a long while, before he

said, "Do you plan on standing there all day, or do you care to join me?"

"S-Sorry," Leah muttered, stepping back. "I didn't mean to. I don't want to interrupt."

Nick cracked his eyes open. "You aren't interrupting, señorita. Come. Sit."

She stepped past the tree and rested on one of the large roots that stuck out of the ground next to him. He carried on playing for a while longer as she stared at the creek, emotions surfacing gently before passing by. Something about the music, or perhaps Nick himself, gave her peace, and all she could do was give him a slight smile as a tightness in her chest finally came undone.

As he finished, she pulled herself out of her thoughts and looked over. "That was great."

"Thank you," he answered, bowing his head. "Always nice to have an audience."

"Last I heard, you were still in Venezuela."

"I was, but with the vote less than a week away, I figured it was time to return. That and you four are reconnecting with the Tree soon, yes?"

Leah nodded and sighed. "Any day now."

"But that's not what brought you here, is it? What's the matter, señorita?"

Leah shook her head. "It's nothing. Just a lot going on."

"I see. Well, I've been told I'm a superb listener, if you'd like to share."

Something about the way he spoke made her believe him completely. She needed someone to talk to. Someone that wasn't relying on her. "Okay, it's about a friend. I messed up. He doesn't want to talk to me."

"Ah, is this about you and Gabe?"

"What?" Leah asked, heat rising to her cheeks. "No. It's not about that. This is a different friend. It's . . . well this is going to sound weird, and you must promise not to tell anyone else."

"You are talking to someone who can heal wounds in seconds but still can't mend broken hearts at a headquarters with people who do things beyond most people's wildest imagination. I think weird is not something to worry about here."

"Fine," Leah said. "It's a ghost. He was sort of a friend before the Academy burned down. Now he thinks I left him on purpose, and he won't even talk to me."

"That is new," Nick nodded.

"See, I told you it was weird."

Nick laughed. "Not weird, only new. Were you close at the Academy?"

"Not particularly, but I was the only one who talked to him."

"I don't know much about ghosts as friends, but as Mystics, we are taught that ghosts are unpredictable. They're slowly corrupting reflections of who they once were, attached to something here and unable to move on."

"But how do you help them?" Leah asked.

"Well." Nick sighed. "We're taught to find the object they're latched onto and burn it. Some Bishops from the seventies tried talking with the ghosts, attempting to get them to move on in a less traumatic fashion, but that was never picked up as standard practice. But I doubt that's what you're asking."

"No," Leah said, eyeing the creek. "I need his help with something, but he won't even materialize."

"And, I have to ask, the corruption?"

"He's got some corruption, but he can control it."

Nick set the guitar aside and played with his chin. "Well, he can't be far from the object he's attached to. I bet he's just beyond the veil, in the first layer of the Astral. Nothing a little *Tiferet* can't find."

Leah looked up at the sky. "Great. The one thing I don't have."

"Not for long," Nick said.

"I just—I need him before the vote."

"Well, if I tell you a secret, you promise you won't tell your friends?"

Leah frowned. "Sure?"

"Your Tree Bonding Trial is tomorrow."

"What?" she screamed, sitting straight up.

CHAPTER 28

TREE BONDING

As Leah and her friends entered the lab the next morning, Eli, Sandeep, and Nick, along with a handful of White Bishops, greeted them. They all stood tall, with several around each pod, hooking up various wires and devices to each one.

"What's going on?" Gabe whispered to the others.

"Today's the day," Eli said. "I've prepared you as best I can. Regardless, the dangers beyond that door are very real, hence why we have our most skilled *Chesed* users here. We only have one shot at this, so let's make it right."

"Yes, sir!" they all said, standing at attention.

"Go get ready," Eli said. "We're on a tight schedule, and you four need all the time you can get."

They marched off to the changing room and dressed. Isaac was pale after he stepped out. "I don't know if we're ready."

Sarah wrapped an arm around his shoulder and pulled him in. "Only one way to find out. Catch you on the flip side."

They each stood next to their capsules as Sandeep injected them with serum. He yawned as he spoke. "We'll be attaching some monitors to you, so don't close your lids when you get in."

Eli clapped his hands together and smiled. "You've been training hard for this day. You all have it in you to reconnect. Trust your instincts, and face anything the Tree throws at you."

Leah slipped into her capsule as White Bishops surrounded her and placed a mesh headpiece on her, attaching her fingers to various sensors. Once the lid closed, Leah slipped immediately into the Astral realm, opening her eyes to the inside of a broken capsule, with sickly orange light filtering through the cracks.

She found Eli waiting for her, and seconds later, Gabe, Sarah, and Isaac stepped out of their pods.

"Pawns, now is the time to step through the white door." He gestured to his left, and the door materialized, the same as it had been since the first time Leah came into this room.

Leah glanced back at her friends, nodded, and stepped forward. She twisted the cold metal knob and stepped through.

Cold air washed over her as she looked up into a night sky overlooking a valley. A full moon, much larger than she was used to, peeked out from the steep mountains, casting enough light to illuminate the path into a looming hedge maze ahead.

"Woah," Sarah said from behind her. "Bit cold in there."

Leah turned to respond, but the door vanished, along with her friends. "Sarah?" she called.

But no one replied.

She shivered and rubbed her arms, contemplating how nice it would have been to be in her jacket. It took just that thought for her White Pawn jacket to materialize around her, shielding her from the icy wind.

"Asmodeus, you here?" she asked. Several moments passed while nothing echoed in her mind. She pulled back her sleeve, noticing that the demon mark was missing.

"Guess I really need to do this alone," she whispered to herself, starting down the path.

She stopped at the entrance to the hedge maze, noting the tall pillars on either side that housed two owls, one white and the other black. They stared down at her, moving their heads from side to side as if inspecting her.

"The moon marks the beginning," the white owl said in a soft, light voice.

"The moon marks the end," the black one spoke, their voice deep and harsh.

"The path ahead is easy for those with minds clear."

"The path ahead is difficult for those filled with fear."

Leah looked past them, eyeing the moon that lined up perfectly with the hedges in front of her.

"Got it," she said, looking back up at them. "Anything else?"

They both remained as still as statues, staring down at her with those piercing eyes.

"Okay then," Leah said, stepping forward. "Here goes nothing."

As she moved inside, the path ahead and behind her stretched far, and the hedges loomed over her. She was alone, again, lost in a maze.

She walked forward, turning left and right down long corridors lined with hedges, trusting her instincts to guide her through. After reaching the third dead end, a sonorous boom sounded overhead. She plugged her ears as the sound echoed through her core.

"What the hell was that?" she asked.

She carefully turned around and headed back the way she came, finding another fork and testing out a different path. She'd gone on for what felt like hours, spotting nothing but corridor after long corridor of hedges. Until, finally, she rounded a corner and spotted two glowing eyes, far down the path, staring at her.

"Uh, hello?" she called out.

The eyes inched closer toward her, still cast in shadows. She stepped back, pressing up against the leaves. "Who's there?"

It took another step toward her and stretched up, as if craning its neck. The thing was tall, taller than any human. Her heart raced, and instinct kicked in. She ran, retracing her steps back through the maze. She could hear it behind her, thudding hard against the ground and rustling the sides of the hedges.

She squeezed her fist, calling on *Malchut*, but nothing came. She didn't feel the serpent uncoiling in her chest or the pool of energy form in her hand. It felt as if she'd never had it at all. Never had a connection to the Tree. She took a left and stopped in her tracks as she faced a dead end. She was trapped with nowhere to go. She pushed up against the hedge, looking for a place to crawl into or hide, but thorns cut into her, digging deeper into her the more she looked.

Heavy thudding sounded behind her as the thing got even closer. Leah fell back against the hedge, cowering as the silhouette of the thing stepped into the moonlight.

Its jaw was long, ending in a snout, with fur that looked dark, almost orange-like. The creature's yellow eyes stared back at her, and she remembered that face. It was the same face she'd encountered in the library, and on the docks.

The same face she'd seen, dead.

"Theo?"

CHAPTER 29
THE BROTHER

Blood oozed from a hole in Theo's chimeric head, dripping onto the ground as he slowly stepped forward. She had nowhere to go. He'd kill her, and she deserved it.

"Theo," she muttered. "Theo, please. I . . . I . . ."

Her back pressed up against something hard. She turned to find a small white door, small enough for her to crawl through, that hadn't been there a moment before. She fumbled for the handle while keeping an eye on Theo. It opened, and she scrambled through it as Theo let out a long, guttural howl.

She was no longer surrounded by a hedge maze. Instead, she stood at the edge of a massive field surrounded by hedges with an octagon platform and stands in the center.

Clouds above parted, and a beam of moonlight shone on the platform.

"Very subtle," she mumbled, pushing herself up and heading to the center of the field.

As soon as her foot stepped onto the platform, a voice called from ahead.

"We meet again, Leah Ackerman." The voice bored through her, and Brandon Roe materialized in front of her, stepping onto the platform, half his face terribly burned beyond recognition. One eye stared at her, glaring as he let in a light wheeze. He bobbed his head from side to side, his neck cracking as he said, "I've been waiting for this."

The surrounding stands filled with people sitting shoulder to shoulder, all pale and with empty eye sockets. Leah's chest tightened as she spun in a circle, meeting the gaze of the sightless people, feeling a sense of judgment and hatred emanating off them.

She faced Brandon once again. "Brandon, I . . . I'm—"

"Save it."

He launched at her, propelled by *Malchut*, his first aimed right at her. Leah jumped to the side, dodging his attack, but he pivoted in the air and landed an elbow right into her ribs.

She gasped, clutching at her side as she fell to her knees, catching her breath. She pulled at *Malchut*, feeling the serpent once again in her chest. Brandon lunged again, punching her right in the jaw. Stars formed in her vision, her ears rung, and her hold on *Malchut* vanished as she fell onto the hard platform. Brandon closed in and kicked her in the ribs, sending jolts of pain through her.

"What were you going to say? I'm sorry? Save it. You killed him. You killed me. Nothing you say or do now will bring us back," he said, ramming his foot into her side over and over.

I can't give up, she said to herself. *I have to fight back. They need me. Get up. Get up. Get up!*

But her body didn't respond. He kicked, and he kicked, and she didn't fight back. The part of her that thought she deserved this kept her still. The pain numbed her bones, creaking against the force.

He landed another blow, and she heard Sarah's voice in her ear. "Stop dwelling on the past." He kicked her again, and she tasted blood in her mouth. "It can't be changed. What's done is done." She didn't deserve this. She'd beaten herself up enough. "But if you let it overtake you, you'll never move forward."

Leah opened her eyes. *I can't let this consume me.*

He kicked her again, her ribs at the edge of breaking.

I must move forward.

Another kick.

"What's done is done!" she yelled, pulling on *Malchut* and releasing it with an explosive force. The platform cracked, and Brandon flew backward, landing hard on his feet as he held onto his side.

"I killed your brother," Leah said, shakily rising to her feet. "He attacked me, and I protected myself. Nykima didn't want me to tell you. She didn't think you were ready. But that's no excuse. You should have known, and I am sorry I didn't get to tell you."

"Stop," Brandon growled. "You don't get to be the self-righteous bitch. Not here." He straightened up, wincing as he shifted his weight, and prepared to launch himself again.

He propelled forward, and Leah braced herself, preparing a *Malchut* fist. She'd already faded a bit from the explosive force she'd used, but she'd have to use it again if she was going to get out of here.

Something massive stepped between them, catching Brandon mid-leap in a long arm embrace.

Ginger fur glinted in the moonlight as Theodore said, "That's enough, brother. That's enough."

"No! Theo," Brandon said, pushing against him. "Let me go."

"No, brother. Let it go." He squeezed tighter, restraining Brandon. "She's not our fight. We're free. We're together."

"Let me go! She must pay!" Brandon screamed, clawing at his brother's arm.

Theo squeezed harder, and Brandon gasped for air.

"You're always looking for a fight, brother," Theo said. "Leah was protecting herself. You hear me?"

Brandon slumped in his brother's arms. Finally, Theo let him go and he stumbled to his knees. He looked up, tears in his eyes. "Why did you leave me?"

"You wouldn't let me grow," Theodore said. "Even at the Outpost, you did everything to protect me. You didn't let me fail."

"But you're my brother. I—I had to protect you," Brandon said.

"You didn't though." Theo kneeled next to Brandon. "No one talked to me at the Academy because you'd bully them. When the chimeras took me, I found peace. I was happy."

Brandon stared at the ground for a long time. Then he slowly got to his feet, tears in his eyes. "Well, I'm here now, and I'll listen, I promise."

Theo stood, wrapping a massive arm around Brandon. "That's all I ask."

Wind blew past Leah, and the people in the stands dissolved into mist. Then, right before Leah's eyes, Brandon and Theodore vanished, leaving her alone on the platform.

A warm hand landed on her shoulder, and a voice she'd thought was long gone spoke in her ear. "Come on, your work here is done."

Leah swallowed, turning to see Eric staring back at her, smiling.

CHAPTER 30
THE UNCLE

Eric waved his hand, gesturing her to follow. Then he turned around, revealing a second white door right behind him.

Leah's heart pounded heavy in her chest. Could this really be him?

She followed him, stepping through the door. Her pain from the fight instantly vanished, and she squinted in a bright morning light and a clear blue sky. She looked down and noted she wore street clothes, not her usual Pawn uniforms. She felt at her ribs, expecting pain, but it was gone. As her eyes adjusted, she recognized the familiar parking lot, and the sign of Flyby Donuts came into view.

Eric waited for her to get her bearings as he stood next to his car. Then, when she finally smiled at him, he rushed in, wrapping his arms around her.

It was him. He was really there with her. Tears streamed down her cheeks, and she whispered, "It's you."

He squeezed her tight, then pulled away, resting his hands on her shoulders. "I have a surprise for you." He pulled keys out of his pocked and unlocked his car, getting in the driver's seat. Leah followed suit and breathed in the scent of freshly made donuts. He reached behind the seat and handed her an unopened box of Flyby Donuts.

"Oh, my god, are you serious? I haven't had this since—"

"Since we left your house. Figured you'd enjoy them."

Leah grinned and opened the box, taking in the sight of Bavarian cream, strawberry, and the one she finally settled on, blueberry glazed. She pulled it apart and popped it into her mouth, the dough still warm and soft, mixing with the sugar and the slight acid from the blueberries.

Eric revved the engine to life and pulled out of the parking lot, turning on to the highway as he drank from a large cup of coffee.

"So, where are we headed?"

He scratched the back of this head. "There's an Outpost in Mystic, South Dakota. It's the closest one I know of I can drop you off at."

Leah frowned and looked up from her donut. Was he serious? Was this just a memory? She looked over at him and caught his gaze. A smile spread across his lips, and a roar of laughter burst from him.

"Sorry," he said. "Had to—for old time's sake."

Leah picked at the donut and spoke, "Honestly, that was one of the worst days of my life."

Eric gripped the wheel and sighed. "I know."

"But even now, I wish I was back there."

"Really?" Eric frowned. "Why?"

"You'd still be alive," she said, looking over at him. She struggled to swallow, and tears formed once again in her eyes.

Eric bit his lip. "Funny how all that works. You were so scared back then, and all you wanted were answers."

"I did," she said.

"Now that you have them, are you happier?"

Leah thought for a moment, then shook her head. "No. Even at the Outpost, things were simpler. I knew who was after me. Now, Legion could be anywhere."

Eric nodded. "I've come to realize we grieve those tough moments. Not from the fear we'd had, but we regret what we could have done without that fear. Such is the irony of life, I suppose."

Leah let her emotions wash over her, contemplating how life would be different if her parents hadn't died. How she'd never have met Sarah and Isaac. That thought pained her. She'd never had friends like them before, and to live life without them seemed so foreign now.

"Even if I could change it, would I still be me?" Leah asked, leaning against the window and staring out at the blue sky. "If I could have saved you."

"I wish I could have been there. I promised your mom I would be. And now, I can't protect you anymore."

Leah looked up from the box of donuts. "You protected me when I needed it. You taught me how to protect myself. Because of you, I'm still alive."

Eric gave her a half-smile. "But I still burden you."

"Burden me?" Leah frowned. "You don't—"

"You're going to tell me you haven't been hearing my voice the past few weeks?"

Go! Get out of here! His last words echoed in her head once again.

"I—I . . ." she started, then she wrapped her arms around herself. "I'm sorry."

"It's not your fault. You're obsessing. Wondering if it could have been different. But there's nothing you could have done."

"But I. I could have—"

"Leah."

Tears streamed down her cheeks, and the weight in her

throat grew tight. "I could have listened to the ghost's warning. I could have trained harder. If I'd just stuck by your side back at the orphanage, then I wouldn't have found that trap. Isaac wouldn't have been half-possessed. And we wouldn't have had that kid with us. If I just—"

"Those are in the past. Things that shaped you into who you are now. They can't drag you down. You said it yourself."

"But they are mistakes," Leah said. "How can I just let them go?"

"It's easy to look back and point out all the wrong choices you've made. But you did what you thought was best at that time. Back at the orphanage, we'd failed so many missions, everyone wanted answers. And you were lured, something none of us expected."

"Yeah but—"

"You need to accept the past and focus on the future. Your friends have told you this; listen to them. Even you just told it to Brandon, but you can't take the advice on as your own?"

Leah bit her lip. "I wasn't ready to lose you."

Eric pulled the car over at a rest stop. One that looked oddly familiar to Leah.

"Come on," Eric said, killing the engine and stepping out. "Follow me."

She followed Eric as he took a path down toward a secluded park bench overlooking the Badlands. The sun had passed beyond the peak of the sky, burning bright overhead.

"Wait," Leah said, looking out at the drop off near the park bench. "Are you going to test me on *Malchut* again?"

Eric turned and smiled while walking backwards, stopping right at the edge of the cliff. "Something like that. Back then, we were testing your control. Today we need to test something more important." He opened his arms. "Your willingness to let go."

Leah's eyes widened. "What? You want me to push you off the cliff?"

"That's *exactly* what I want you to do."

Leah shook his head. "No. I can't."

Eric's face softened. "You need to reconnect with the Tree. And to do that, you must push me."

"But you died only a few weeks ago! How can I just let go?"

"I'm not asking you to let go of grief. But the resentment you have with yourself over what happened. The pain that causes you. You have to let that go. Make peace with the choices you've made."

Leah turned away. "I don't want to lose you again."

Eric wrapped his arm around her. "I haven't left though. None of us did. We're still around. Watching. Cheering you on."

"But—"

"You won't lose me by letting go. But you'll miss your chance if you keep holding on. The Tree only bonds with those who can move past their old bonds. You must do this. You have to move on."

Leah looked up at him and nodded. "Okay. I'll try."

Eric walked back to the edge and grabbed something from his pocket. He tossed it over to Leah's feet. They were his keys, glinting in the light. "Go for a ride once this is done."

"Where?"

"Anywhere," Eric shrugged, holding out his arms. "You're the driver now."

Malchut uncoiled from her chest and slithered down into her hands. She stared at him the whole time, extending her hands and letting out a wave of energy.

He smiled as his feet left the ground. As he vanished, she fell to her knees, a weight she didn't know she'd even had lifted off her.

She picked up the keys, slowly making her way back to the car. She drove for hours on an empty highway, then into a forest, and onto a gravel road. She couldn't say if she knew where she was going or not, but each turn shed away her doubts, and soon enough, the woods towered overhead.

Leah drove by boarded-up homes, and she slowed as she spotted the wooden cabin she'd stayed in after her parents had died.

She shut off the engine and looked onto the porch, spotting a tall woman, thin with high cheekbones and long black hair.

As she stepped out, Black Bishop Alma Sachs raised an eyebrow. "Come, Pawn Ackerman, you're late. And we have work to do."

CHAPTER 31

THE MENTOR

"It's good to see you," Leah said as she stepped onto the porch.

Alma reached out and squeezed Leah's shoulder. "You've grown so much. Come. Follow me."

The Outpost looked the same as she'd remembered it, with the three large leather couches surrounding a low table positioned at the middle of the living room, the enormous stone fireplace, and the log walls and high ceiling above her. She smiled as memories of her and her friends playing cards on the couch came to mind.

They walked through the crowded dining room, with the two dinner tables placed side-by-side, and out through the glass doors into the backyard. Leah expected to see the training field, but instead they were transported into the middle of a dark forest.

"Black Bishop Sachs? Where are we going?" Leah asked as she followed.

Alma waved her on. "Don't stop now. We're close."

Each step led them deeper into a dark forest, far from the Outpost. Lights pulsed and dipped behind trees. Too big to be fireflies, but they moved the same way.

"Beautiful, isn't it?" Alma asked.

One light approached Leah, brushing up against her skin.

A buzz of energy traveled up her arm, followed by a voice that echoed softly in her mind. *Lost. Elsa. Trapped.*

Leah pulled her arm away. "What is that?"

"Essences. Or what some people call souls."

Leah looked out into the woods, spotting hundreds of lights dancing through the woods. "There's so many."

"We're here," Alma said, stopping in her tracks.

Leah looked up, noting a small clearing ahead the little orbs of light didn't seem to float into.

Alma kneeled and pulled off her shoes. "This is a sacred place. Take off your shoes."

Leah complied, feeling the soft sandy earth beneath her. Ahead, small stones formed a spiraled path leading right into the heart of the clearing where something large stood.

"So, I just follow the path?"

Alma nodded.

"What happens when I get to the center?"

"Then you've made your decision," Alma answered.

Leah frowned, more questions surfacing, but she could sense she wouldn't get any more answers from Alma.

She stepped onto the first stone, feeling its smooth form beneath her. Pausing, Leah noted how it was also warm. She took another, and another, starting the path that wound around the center, a tingling sensation floating up her body and into her fingertips. With each step, a brief surge of power filled her extremities and pulled the weight off her shoulders.

She'd made it halfway through when a scream sounded from behind her. "Leah!"

Leah peered over her shoulder, toward the other end of

the woods than where she'd come in. She found another path, which seemed to bubble up out of the ground, winding in an opposite direction to hers. At the edge of the woods, and the start of this other path, was a statue made of obsidian stone with red, glowing eyes.

"Don't stop!" Alma yelled. "You must reach the center. You can't stop. Not now!"

She looked back at Asmodeus, who stepped onto the path for a moment, screamed, and lunged off it, smoke billowing from the bottom of his feet.

"Great power awaits you," Alma said. "You need to reach the center."

"What about Asmodeus?" Leah asked, trotting down the spiral path to get closer to Alma.

"You mean the Demon who killed your parents?" Alma spat.

Leah bit the inside of her cheek and took another step, entering now the closest ring to the center of the circle. The buzz of energy flowing through her was almost too much to bear, too much to have, and to think about anything else. She wanted more; she needed more. She kept moving closer, and all her pain and fear seemed to vanish. This is the energy she needed, the power she needed to take down Legion.

Asmodeus let out another scream and collapsed on the ground. He reached out for the stone, only for it to sear his hand.

"I . . . I can't let him die," Leah said, stopping in her tracks.

"That demon has been living in you like a parasite after he attacked us. You really think he is worth saving? After everything he's done? The lives he's taken? Isn't it exhausting to carry all his burdens with you? Without him, you're free. You are powerful."

Leah eyed the massive smooth stone at the heart of the clearing. It was so close, just a few more steps and she'd reached.

But.

She looked back at Asmodeus. He was reaching for her. Calling to her. By the looks of it, he'd die if she moved any closer.

"Just one more step, and you'll bond with the tree," Alma said.

Cracks formed in Asmodeus's obsidian arm, and bright molten glass shone through as he gripped the stone path. Memories flooded her brain, and with each one, shards of glass fell off the demon. They were memories of them. All the countless times Asmodeus had helped her, had given her council, or had single-handedly saved her or her friend's lives. And all the times she'd stopped him. All the times she'd saved him and had shown him what it was like to be human. If Alma was right, this was her only chance to bond with the Tree, but in doing so, she'd kill Asmodeus.

"No." Leah stepped off the path, the cold ground welcoming her feet.

"What are you doing?" Alma screamed.

Leah raced toward Asmodeus, the energy sapping out of her with each step. By the time she reached him, all the obsidian glass had broken off him, and instead, he was the man Leah had seen in her dreams. The human version of Asmodeus.

"What? You . . . you came back," he murmured.

Leah grabbed his arm and pulled it over her shoulder. He wheezed as she brought him up to standing, his frame thin and frail.

"We're in this together," Leah said, stepping forward.

"No," Asmodeus pushed back weakly. "The path. It burns."

But as he said it, his bare feet landed on the stone. He gasped and stood upright. Color filled him once more, and he stared at Leah, eyes wide.

They stepped forward, down the path, but Alma stood in their way, blocking them from moving forward.

"What are you doing?" Alma asked.

"He saved my life," Leah said, holding Asmodeus up. "More than once."

"But he's killed so many. You have the chance to finally rid yourself of this parasite. Why save him?"

"I wouldn't be able to forgive myself. I need him, and he needs me. I can't betray him. Not now."

Wind blew through the trees, swirling around them as a deep red sand picked up from the ground. Before they knew it, the three of them were caught in the center of a sand-storm, with balls of light spinning around them.

"Very well," Alma said, stepping back. The sand engulfed her in seconds.

"Wait!" Leah screamed, but it was too late.

The red sand closed in, scraping against her skin and digging in. The light from the orbs grew bright, too bright, and she shut her eyes. She couldn't breathe, the sand wriggling its way into her nose and mouth. She was going to die here, holding Asmodeus in the middle of this storm.

Then the light vanished, along with the wind. She opened her eyes to a small clearing, with the mood over-head. Asmodeus was no longer in her arms, and Leah wobbled on her feet, her stomach turning. Alma caught her, holding her shoulders as she looked into Leah's eyes.

"Easy now. It's still settling."

Leah blinked a few times, noting that the spiral path and the center stone was missing. "What? What happened?"

Alma smiled. "You passed the Tree's test. You are bonded."

Leah frowned. "What? How? I didn't get to the center."

"True. But that wasn't the test, was it?"

"I don't understand. The tree wanted me to save Asmodeus?"

Alma shrugged. "I wanted you to become whole without him. But looks like the Tree has other plans for you. I believe your selflessness and sacrifice is what it wanted from you."

Leah sensed the power of the tree within her once again as she looked down at her hands. She could also see the demon mark, clearly imprinted on her arm. "I know he's just an unredeemable demon to you. But he's different now."

Alma drew a deep breath. "Perhaps one day I will understand. But what matters is that you are bonded once more, and Asmodeus is still within you. I suspect the Tree trusts you with him, so I must too."

Leah nodded and lunged forward, hugging her mentor. "I wish—"

"Me too," Alma said, cutting her off. "But it's time to go back."

Silver moonlight washed over them, growing brighter by the second.

"We're all still with you," Alma said. "Don't forget that."

Leah couldn't keep her eyes open any longer, the light washing over her in one last bright flash. As she shut her eyes, the ground beneath her gave way, and she slipped into darkness.

CHAPTER 32

UNBOUND

Leah pushed open the lid to her capsule, pulling off the mesh netting around her head as machines beeped around her.

"Easy there," Sandeep said, taking the wires from her. "Take some deep breaths."

She sensed the rush of *Malchut* flowing in and out of her hands while she opened and closed her fists.

"How are you feeling?" Sandeep asked.

"I feel amazing," Leah said, grinning at the Sage.

Sandeep smiled. "Excellent! Looks like the bonding was a success."

"Congratulations, Pawn Ackerman," Eli said, walking over and assisting her out of the capsule. "You've done what other Mystics have never been able to achieve."

Leah looked out toward the other pods, noting that each of them were already opened. "Was I the last one back?"

Eli shot a glance at Sandeep before saying, "Yes."

"And how did they do?"

Sandeep cleared his throat. "Bonding to the Tree is difficult. We do everything we can to prepare you, but there's no guarantee that it'll actually work."

"What happened?" Leah asked.

"Gabriel Tate didn't secure a bond," Eli said flatly. "He was the first back. A bit shaken from whatever he saw, so Nick took him to the hospital wing. Nothing physically wrong with him from what I saw."

"Wait," Leah said, her mind reeling. It had always been a probability that they wouldn't all make the bond, but she hadn't thought about it. And now what? "What can we do? There's got to be something."

Sandeep shook his head. "There is nothing we can do. The trial can only be performed once. But the others made it through, beating our expectations."

"No," Leah whispered, balling her hands into fists. "He has to connect. I mean, what'll happen to him now?"

Eli eyed the ground. "He'll be tested on his abilities with *Malchut* again. I can put in a good word, but a kid at his rank with a broken bond really has only one place to go." He gestured for Leah to head into the changing area. "You need to focus on yourself now. You've got your bond back, and we need to prepare you for the fight ahead."

Leah shook her head. "No. Which room did Nick take him to?"

"Leah, you—" Sandeep started.

"Which room?" Leah shouted.

Leah rounded the corner and found Isaac and Sarah sitting on the floor, outside Gabe's room. They rushed to their feet, a spring in both of their steps that she hadn't seen in weeks.

"Any news?" Leah asked.

Isaac shook his head. "No, they won't tell us anything."

"Did you make it?" Sarah asked, leaning in. "Did you bond with the Tree?"

Leah nodded, a lump forming in her throat as she eyed the door. "I hope he's okay."

"Me too," Sarah said.

The doors to Gabe's room opened and Nick stepped out, his face cold and distant, which was a stark difference from his usual jovial look.

"How is he?" Isaac asked.

"Stable. Resting now," Nick said.

"Can I see him?" Leah asked, attempting to step around Nick.

Nick blocked her. "He's finally asleep. He needs to recover before he can talk."

Leah didn't back down. She wanted to see him. Wanted to be sure he was okay.

"Go get some lunch," Nick finally said. "Come back this evening, after training. I'll allow that, okay?"

After hesitating, Leah nodded, backing up and heading to the elevators without another word.

As the doors to the elevator closed, Leah said, "We need to get the ghost on our side before they take Gabe away."

"Hey guys! Congrats on bonding," Yuki said, sporting a long winter coat and clapping her hands as she smiled wide. "Zafirah and Desmond are back, and they asked to join us today." She gestured to the woman next to her, who was wearing a light sports bra and shorts, as if the cold air had no effect on her.

Leah frowned, looking around until she saw the man

leaning up against one of the trees beyond the field in a thick leather jacket.

Zafirah stepped forward and stretched, her arms and legs bending over one another. "I'm impressed so many of you bonded with the tree again. I'll admit, I didn't have much hope. But here you are. Hope you're ready for some sparring, cause I'm not going to hold back."

"Wait, what?" Isaac asked. "We're not ready to spar. We just—"

"Yes, you are!" Yuki shouted. "You're bonded and ready to go. You need all the practice you can get. And, if things get hairy," she pointed her thumb back at Desmond. "This guy will step in and help."

Leah looked over at her two friends and frowned.

Zafirah snapped her fingers. "Yallah, yallah! We don't have all day."

"So, do you want all three of us sparring you at the same time?" Leah asked.

Zafirah snorted. "What? Are you scared, little Pawn? Go, stretch with your friends and come up with your best plan to fight me."

Leah clenched her teeth and nodded at Sarah and Isaac. "Let's do this."

The three of them huddled together, stretching. Distracted, Isaac kept looking back at Zafirah and fixing his hair.

"Hey, focus. Any ideas?" Leah asked.

"What?" Isaac asked. "Oh, I don't know. I mean, she's the Sage of *Gevurah,* so we have to look out for roots or fire. Given that she is the Sage, we'd probably need to watch out for air and water too, but even Sid said he'd never seen anyone use those before."

"Well, I'm happy to fight fire with fire," Sarah said, little sparks shooting out of her hand. "Been dying to use that again."

Isaac shook his head. "She'll be stronger than you. Fighting her head on won't work. If you come at her with *Netzach,* then Leah and I could use *Malchut* to close in and knock her out."

"Time's up! Get in position!" Zafirah yelled from the other side of the field. "And Pawn Ackerman, use some of that Tree of Death. I'd love to test it out in a fight."

I don't like this one, Asmodeus mumbled. *Too cocky.*

Asmodeus, you're awake!

For now. Let's show this Sage who she's up against.

Leah grinned and clenched her fists. "Oh, I'm ready."

CHAPTER 33

THE ELEMENTAL

"Begin!" Yuki yelled.

Leah and Isaac launched themselves up into the air on either side of Zafirah while Sarah raced forward.

"A direct attack? On a Sage? What a shame," Zafirah said, standing still with her arms crossed.

She didn't even move as three large roots exploded up from the ground. They caught Sarah and Isaac, but Leah broke it apart with a quick kick of *Malchut*. Leah landed right next to the Sage and punched.

Zafirah shifted to the side, dodging Leah's fist as more roots sprouted from the ground and curled around Leah's hand. She'd barely paused when small roots wrapped themselves around Leah's feet and legs, holding her in place.

"Not bad," Zafirah said before turning to Sarah and Isaac, who had cut the roots with a *Malchut* blades and launched an assault of energy waves at her.

Additional roots formed a barrier, absorbing the attacks as they chipped and flaked off. Zafirah tilted her head, and Leah flung herself forward, over the makeshift barrier and to the tail end of a *Malchut* blade that cut into her chest.

"Shit, sorry!" Sarah yelled.

The ground trembled, and the earth around Zafirah split as a giant root tossed her into the air. She flipped over the three of them, landing right between Leah's friends. "You're letting your guard down."

Two massive plumes of fire burst from her hands, aimed at Isaac and Sarah. They both tumbled back, blinded by the light.

She used that opportunity to punch Isaac in the ribs, sending him tumbling back, gasping for air.

Leah wheezed, trying to stand, but the cut from *Malchut* was too deep.

"My turn!" Sarah screamed, unleashing a torrent of fire toward Zafirah.

The fire washed over Zafirah entirely. Leah half expected Desmond to step in and stop them, but he was still leaning against the tree as Sarah's fire blazed.

Once the fires stopped, and Sarah hunched over, they saw that the spot where Zafirah had been standing was completely empty.

Sarah frowned and looked around. "Where did you—"

"Sarah, look out!" Leah shouted.

A slender root sprouted from the earth and wrapped around Sara's neck, pulling her down to her knees.

"Sarah!" Leah yelled, but roots burst from the ground in front of Leah, wrapping around her wrists.

"Let me go!" Isaac yelled, struggling with his own roots holding him down.

Zafirah appeared between them, slipping up from the ground as if it were water. She brushed off her hands. "Too easy."

Leah clenched her jaw and pulled against her restraints,

which wrapped around her body. Blood stained her shirt, the cut in her chest now freely bleeding, sharp pain pulsating from it. Was she really this weak? She couldn't be. Not if she was going to fight Legion.

Her body went rigid, and Asmodeus whispered, *My turn.*

Asmodeus jerked her arms up, ripping the roots up out of the ground before they had a chance to pull back. Then he pressed their right hand's knuckles into their left palm, with right hand fingers pointing toward Leah and left aimed at the roots. Anger filled them, and with each slow breath, Leah noticed the pain in her chest subsiding, the hold from the roots weakening. She was healing, and the roots were drying and cracking away.

Zafirah eyed Leah, arms crossed. "Interesting." Little roots peered out from the ground, readying for another attack. She shot two quick glances at Isaac and Sarah. "You two. Sidelines. Don't want anyone getting hurt."

Asmodeus smiled, outstretching his hands and letting in a quick, deep breath. The surrounding ground turned to ice, and the little roots cracked and snapped.

"You wanted a fight, right?" Leah asked, launching forward with *Malchut.*

Thick roots erupted from the ground, forming a wall between Leah and Zafirah. Leah's energy proved strong enough to break through, but the roots quickly knit together. Something moved in the corner of Leah's eyes, and she turned to find Zafirah closing in with a punch aimed at Leah's face.

Leah called on *Netzach*, and the punch slid off her like she was made of metal. She took her chance and landed a punch to Zafirah's stomach, though it felt like punching a concrete wall. Zafirah grabbed Leah's arm and turned, aided by roots, as she twisted and pulled Leah up and over her head, swinging her onto her back.

Leah still had *Netzach* active, landing hard on the ground without feeling it. She called on *Malchut* and thrust herself up to her feet. She launched forward, and Asmodeus called on *Thagirion,* turning them invisible just in time for Leah to land a surprise blow to Zafirah's side. It still felt like hitting a wall but the Sage stumbled back, a smile on her face. Leah took her chance and leaped forward.

Zafirah raised both her hands and dozens of roots shot from the ground, winding around Leah and pulling tight. Asmodeus dropped *Thagirion,* as he joined Leah in fighting against the restraints. Anger bubbled up inside them, and an energy seared through her stomach, spreading up like acid in her throat.

Kill. Burn. Kill.

Blue flames burst from her chest, spreading to the roots like a hungry, devouring creature. Heat surrounded Leah as she fell to the ground, the heat from the fire singeing her skin.

Burn. Kill. Burn.

"Asmodeus stop!" she yelled.

I can't! I can't!

"Desmond!" Zafirah yelled.

Leah shut her eyes tight, curling up into a ball surrounded by flames. Arms wrapped around her, pulling her up and away from the nest of flames and burning roots. She gasped for breath as she and Desmond landed on the ground.

Leah screamed as more blue fire expelled from her chest. She gripped Desmond's jacket and pleaded, "I can't stop it! run!"

"It's okay Leah." Desmond said, his arms tightening her body against his as the fire engulfed him.

Zafirah stood in front of them, hands held out as she strained against some invisible force. A speckle of light caught Leah's eye. A drop of water appeared out of thin air, and grew in size, reflecting the sunlight. More droplets followed, surrounding Leah and Desmond, hovering in the air around them. The blue flames jumped and formed a tight ring around Desmond as if it could see the water threatening its life.

I can't hold it back! Asmodeus yelled as more blue flames slithered out of Leah's chest.

"I . . . I can't stop it!" she yelled.

Desmond looked back at Zafirah and shouted, "Any minute now!"

Zafirah fell to her knee, the drops around them growing denser. "Calling the humidity in. Almost there!" she gasped.

More and more drops formed, congealing around them. As water met fire, vapor rose and the fire seemed to scream. In the blink of an eye, the drops merged together, forming a massive globe of water around Leah and Desmond.

Steam burned Leah's throat as she breathed. Inside the water, with the fire still fighting, it felt like a hundred saunas. "I can't—" she started, but the steam took her words. She gasped, but instead of air, water rushed into her lungs, the globe collapsing and submerging her and Desmond. Bubbles blurred her vision, and darkness took her as she gasped for air.

CHAPTER 34

GOLOHAB

Leah came to, gasping for air, and coughing up a mouthful of water. She blinked, and the silhouette of people hovered over her. All she could mutter was, "Wa . . . Wa."

"She's up," Sarah said, leaning in close.

Her vision cleared, and she noted the same ceiling and wall from the room she'd woken up in all those weeks ago.

Nick appeared in her vision and helped her sit up, then offered her a small cup of water. "Slowly, señorita," he said as she tried to gulp the whole thing down.

When she finished, she looked at Nick. "More please?"

Nick shook his head and nodded to the IV bag handing next to her. "Not until you get some more fluids in you. Don't want you vomiting it all up."

She lifted her arms and frowned. "There was . . . fire. I felt like I was burning."

"I healed them before they did any major damage. The fire was centered mostly around your chest. And it caught some of your hair."

Leah grabbed her hair, expecting it to be completely

gone, only to feel at the uneven strands that hung just short of her shoulders.

"We can get that evened out," Sarah said.

Leah gave her friend a half smile as she tried to swallow again. She looked up at Nick. "What happened? It's like I lost control over *Gevurah.*"

"It's called *Golohab,*" a familiar voice said from behind Nick.

He stepped aside, revealing Zafirah, sitting in a small reclining chair, both arms hooked up to IVs. Her skin was dry and flakey, and her eyes were sunken. "It's a well from the Tree of Death."

Nick looked down at his watch. "Well, I need to check on the others. Sarah? Isaac? Why don't you two come with me and see Gabe? I'm sure he'd like that."

The pair eyed each other.

"I'm fine," Leah said. "Focus on Gabe. He needs you more than I do."

They both nodded slowly, then Sarah rested a hand on Leah. "We'll be back. Okay?"

Isaac squeezed Leah's hand and headed to the door with Nick and Sarah. "We'll bring some food back to the apartment, okay?"

Leah and Zafirah sat silently for quite some time before Leah spoke. "I've seen those flames before. Back at the Academy. The dean, White Knight Wright, used them."

Zafirah uncapped a bottle of water at her side and took a sip. "*Golohab* is a very dangerous well. That demon in you is a moron for trying to use it. If Desmond hadn't been there—if I hadn't been there—there would be no headquarters left."

I used what seemed right. How was I supposed to know it would be unwieldy? Asmodeus whispered. She could picture him now, resting his head in his hands, his usual crisp suit now charred along with his arms.

"I'm—we're—sorry."

Zafirah waved her hand. "I told you to use the Tree of Death. I didn't think you, or your demon, had it in you to reach that high." She chugged the rest of the water and tossed the bottle into the bin next to her. "*Golohab* is an untamed fire, one that consumes. Only a few Mystics have used it and lived."

"I never want to use that again. Any of the Tree of Death."

Zafirah eyed her IV bags, both of which had emptied. She pulled the needles out of her arms and applied bandages that were laid out on a table next to her. "No, you will. We need it. We're at the start of war. And if this Legion is as big of a threat as you say, then we are fast approaching two wars. We need all the power we can get."

"Every time I use it feels like I'm losing control. What if it happens again?" Leah asked.

Zafirah picked up a bottle of lotion and started applying it to her skin. "You lost control, that's all. Wells have limits and consequences on both sides." She paused and stretched out her hands. "Hell, just look at me. Look at all the Sages and you'll see."

"You mean the dry skin?"

Zafirah lathered on another coat of lotion and nodded. "Dry skin. My choice of attire. Do you think I like looking like a snowman half the time? If only I could control my body temperature, but I lost that when I gave myself to *Gevurah*. We push the limits. That's why we're Sages. That's also why Nona is permanently blind, why Eli can't seem to pick up on emotions, why Sandeep is always so tired but is never able to sleep and why Nick is so depressed he can barely get out of bed some days."

"Wait," Leah said. "But Nick is always so happy."

"Some of us wear our masks well. Even Yuki is seeing the effects of *Malchut*. Soon enough her muscles will be so cramped she'll require a wheelchair most days just to get around. But these connections to the wells let us push boundaries we've never seen before. Desmond has it the worst, though, in my opinion."

"Why is that?"

"Sage of *Netzach* makes you the last one standing. He can't help but feel invulnerable, risking another scar that cuts too deep while his fellow Mystics perish around him. It's a lot to carry."

"And you?" Leah asked. "Too much *Gevurah* and you dehydrate to death?"

Zafirah eyed her with her big brown eyes. "With water, yes. But *Gevurah* is more than that. Too much earth, and I calcify. Too much fire, and I could die from heat stroke or hypothermia. And I lose oxygen in my blood with too much air. But a little self-care and awareness, and my ailments are nothing compared to others."

Leah rubbed the back of her neck. "I wish I could gauge the Tree of Death like that. It seems like every time Asmodeus, or I use it, we use too much."

Zafirah nodded. "We need you practicing it more. Not only calling it when you need it."

"But we don't have time," Leah said. "Legion—"

Zafirah tutted her tongue. "We would not throw a White Pawn at Legion without proper training. You have not even practiced with the Tree of Death. All you do is react with it."

"But—"

"No," Zafirah cut her off again. "You will practice. And for now, you will not use *Golohab,* or the other upper wells. Not until you have proven to me and the others that you have control. Even then, there is so little known about any of these wells. They are dangerous, and you must use them with caution. And your demon should never use *Gamaliel*, the opposite of *Yesod*, on another Mystic. Understand?"

"Why?" Leah asked.

Zafirah crossed her arms. "It forces a bond between you and another, allowing you to control them like a puppet. There are reports of its use, most where the caster has permanently destroyed their vocal cords. Doing this to another Mystic may damage their bond to the Tree."

"It's all dangerous," Leah said, shaking her head. "I can't see how I can use any of it unless it's a last-ditch effort."

"*Nehemoth*, *Samael*, and *Thagirion*. I want you to practice those with your demon. The corruption does not ail you, and those three could turn the tides of war if a Mystic isn't lost from them. This is decided." Zafirah nodded. "We will work together to prepare you."

"Do we have time for that?" Leah asked. "With the upcoming vote and all?"

Zafirah looked past Leah for a moment before answering. "Not before the vote. Rooks should begin arriving tonight for Friday's vote. We'll resume training after. No matter which way the vote leans, we will depend on every ounce of help available."

"Shit," Leah murmured. That meant she had less than two days to communicate with the ghost. Two days to discover the possessed Rooks trying to sway the election. Two days to stop them.

CHAPTER 35

UNCERTAINTY

Leah rubbed at the bandage on her arm, fresh gauze covering where they'd inserted the IV needle. She paused outside the apartment, listening to the muffled voices of her friends on the other side, before turning the knob. The smell of rosemary and garlic hit her nose as she saw a steaming plate of chicken and potatoes waiting for her.

"Finally," Gabe said, hopping to his feet. "I was worried they were going to keep you overnight."

"Gabe!" Leah rushed and gave him a hug. He returned it, and for a second it felt like the old times, as if all their differences had never been there.

"You're out early," Leah said, finding a spot at the table. "Figured Nick wouldn't let you go."

"Yeah, well," Gabe said, rubbing the nape of his neck and joining her at the table. "Nick said they'd probably need a few beds tonight, with the Rooks coming and all."

"Sounds like we're going to have double duty at the Mystic's Corner tomorrow," Isaac grumbled from the living room.

Leah cut a piece of chicken and popped it into her mouth. "I'm sorry for what happened," she said to Gabe.

He gave a half-smile and looked down. "It was always a risk. But you, are you okay?"

"Doesn't look like Zafirah incinerated you," Sarah said, peeking up from the couches.

Leah rolled her eyes at Sarah. "Ha. Ha. I'm fine." She looked up at her singed hair. "Although I'm sure I look like a mess right now."

Gabe laughed. "You're just going for that asymmetric all over the place look."

She grinned and shook her head. "If only I were that cool." She spotted the slight drop in his shoulders as he looked down at his hands. "Do you want to talk about what happened?"

Gabe shifted on his seat, and fidgeted with his hands, until he finally said, "I think I should. I mean, if you want me to unload all my emotional baggage."

Leah opened her arms. "Go right ahead. I do it all the time." She chuckled.

He smiled and opened his mouth, but the words seemed to drown in his throat. His eyes watered slightly.

Leah grabbed his hands. "It's okay, just take a breath."

Gabe nodded and wiped his eyes. He cleared his throat. "I saw my dad. He was proud of me. Said I'd become the Mystic he'd always hoped I would be. We caught up. I told him about you three too." He paused and frowned. "He told me he was sorry. He admitted I never had a choice, and that me being a Mystic was always his and mom's want for me."

Leah squeezed Gabe's hands and nodded slowly. "Sounds like exactly what you needed to hear."

"He said I didn't have to do it anymore. That he wanted me to live the life I wanted. And I . . . I believed him." He pulled his hands away, hunching his shoulders. "I'm sorry."

Leah leaned forward. "Hey, you got to choose. Just like we did. If this is what you want, then you don't need to apologize to us."

"Yeah," Isaac added. "We're friends, and we support you."

"As long as you keep making us food," Sarah said.

"Sarah!" Isaac yelled.

"Oh whatever, you know I didn't mean it."

"But what now?" Leah asked.

Gabe rested his elbows on the table. "Nick said I won't be training with you guys anymore. The rest is all up in the air. Maybe the Shadow Board. Maybe a job here. They have a meeting tomorrow, and Nick said the Shadow is desperate for recruits right now."

"Would you really go, though? If you had the choice?" Leah asked.

Gabe shook his head. "Hell no! I have a real chance of getting out now."

"You could go to college," Isaac said. "Or culinary school."

Gabe nodded. "If they let me go, that would be nice. Maybe live with my grandmother for a bit."

They remained quiet for a while after that, the rest of Leah's food getting cold as she imagined what her life might be like if that night hadn't occurred. She was the first to free herself from her thoughts, and she smiled at Gabe. "Hey, I'm proud of you, too."

"Me too," Isaac said.

And after an elbow from Isaac, Sarah said, "Yeah, yeah. Me too. Obviously."

The sound of an alarm going off made them all look up.

"Oh, the brownies are ready," Gabe said.

Gabe stood and went to the kitchen. Her eyes trailed after him, a deep heaviness settling in her chest and limbs.

A hand rested on her shoulder and Sarah spoke, flashing some kitchen scissors. "Come, let's even out that hair."

Leah nodded, stood, and followed her to the bathroom while biting the inside of her cheek. She became aware of the sensation of her body being somewhat cold. She had a hard time swallowing, as the fact slowly hit her: whatever the path Gabe chose tomorrow, it meant he would leave them—leave *her*—for good.

CHAPTER 36

HIGH POTENTIAL

Leah walked back into the living room and tossed the red book on the table. "I think it's time I get this ghost on our side."

"Uh, you sure?" Sarah asked, sitting up from the couch. "After everything that happened today, don't you think you should sleep?"

"The Outer Council meets in two days," Leah said. "We don't have time. I've got *Thagirion* now, and we need him on our side."

"How can we help?" Isaac asked.

Leah sat down on the couch between her friends and eyed the book. "Maybe just keep an eye out in case something happens. You won't see me, but knowing you're here will help."

"Want coffee?" Gabe asked, heading into the kitchen. "I'm sure we could all use a little energy before you dive in."

"Sure," Leah said, after seeing his expression. He seemed desperate to offer assistance in any way he could, and Leah couldn't refuse.

A few minutes later, she sipped on a perfect cup of

coffee, along with the rest of them. She leaned forward, setting down the mug and picking up the book.

"Okay," she said, taking in a deep breath. "I'm ready."

"Please, be careful," Gabe said, his eyes shifting from Leah to the book.

"We'll be here if you need anything," Sarah said.

Leah nodded and closed her eyes. *Asmodeus, you ready?*

Yes, he said. *Be quick. We shouldn't linger in the Astral Plane.*

The sensation of cold gel flowed over the top of her head, muffling the sounds from the living room. When she opened her eyes, the incandescent lights had vanished, replaced with the sickly yellowed moss that seemed to glow. The room had deep fissures and cracks that cascaded up the walls and onto the ceiling. Everything looked as if it had been sitting there for decades, untouched and covered in dust. She turned and saw the outlines of her friends, faint shadows but still there if she needed them.

A sharp screech and a crash sounded behind her, and she jumped up from the couch. Behind her, a plate had smashed to the floor, her plate from dinner.

I don't like this, Asmodeus whispered.

She slowly approached the kitchen, stepping over a patch of moss and using the orange light from outside to guide her.

"Hello?"

A door to her right slammed shut. She jumped, eying her now closed bedroom door.

"I know you're here," Leah said. "Please. Can we just talk?"

Footsteps ran past her and into the kitchen. Whatever it was, it kept close to the walls, hiding in the shadows. She peered into the dark and found two white eyes staring back at her.

"Hey," she whispered.

"So hungry," the ghost moaned.

"It's okay, let me help you—"

Her voice caught in her throat when the ghost lunged out from the shadows in his full monster form, fangs bared.

"You left us!" he screamed as he descended on her. She lifted her arm, and his needle-like teeth punctured through her skin. "You left us to burn," he growled, mouth full of her arm.

That's it! Asmodeus yelled.

Leah's arm contorted into a fist, and black ooze pooled out of the puncture wounds. In an instant, several of the teeth cracked, and the black ooze changed into hard obsidian armor.

The ghost pulled away, yanking intact teeth free from her arm as Leah's arm turned into a black gauntleted fist. The arm lunged out, wrapping hard around the ghost's neck.

"What the hell?" Leah shouted.

I won't be food for some ghost, Asmodeus said.

The ghost clawed at her arm, sending sparks, but the obsidian remained firm, squeezing harder and harder.

"Stop! We can't kill him!" Leah yelled.

"It can't be reasoned with. It's either him or us!" Asmodeus yelled, his voice tearing through her throat.

Leah focused on her arm, trying to take control over Asmodeus. The fingers loosened, and the ghost smiled.

It lunged, swiping a claw at her head. Leah ducked, but one claw slid across her face, tearing flesh. The ghost attacked with the other arm, and she lifted her right arm in defense.

She gritted her teeth as the claws broke through her palm, scraping against bone. "Please," she pleaded with the ghost. "Stop. I'm trying to help."

Asmodeus regained control and squeezed harder. The ghost growled and writhed in her hand.

She couldn't reason with him. Not like this. Not with Asmodeus holding him like that. But if he let go, she wouldn't make it.

"*You simply have the potential. Your connection to the Astral Realm is higher than most witches. Here you are—a one-in-a-millennia prodigy . . .*"

If she was like Cora said, then the Astral was her domain as much as it was the other witches. Which meant . . .

Something clicked in Leah, and the ghost in front of her froze. She felt the energy boiling up inside her. It was similar to the energy her reflection had used, and a violet hue glowed around the ghost. Leah carefully pulled her hand back out of the ghost's claws, wincing at the pain, but when she looked down, there were no holes or punctures in her skin, only blood. She opened and closed her fist, the pain subsiding as if it hadn't happened at all.

She eyed the ghost and the violet barrier that encapsulated it. The energy rippled around the ghost, and brief flashes of light formed and expanded into small frames that seemed to play some kind of blurry videos. She reached her right hand forward, gently pressing against its energy. It was cold, giving way like sand in the ocean.

No, Asmodeus whispered. *Don't—*

She pushed harder and the little films came into focus. With it came the roaring sound of the ocean and a child's laughter. The images grew bigger and bigger until suddenly she lurched forward, pulled right into the glowing violet barrier.

CHAPTER 37

TOM

Leah fell through a bright violet cloud filled with clusters of massive orbs of light, each of them flashing with images. Her descent slowed and the orbs hovered and circled around her.

One was of a little boy, opening up a present next to a small and misshapen Christmas tree, smiling as he held up a small wooden figure. Another was of the same boy, a few years older, inside an elementary school, holding up a piece of art, his face scrunched on the verge of tears as the rest of the class laughed. She'd didn't have time to react as one of the orbs raced up to her and she slipped inside. Violet light transformed into a starry night with half the moon shining down on her.

She lay on cold stone, no longer falling from the sky. As she pushed herself up, she noted she was right outside the Academy.

A masculine voice shouted from behind her. "What the fuck is that?"

Leah spotted a small group of kids, not much younger than her, all in Black Pawn attire and all facing the outside wall of the academy. Well, *almost* all of them. She noted one boy who was much smaller than the other kids, with short dark hair, standing with his back against the wall, surrounded by four other students.

One of the taller students, with blond hair and broad shoulders, waved a piece of paper in the air, then shoved it toward the smaller kid. "Look at me! What the hell is this?"

"Alex, stop. He can't answer you if you smother him with it," a girl with curly black hair said.

Alex turned and frowned before pulling the paper away. "Fine." He turned back to the kid. "Now, speak."

The kid looked at Alex and the piece of paper. Then he spoke with a small, mousey voice, "I'm sorry. I didn't know."

"You didn't know what? Really?" Alex growled.

"I got it wrong too. I thought it was right!" the kid shouted.

"We shouldn't have trusted this idiot," another guy, shorter than Alex and with a rounder frame, said. "Now Bishop Hannon's got us coming in after lessons for a week."

"I say we beat him up," one of the other boys said. "Show him not to talk about things he doesn't know."

"Hey!" Leah shouted, stepping forward. "Leave him alone!"

None of them reacted to her shout, not even the kid. She moved in closer but froze as the whispers of disembodied voices filled her ears. They were all around—whispering behind her, in the trees, and behind the walls of the academy.

"Why are you so stupid, Tom? Did your mom drop you on the head as a kid?"

The kid, Tom, wasn't looking at his bullies anymore. He focused on something past Leah, something she couldn't see when she looked over her shoulder.

Alex slammed his hand against the wall beside Tom. "Hey! I'm talking to you!"

Tom straightened, his gaze turning to Alex. "Why don't you do it yourself? Or are you so stupid that you need others to help you?"

The girl with loose curly hair let out a laugh, and Leah saw Alex's fists tighten. Tom must have seen it too, since the color drained from his face.

Alex balled the paper up in his hands. "You're gonna regret that." He pushed Tom hard against the wall. "I'm gonna make you eat your words."

Tom grabbed at Alex's arm, trying to free himself, but the others pulled his arms back and held him against the wall, laughing as they did.

"Show him who's boss," the guy next to Alex said.

Alex moved his hand to Tom's jaw, wrenching his mouth open with his thumb and fingers. He then started pushing the wad of paper into Alex's mouth while saying, "Eat up."

"Hey! Stop!" Leah screamed, running toward them.

As she approached, they all dissolved in front of her eyes, leaving her alone in front of the academy. She froze, turning in circles. "What the—"

Voices near the entrance to the academy caught her attention. She rushed toward them, and the sun seemed to move with her, rising into the middle of the sky. Cool air blew by her as she spotted students walking through the doors and to the cafeteria. She stepped inside, finding Tom slowly descending one of the double sets of stairs with the stained glass window shining in behind him. Her own memories flooded in.

She saw the parchment scoreboard, the same as the one she'd had during her trials, with a list of names she'd never seen before.

Margaret Bateman +8

Holly Daniels -1

Tom Davis: +12

Alex Emerson: +3

A tightness formed in Leah's chest for a moment, remembering how stressful those numbers had been to her and her friends so long ago. And how her fellow classmates would vanish if they didn't make the cut.

Tom reached the bottom of the stairs when the disembodied voices trailed off from the library, right past Leah and to Tom. He blinked slowly and his shoulders slumped as if he fell into some kind of trance.

"Move!" Alex shouted, ramming right into Tom and knocking him over as he and his group of friends walked by. No one stopped to help Tom up, not even the other Pawns, who rushed away, pretending they didn't see.

Leah clenched her jaw, knowing that anything she said or shouted to the cowards who walked away or to Alex wouldn't be heard. Still, Leah started toward Tom, but a shorter girl with platinum blond hair and blue eyes raced over to his side.

"Again?" she asked, helping him up.

Tom nodded, his face red as he kept his eyes on the floor.

"He's such an asshole. Come on, brush it off and let's get some food."

"I'm not hungry," Tom mumbled.

"I wasn't asking," the girl said, locking arms with him and pulling him toward the cafeteria.

Tom pulled back, his eyes drifting up toward Alex, who stood in the cafeteria entrance. "Anat, stop."

"No, you stop. You've got to eat. The last thing you want to do is pass out during practice."

Leah gave a half-smile, remembering how much Isaac

had struggled during his time at the Academy and how she and Sarah had refused to let him give up.

Leah followed as they headed off into the cafeteria, but everyone vanished again. The light from outside slipped beneath the horizon, and the lights in the academy turned on. Cold swept past her, ice forming at the edges of the windows and snow falling outside.

The parchment scoreboard now displayed fewer names. Leah traced down and found Tom with +15 next to his name. She was happy to find Anat's name as well, though she had a -6 next to hers. And Alex had a minus two next to his, which she laughed at, happy to see that he struggled.

Leah felt a draw to the library, as if something was gently pulling her in that direction. She followed, pushing through the doors and sporting several tables filled with students up late, studying. She immediately spotted Alex, with tousled hair and a gaunt face, alone at a table and nose deep in a massive tome. Leah guessed, by his lack of friends, that everyone else in his group had been cut.

"You got this," Leah heard Tom say over on the couches near the windows. "Just let the serpent flow freely."

"It doesn't work like that for me, Tom. I've said it like a hundred times, I don't feel it. At all. Not even a little worm." Anat slammed shut a thick green leather book titled *The Metaphysical Sources of Malchut* and let out a groan.

"But you *are* improving, whether you feel it or not. I mean, you said so yourself when we were practicing in the fields yesterday."

Anat stared up at the ceiling. "I hate these stupid tests. I can't work under this pressure, not with the rumors of what happens to the people that fail. They . . ." She slid her thumb across her throat.

Leah smirked, remembering how she'd also believed that rumor during her trials.

"They don't just off kids that don't make it through. They can't." Tom's voice trailed off, then he shrugged. "Besides, you aren't going to fail out. I won't let that happen. You'll make it, and we'll both be White Pawns with bonds." Tom hopped up and grabbed Anat's arm. "Come on. We're not giving up."

Anat rolled her eyes and slowly got up. "How do you do it? How do you keep your calm during these tests?"

Tom paused. "I donno. They just want to see the best that you can do. If I get stressed over what I can't do, then I'd fail over what I can. At least I have control over the tests. Not like—"

The whispers picked up, louder than before, right behind Leah and deep into the library stacks. Tom peered at them, his face going slack.

"Not like what? Tom?" Anat asked, snapping her fingers in front of his nose. "Earth to Tom. You there?"

He shook his head and blinked. "What? Oh . . . come on, we've got more studying to do."

"No, you don't. You don't get to do that," Anat said, crossing her arms.

"Do what?"

"Every time you talk about yourself, you do that zone out thing."

Tom peeled his eyes away from the stacks. "Maybe I'm just not that interesting."

Anat rolled her eyes. "Says the one who doesn't get stressed with tests or bullies or anything. You just take it. You know all about me, but I know nothing about you."

"Fine. I'll tell you," Tom said.

"Finally!"

"After the trial," Tom continued. "We need to keep studying tonight. Deal?"

Anat let out an audible sigh. "Fine. Ugh. Promise?"

Tom cracked open another tome. "Promise. Now let's work on that form of yours."

They vanished again, dissolving into fine particulate matter as the sun swooped up from the ground and illuminated a gloomy gray sky.

Leah felt the pull again, following her instincts and stepping out of the library and into the hallway. There she found Anat, tears streaming from her face as Tom came rushing in from outside, snow covering his boots.

"There you are!" Tom shouted.

"Stop," Anat said, holding up a hand. "I don't want your—"

"It wasn't that bad," Tom cut her off. "The judges—"

"Don't lie, Tom. It was awful."

"That's what you said last time, and they scored you at a seventy-five!"

"Stop! You and I both know this is different. Just leave me alone." Anat turned and ran.

"Anat! Stop!" Tom yelled, jogging behind her.

Leah followed, stepping out into the main entrance. Students had already huddled around the parchment, and Anat was nowhere in sight. One by one the students vanished into mist, leaving behind Tom, his head dropped low. Leah traced down the parchment until she found the name:

Anat Reeds: -68

There was no way she'd come back from a score like that. It was the same thing that had happened to Buck, back when Leah was at the Academy. She reached an arm out but stopped inches away.

The whispers started again, calling from the library. Tom lifted his head, eyes losing focus.

"Aw, there's the lost little puppy," Alex shouted from

the top of the stairs. "Too sad now that his bitch has been cut."

Tom didn't move, his eyes glaring up at Alex until the taller boy waved a hand in dismissal and headed down the hallway.

Tom stood still as the light shifted around the windows, falling under the horizon. He vanished as rain pattered against the glass, and the lights inside the academy came to life.

Leah took a step forward, and the world shifted. Now she stood inside the library, facing the dark stacks of books, late at night, alone. The pull into the dark was strong, as if something had caught her around the waist and was reeling her in like a fish.

Tom stood deep in the stacks of books, even paler and skinner than before, with bruises around his arms and neck. He reached up, the voices all around them, right at the edge of Leah's hearing, and touched a red book on the shelf. The whispers stopped immediately as he pulled the book from the shelf and sat, flipping through the pages. Time slipped by, the library brightening from a rising morning sun as Tom flipped through the pages. He hunched over, more and more, his skin becoming paler as black veins trailed up his neck. Finally, Tom breathed and leaned back, whispering under his breath.

"What's that?" a voice sounded from behind Leah. She turned to find Alex, half-asleep and still in his pajamas. "How the hell did I get here?"

"I called you," Tom said, his eyes still on the book.

"How? What are you doing, you fucking weirdo?"

"What's wrong, Alex? You scared?" Tom spoke flatly.

"Fuck this," Alex said, turning around.

Tom snapped his fingers and let out another whisper.

Alex spun around on his heels, his eyes wide. "What the fuck? Let me go!"

"This place is cruel. It rewards monsters like you and punishes good people like Anat." Tom stood, his eyes still locked on the book.

Alex snorted. "You're still on about that? Let it fucking go."

"No. I don't want to let anything go. Not anymore." Tom crooked his finger.

Alex's body responding, taking one step, then another toward Tom. "What the fuck are you doing to me? They'll expel you for this."

Tom finally looked up, his eyes bright red with bulging veins snaking to his temples. "*You* are what's wrong with this place. What is wrong with everything. I'm going to fix it. I'll fix it all."

Alex groaned against his invisible restraints, but every time he pushed, it seemed to squeeze him tighter until his lips turned purple.

"Stop!" Leah shouted, reaching for the book. Her hands passed through it, and neither Tom nor Alex seemed to notice.

"Truth is," Tom continued, "I don't care what happens to me anymore. The world is broken, and I'm going to level the scales."

Alex's eyes bulged as Tom raised a finger to Alex's forehead.

Tom let out one soft whisper, barely audible as he touched Alex. "Die."

Alex's gaze shifted toward the ceiling as bones snapped and cracked, breaking through skin. Blood poured out onto the ground, and Leah turned away as the squelch of Alex's remains splattered onto the ground.

CHAPTER 38
CURSED BOOK

Tom dropped the book, blinking and rubbing at his eyes. Color slowly came back into his cheeks, and the dark veins receded. When he finally looked at the mess in front of him, he started hyperventilating and looked down at his bloodied hands. "Oh no. No. No. No. What? What did I do?"

He slumped to his knees, shakily touching Alex's corpse. "Help! Somebody, help me!"

The book on the floor fluttered open, and disembodied voices spilled out, filling the air with promises of revenge and death. Tom froze, his screams caught in his throat as his shoulders dropped and his eyes rolled back. His back arched, and he collapsed to the ground, a last gasp of air leaving his body.

Glowing gold particles drifted up from Tom's body, forming a translucent version of him that hovered, looking down at his resting self. A black tendril, dripping with an inky darkness, slid out of the book, wrapping around this floating version of Tom, and pulled him to the ground and toward the book.

"No! Stop! Please, no!" Tom shouted, clawing at the ground.

Another tendril slid out and wrapped around his arm. Then another around his neck. Leah tried reaching again for Tom or the book, but her hand slipped through everything as if she weren't there. Tendrils dragged him toward the open book, and his body stretched and contorted as it slipped into the pages. His screams echoed off the walls until his hands slipped under the pages.

The book shuddered, and the pages flipped until it slammed closed, then it slowly lifted off the ground and slid into place on the shelves, out of sight. The doors to the library burst open, and people came racing over to the stacks, stopping in their tracks as they came across the two bodies lying on the ground.

"Now you know what happened," a voice echoed out from the shelves.

The library burst into flames in an instant, books crumbling to ash and shelves collapsing as the ceiling caved in. Leah ducked as rubble fell, but it passed right through her, as did the rain that slowly put out the flames. Yet, the shelf with the leather book remained unburnt. Tom appeared a few feet from her, skinny with burns charring his clothes and flesh.

Leah shook her head. "That wasn't you. It was the whispers and the book."

Tom raised an eyebrow at Leah. "But you've had the book for a week now, and it hasn't called you. You haven't even heard the whispers."

Leah pulled the book off the shelf and turned it over. "No, but maybe that's because it already has you."

"I wanted to hurt him," Tom snarled. "He deserved it after everything he did. And then they took Anat, but he got to stay." He closed his eyes and took a deep breath.

Leah stepped forward, but Tom recoiled. "You were angry," Leah said. "It took advantage of that."

Tom turned and found a burned bench to sit on. He opened his mouth several times, but nothing came out.

Leah took the opportunity to join him, and this time, he didn't recoil. "I see you, Tom. And I'm not afraid."

"The book won't let me go. I see others passing on deeper into the Astral, but the book always pulls me back, turning me into this . . . this monster. But you . . . you move easily between the spaces, going deeper than I can even reach. How?"

"It's part of who I am, I guess," Leah said. "There are these witches who are born with the ability to use the Astral, and I'm apparently one of them. Or I could be."

Tom pulled his legs up to his chest and held them, slowly rocking. "I'm sorry. For everything."

Leah looked back at the burned stacks. "I've had worse. Trust me."

"Will you still be my friend?" Tom asked.

"Yes, but," Leah paused, "I do need to ask something of you. Something no one else can do."

Tom nodded. "I know, but I need to ask something from you too. Something you're not going to like."

"What?"

Tom looked at her and said, "I need you to destroy that book. Now."

Leah sat up straight. "Tom, I . . . we—"

"I know." Tom sighed. "You need us. But I can't keep doing this. The book is eating me alive. Each time it takes over, it's like a piece of me chips away."

"But if we destroy it," Leah said, "then what happens to you?"

Tom shrugged. "I'll be free. One way or another."

Leah stood up and paced. "Tom, there's something coming. Something that might kill a lot of people."

"And you want me to find them? I know. But if I do that, then I have to let the book in again, and I'm tired. I've been tired since they killed Anat."

"Wait," Leah said. "You don't still believe that, do you?"

"She failed the trials."

"But that's a rumor," Leah said. "They send them off to the Shadow Board for training. My friend Buck was sent . . ." Suddenly the name hit her, and her eyes widened. "Anat is his mentor!"

Tom looked up, a frown on his face. "No, it can't—she's dead."

"No, Tom," Leah said, catching his gaze. "That has to be her."

"No!" he screamed, a vein popping in his temple. "I already lost her once!"

Leah held up her hands. "Okay, okay. But even if it isn't her, my friend failed the trials and went to the Shadow. He was just here. I saw him with my own two eyes. That means that rumor isn't true."

Tom sat for a long time, frowning as he thought. Then he exhaled and said, "Okay. If there's a chance that she's still alive, then she's still in danger. I'll help."

"You will?" Leah asked.

He nodded. "Maybe I was the injustice back then. Maybe not. But this is my chance to make it right."

CHAPTER 39
GHOST EYES

Leah opened her eyes, finding herself still in the Astral, but back in the living room of her shared apartment, the orange hue and yellowed moss lighting up the space.

"You should go back," Tom said, standing next to the coffee table. His face was contorted, slowly stretching. "I can't hold it back for much longer."

Leah carefully picked up the book from the table, partly thinking the black tentacles might spring out at any second. "I'll be carrying this with me. Is there anything else I need to know?"

Tom shook his head. "It doesn't like those demons. The ones that hide. It should cooperate for a bit if you're hunting them too."

Leah nodded. "Good. I'll see if I can get Buck to help me find Anat. Maybe she'll help us?"

"Maybe." Tom nodded.

"Okay," Leah said. "See you around." She sat down and let *Thagirion* go. A wave of sound washed over her, and the orange light melted away, replaced with incandescent bulbs.

"You're back!" Gabe said, rushing over to her from the kitchen.

"Any luck with the book?" Sarah asked, yawning and rubbing her eyes.

"He's going to help," Leah said, holding up the book.

"Nice!" Isaac said, pushing himself up from the couch.

Leah looked at her friends, who all looked to have woken from a nap, and frowned. "How long was I gone?"

Gabe checked his watch. "Almost four hours."

Leah pushed herself up off the couch. "Then we don't have a lot of time. Think they're all still at the bar?"

"Probably," Sarah shrugged. "But it isn't our shift."

"I'll hide," Leah said. "I just need to get close enough for Tom to spot any dormant demons."

"Tom?" Gabe asked.

"That's his name. He was a Black Pawn. Decades ago. Got tangled up in something in this book. Dark magic or something."

"Okay," Isaac said. "So, you are just going to run in there, and what? You need a plan."

"I have a plan." She held up the book. "Go to the bar, let Tom do his thing, and report back to Nykima."

"But what if one of them catches on?" Gabe asked. "You'd be putting yourself in danger. If they know what you're doing, then they could just wait around and kill you when no one's looking."

"I might have something," Leah said, racing off to her room. She pulled the corked mandrake potion she'd taken from the forensic lab from her bedside table and held it up. "This is a last resort, but the druids gave me this. It'll work if we need it."

"We should go with," Sarah said.

"No," Leah said, heading for the door. "The more of us, the more likely they'll catch on. Try to find Nykima and let her know what we're doing."

"Fine," Gabe said, then paused. "Anyone in particular you're hoping to check?"

Leah grabbed onto the doorknob and turned back. "The person who opposed the fortress from the start. Black Rook Jaime McMillan."

CHAPTER 40

POSSESSED

If there was one shot at finding Black Rook McMillan at this hour, it was at the Mystic's Corner. Leah called on *Thagirion* and she approached the bar, in hopes of not raising any untoward attention to herself.

Leah held out the book, and Tom materialized a few feet from the bar, his back curved more so than it should be and his chin hanging lower than normal.

"Hey," Leah whispered. "I need you to check someone here. He's got ginger hair, a bunch of scars, and he's missing half a finger. Should be easy to find. I need to know if he's possessed or not."

The ghost gave a curt nod and slipped into his own shadow, a dark blur that traced along the ground. She crept closer, doing her best to stay silent as she reached the entrance to the bar. She rounded the corner and ran face first into a stumbling Rook who reeked of alcohol.

Thagirion dropped immediately as she fell back, and the Rook tripped, holding himself up against the wall as he eyed her. He was fairly tall, with a thin frame and slurred speech. "Oops, didn't see you there."

"It's okay," Leah said, helping herself up.

"Hey." The man frowned. "You're that Ackerman kid, aren't you? What are you doing—"

"Covering a shift," she said, looking past him and noting that the place was completely packed. "Or I guess coming in to help by the looks of it. I don't really know; they didn't tell me."

"Ah, well, good luck with that. It's a madhouse in there," he said, stumbling away.

She couldn't risk hiding again with *Thagirion*, not this close to the bar, so instead she slipped inside, maneuvering between Rooks, Knights, and Bishops until she came upon Jaime, sitting at his usual table, surrounded by Rooks and drinking scotch.

She looked around, hoping to glimpse Tom's shadow, but before she could find him, she heard Jaime's booming voice over the crowd. "Well, well, well! Looks like Miss Ackerman has come by for a late-night drink!"

The crowd around her fell silent, heads turning toward her. "No," she said. "I'd heard it was busy and I—"

"Relax." Jaime laughed. "Come, sit with us, Mizrahi."

With all the eyes on her, Leah couldn't help but comply. She approached the table slowly, sitting between a short woman and a young Rook with a long blond beard. She noted several empty glasses in front of Jaime and said, "Looks like you're having fun."

Jaime lifted his glass to her and smiled. "Indeed, I am. Soon enough, we'll have the numbers we need to take down the shifters completely."

"Aren't you celebrating a little early?" Leah frowned. "You haven't had the vote yet."

The man next to her turned and hissed. "Show a little respect to your elders, Pawn."

"Now, now. No need to get testy, Tim," Jaime said. He looked at Leah and continued, "I have the upmost faith the Board will cast their votes on the right side of history."

Heat grew in Leah's cheeks. "I wouldn't be so sure about that. The threat of Legion—"

"Is nothing compared to the fight down in the south," Jaime cut her off. "It's only gotten worse since our last vote, yet your demonic threat hasn't had a single recorded incident since the events at the academy."

"Legion is smart. If he caught wind that we were casting a vote, then getting us tied up in your Brinkmate would be exactly what he wants."

Jaime scratched his chin and said, "I'm sure that's what your Queen will use to try and swing the vote. She's always got something up her sleeve."

Tom's voice hissed in Leah's ear, and she jumped. "He's not possessed, but—"

"Everything alright, lass?" Jaime frowned.

"It's not you," she said before leaning forward. "Black Rook McMillan, please, this is a mistake. Trust me."

Jaime's smile dropped, and he took the last swig from his scotch and pushed himself up. "Come with me, lass. I'd like to have a word with you, in private." He snapped his fingers at the man next to Leah. Tim. "Get another round for the table. I'll expect another one of these when I'm back."

He started away before Leah could say anything, so she pushed herself up and followed him out of the bar and into the empty hall.

He turned and frowned, thinking for a moment before asking, "Have you ever seen a shifter?"

Leah raised an eyebrow. "No."

Jaime leaned forward, and suddenly Leah realized how very alone they were. His breath reeked of scotch, and even though Tom said he wasn't possessed, she still wondered if following him out of the bar was her best decision.

He pulled down his scarf, revealing a tight iron chain that cut into a deep bluish gash with dark veins spidering under his flesh. "Now you have."

Leah stepped back, *Malchut* filling her fists as her heart pounded. "What? So, you—"

"Infected," Jaime said, pulling his scarf back up. "Spreads within minutes. The bastard who did this came with a group at night and took my son, a young Black Knight on his first major mission. I only had enough chain to help myself. It's an old alchemy trick I'd picked up. Infuse iron and keep the infection at bay. By the time I came out of it, the rest of the camp were part of the shifters, and my boy was gone."

Leah took another step back. "Do they . . . do they know?"

Jaime laughed. "Of course they know. The chain only slows it down so much. The treatments down in the lab help, but it won't last forever. I just need one last push. Something to take those fuckers down before I go with them."

"I'm sorry," Leah muttered. "I didn't know."

"Good," Jaime said. "I didn't want you to. Now, if you'll excuse me, I'd like to drink amongst friends, and maybe forget about all this bureaucratic bullshit for a minute." He brushed past her, making his way back into the bar.

"Tom," Leah whispered after a while. "You there?"

A shadow crept along the floor, and Leah called on *Thagirion*, the world around her muffling and turning a slight shade of orange. "Did you scan anyone else in there?"

"I did," Tom said, materializing behind her. "The entire room was clear, except one."

"Who?" Leah asked.

The door to the bar swung open, and Black Rook Skyler Barnes, an ally to Queen Helen, sneered as he looked up and down the hallway, peering through Leah.

Tom quivered, a look of hatred shot at the man, before pointing a long bony finger. "Him," he mouthed.

CHAPTER 41
A DARK PLAN

Rook Barnes rushed past Leah and Tom, unable to see them, and down the hall.

"Are you sure?" Leah asked.

Tom nodded, a snarl on his face. "It's the same aura as the kid. Wrong. Twisted."

The door to the fire exit stairs burst open, and Leah chased after the man, her heart pounding. She needed to know more. Needed to know what he was doing. She caught the door before it closed, slipping through and slinking down the stairs.

He'd traveled up several flights before opening another door. Leah followed, finding herself in a long hallway.

She didn't know this man personally, but he'd been vocal about his support to Queen Helen. Did that mean Legion got to him to sway his vote, or had he been possessed this whole time? If he was possessed, wouldn't he want to divert the attention from Legion? Or was it something else? Maybe trying to sow discord?

Rook Barnes stopped in front of a large wooden door, knocking twice, pausing, and knocking once more. The door opened, and he stepped inside.

"You're late," a woman's voice called from inside.

He stopped, the door wide open, granting Leah just enough time to slip inside.

The office inside was round, with vaulted ceilings, golden curtains, and a navy-blue carpet that muffled Leah's steps. Seven hooded figures stood around, statuesque and staring at Rook Barnes. Leah kept herself close to the door, against the wall.

"Shut the door," the woman standing by the window said. "We have much to discuss."

Tom's voice growled in Leah's ear, straining to whisper. "They're all possessed."

His form undulated, his arms and fingers longer and more monster-like than he had been. Still, he remained by her side, resisting the urge to attack.

Rook Barnes closed the door as the woman turned around. Her face was obscured by her hood, but long black curls dangled through and onto her shoulders.

"Was finishing up some work at the Corner. Saw that Ackerman kid," Rook Barnes answered.

"There's been a change of plans," the woman said.

"Again? What now?"

"It will happen during the vote."

A low growl came from Tom, who twitched and muttered, "Disgusting. They don't belong here. Kill them. Kill them. Kill them."

"Tom," Leah whispered. "Stay with me. Not here. We can't attack here."

Rook Barnes placed his hands behind his back. "The Brinkmate will spoil our plans if we don't get control of it. We should have dealt with him after the first vote."

A shorter, robed figure stepped forward and spoke in a low voice. "The Rook is a tough nut to crack. Our efforts to take him down south nearly gave us away."

Tom spasmed again, and the lights in the office flickered. He stepped forward, his breathing increasing.

Leah grabbed his arm. "Tom. Please, not here. Think of Anat. They'll kill me if they find us."

He shivered, his form shrinking as he took a shaky step back. "I," he whispered. "I can't hold on much longer."

"And now that you've failed," Rook Barnes said. "We have to change our plans."

The short man's hands curled into a fist, but the woman at the window cleared her throat. "This second vote grants us an opportunity we can't pass up. Everything was already prepared. We just need to put our focus here and move swiftly."

"But it's a gamble," Rook Barnes said. "The Queens and the Sages are here. If they catch on, we could sustain heavy losses."

"I've spoken with Legion personally," the woman said. "The rewards will outweigh the risk. We must move before the Brinkmate prevails."

"But—"

"Do you defy Legion?" the woman hissed. "No? Then obey your orders. We strike at the vote."

Leah followed close behind Rook Barnes, sneaking out of the room and into the hallway. She slipped past him into the stairwell and ran down the stairs.

Moments later, she closed the door to her apartment and dropped *Thagirion* as she leaned against the door. She caught her breath, focusing on Nykima, who waited at the table with her friends. They listened as she recounted the last couple of hours.

"I don't get it," Sarah said once Leah had finished. "So, the demons want the Fortress to pass? How does that make sense?"

"Unless Queen Helen is possessed and they want her in complete control," Nykima said.

Leah shook her head. "I find that hard to believe. We fought beside her in the Academy. She gave her all to protect us."

"But she could have been taken after," Isaac said, leaning forward and interlacing his fingers. "I mean, we haven't been with her this whole time. If there are demons already here, then one of them could have gotten to her."

Leah stood and held up the book. "We have Tom now. We can just check right now."

"No," Gabe said, grabbing her arm. "You almost got caught twice from the sounds of it. And now we know there are at least eight people possessed by demons in headquarters. We have to be smart about this."

"We need to act fast," Nykima said, pausing for a moment before speaking. "The integrity of the Infinity Board has been compromised."

"Can Tom get us the name of every Rook compromised? I mean, we could go around HQ or wait in the cafeteria or something," Sarah said.

"No," Nykima said. "That will take too much time. We don't know how widespread it is, or how quickly it's spreading."

"So, going to Queen Helen right now and checking that all the Queens are in the clear should be the first priority, don't you think?" Leah asked.

"Sages first. They'll be less guarded," Nykima said. "Getting the Queens now could tip the demons off before we have the numbers to fend them off."

"And do what with them?" Isaac asked. "Bring them back here?"

Nykima pulled out the black tome from the bag hanging off her wheelchair and flipped open a page with a simple circle and some scrawled notes. "We make a circle of protection. Not here, but outside in the woods, where we have a better vantage point. We'll need a lot of salt, some herbs, brick dust, and blood."

She looked up at Gabe and he sighed. "Yeah, I know where they keep the bags of salt. Just give me the list."

Nykima eyed Isaac and Sarah. "You two know where the maintenance shed is? They have an old bin in the back for replacement bricks. Unless the groundskeeper changed his tune, there's a ton of brick dust in there. You should be able to scoop some up."

"Then what?" Gabe asked. "Say we get them all up and into the circle. What then?"

"We tell them Leah's findings," Nykima said. "We'll have Tom on our side to confirm. After that, we must defer to them to make a plan. They are the voice of the Infinity Board, and we must abide."

"Okay," Leah said. "Tom and I will go get the Sages, confirm they're clean, and send them out into the woods to find you."

"And if they're not?" Gabe asked.

"Then I have Tom and Asmodeus to help me," Leah said. "I can't imagine they'd want a full-on fight before they're ready."

"And they won't be able to possess you," Nykima said. "Not with Asmodeus already in you."

Leah nodded. "After the Sages I'll use *Thagirion* to slip by the Queen's guards too and bring them with me to find you."

"You'll need a key to get into the Sage's wing," Sarah

said, her face reddening as she pulled out a small silver key. "East wing, top floor."

Nykima raised an eyebrow. "How did you manage to get that?"

Sarah bit her lip. "Yuki gave it to me." She looked at Leah. "She's the first door on the right."

Leah nodded and pocketed the key before grabbing a backpack and stuffing the book inside along with the Mandrake potion. "Where will the circle be?"

"Behind the sand training field," Nykima said. She held up a cup toward Leah. "Before you go, I need a little bit of blood. Left arm."

"Blood?" Leah frowned.

"You've got a demon in you, so you shouldn't be able to cross unless I work your blood into the circle."

"Oh, right." Leah grabbed a knife from the kitchen, holding the edge to her skin. She paused, looked away, and slit her arm open. "Ow!" she said, bleeding into the cup.

"That's enough," Nykima said, holding up the cup. "Get some pressure on that and go. Good luck."

Leah ran off to the bathroom, applying some bandages to her arm, then smiled at Sarah and Isaac and nodded at Gabe.

"Please be careful," Gabe whispered.

"I could say the same to you," Leah said. "See you all in the circle."

CHAPTER 42
GHOSTLY VENTURE

I hope you know what you are doing, Asmodeus said as they rounded a corner full of Rooks. Luckily, Leah had already called on *Thagirion*, and the Rooks appeared to be intoxicated enough that she could probably be visible and they wouldn't even care.

She reached the elevator lobby of the east wing and used Sarah's key to reach the top floor. The doors opened into a large hallway filled with ornate vases, tattered tapestries, and cushiony rugs on the hardwood floor. She reached the first door on the right, Yuki's room, and activated *Tiferet*. Warmth filled her eyes, and she peered into the door. There was no light or sign of life on the other side. She turned, looking through the other doors one-by-one. Of the seven rooms, only three had the golden silhouettes, all of whom seemed to be asleep.

"Tom, are you here?" Leah whispered.

"I am," Tom said, materializing next to her. He was completely in his human form, with no distortion.

Leah dropped *Tiferet* and rubbed her eyes, approaching the door closest to them with a person sleeping inside. "Can you check if that Sage is possessed?"

Tom nodded and carefully approached the door.

Before Tom could pass through the door, a pale face phased through the wood.

Leah jumped back as Eli, in his Astral body, glared at her. "Care to explain what you're doing, Pawn Ackerman?"

"Who are you?" Tom asked, stepping back, eyes wide. "You see me too?"

"Silence, ghost. I asked this Pawn a question," the Sage said as his body came through the door and floated in front of Leah.

"How are you—?"

"Astral Projection. You shouldn't be too surprised. I am the Bonded after all. Care to explain why you're outside my room using *Thagirion* with a corrupted ghost?"

Leah looked back at Tom, who gave her a nod. "We need to talk."

"I'm listening," Eli said, crossing his arms.

"Tom isn't corrupted. He can see demons. Specifically, the ones we saw at the Academy. The ones who got past *Tiferet*. He's bound to a book they had down in the labs. Once I got it, I asked him to help me check if any dormant demons were here. There's at least eight of them, including Rook Skyler Barnes. I overheard a meeting where they said they were going to do something during the vote."

Eli simply stared, taking in the information before slowly descending, his feet touching the ground. "Then we have no time to lose. Is using your ghost the only way to tell if someone is possessed?

Leah blinked, off guard by how easily Eli had taken this information. "*Tiferet* doesn't work. He's the only one who seems able to see them."

Eli turned to Tom, who stepped back. "You, boy . . . what do you see when you spot these demons?"

Tom looked at the floor, his shoulders hunched. "It's more of a feeling. Disgust. And the thing inside me wants to attack."

"The book he's bound to is cursed or something," Leah said. "I think it's using Tom somehow. I've got it here in my pack if you want to see it."

"Perhaps later," Eli said. "I'm assuming you came up here to collect us?"

"Yes," Leah said. "There's a circle in the woods. We need the Sages and the Queens."

"Understood. Zafirah and Desmond are asleep next door. Scan them, and we'll go."

"Tom?" Leah asked. "Can you check them quick?"

Tom nodded and slipped through the walls.

"What about the others?"

"Yuki is probably trying to snag a drink at the bar. She can't resist with so many Rooks here. Sandeep doesn't sleep much. I know where to find him. But Nona and Nick, I don't know."

"Can you get them?" Leah asked. "Don't tell them anything, not until we know they aren't possessed. For all we know, those Rooks are spreading more demons tonight."

"You shouldn't underestimate us."

"I'm not. Once we're all together, we can form a plan."

"What about you? Where are you headed?" Eli asked, raising an eyebrow.

"The Queens. I can get past the guards with *Thagirion* and then Tom can get a closer look."

Tom materialized next to Leah and said, "They're both clean."

"Good," Leah said.

"I'll gather them and the others. You just go and get the

Queens." Eli placed a hand on her shoulder and added, "Trust yourself, Pawn Ackerman. Your intuition might save us all."

He slipped back through his door as Leah turned and rushed to the elevator.

Leah slipped past two sets of guards and leaned against Queen Helen's office doors, activating *Tiferet*. Only one person was inside. *Perfect.* She nodded at Tom, who slipped inside while she leaned against the door, catching her breath.

What if they were too late? What is Queen Helen was already taken? Thoughts filled her mind as she waited, until Tom's ghostly form slipped back out the door, his gate wider and more haggard.

"What is it?" Leah whispered.

"She's clean," Tom said, with a raspy voice. "It hungers. I hunger."

"Just a little longer," Leah said, letting out a sigh as she pushed open the door.

She dropped *Thagirion*, materializing in front of the Queen Helen, who wore a long white shirt and black dressing pants, with high boots.

Queen Helen jerked her head up, dark circles around her eyes and her hair slightly out of place, and a pressure popped in Leah's ears and her arms squeezed against her sides for a split second before releasing. The Queen relaxed her shoulders and said with a smooth voice, "Leah. I wasn't expecting you."

"I'm sorry," Leah said. "It's important."

Helen frowned and gestured to the chairs. "Please, sit. What is it?"

Leah recounted the evening's events as quickly as she could. When she was done, Helen stood and walked toward the glass window overlooking the dark forest.

"And you are certain about this? This ghost can be trusted?"

Leah nodded. "He warned me about Joanna back at the Academy. I trust him. Which means you and the others are at risk." Leah stood. "Nykima is making a protection circle outside as we speak. We need to find the other Queens."

"Queen Jan Xie should be returning tomorrow morning, and Queen Micah will be—"

There was a knock at Queen Helen's door. Helen raised an eyebrow and stepped near her coat rack, wrapping her hand around one of the two katanas resting behind it.

"Come in," she said.

Reginald Platt opened the door, his gray-peppered beard a bit longer than Leah remembered. He sported a crisp black suit and held his pristine black cane with the golden crow head topper. "Ah, Pawn Ackerman, pleasure to see you. I wasn't expecting an audience."

Leah opened her mouth to speak, but Helen cut her off. "Pawn Ackerman came here after she was dismissed from the hospital wing by Nick. He wanted me to have a personal examination of her injuries."

Reginald closed the door behind him and beamed down at Leah. "Ah, I see. Training with the Sages can be tough, but with a little elbow grease, they'll get you back in shape for what's coming." He grinned.

"Did you have any luck?" Helen asked. "Convincing the others?"

"Oh," Reginald chuckled, looking up at Helen. "I think

they'll come around. Come tomorrow, we should have the vote."

A hand wrapped around Leah's arm, invisible, but tight. She called on *Tiferet* and saw Tom, his face undulating and contorting. "That's him," he growled. "That's Legion."

CHAPTER 43

DECEIVER

ausea washed over Leah, and time slowed. Reginald Platt? The Black Rook who was part of the Administration at the Maimonides Academy? The man who had fought William alongside the others? The man who supported Queen Helen's cause to hunt down Legion? He *was* Legion?

She shook her head. *No, Tom must be mistaken.* She looked at him again, but his eyes rolled back into his skull and his teeth grew long and sharp.

How? Asmodeus hissed, his voice trembling inside her head. *I don't see anything. How could he hide from me?*

Reginald looked back at Leah and frowned. "Everything okay? You look pale, Pawn Ackerman."

"I . . . yeah," Leah said wrapping a hand around her arm in the same spot Tom was squeezing, willing everything in her being for him to remain calm. "I'm just . . . tired. It's been a long day."

Her heart pounded, and she could feel Tom trembling. She had to run. Get out of there before Tom turned. They weren't ready to face him. Not again. Not without a plan.

Helen made eye contact with Leah and stood up tall,

stepping away from the coat rack. "You came just in time, Reginald. Leah and I were just finishing up. Best for her to get some rest. Big day tomorrow."

"Ah, yes." Reginald smiled. "If they make any more of those tequeños, could you put a few aside for me?"

Leah glanced over at Helen, hoping to convey her some kind of message or clue.

"I'm sure they will, Reg," Helen said. "Go on, Leah. Reg and I need to talk."

Leah carefully stepped forward, willing Tom to come with her as his body undulated and shifted beneath her hand. She reached the door, feeling the pull of the book in her backpack, slipping off her shoulder, trying to resist her from leaving. She paused, looking back at Helen, who gave her a slight nod. She didn't want to leave Helen with him.

"It's okay, Pawn Ackerman," Queen Helen said. "We'll talk more tomorrow."

Leah stopped, her hand hovering over the doorknob. She couldn't let him do this again. He'd killed so many people she cared about. She slipped out of the room, her mind reeling. He'd killed them. Constance, Grace, Sid, Miranda, Ricardo, Brandon. Her uncle. She couldn't let him kill again. Not if she could help it.

Her hand slipped into the pack and wrapped around the corked mandrake potion. She could end this. Right here.

Leah, stop. We're not ready to fight him. It'll be suicide, Asmodeus hissed.

I'm sorry, Leah said back to him, pulling out the bottle. *I must protect the Queen.*

She turned, and Reginald no longer stood beside Helen. Instead, he was lunging at Leah, eyes locked on her hand as his sword stripped free from his cane and aimed directly for her neck. She couldn't think. Couldn't pull on *Malchut* fast enough to stop him. He'd already crossed half the room and, in another second, he'd be at her throat.

The space between them blurred and contorted, and a popping pressure pushed against Leah as Helen materialized in front of her, two katanas drawn and clashing against his sword. He stumbled back and Queen Helen turned, landing a hand on Leah.

The world around her collapsed and squeezed, a sensation she hadn't experienced since that night at the academy. One moment they were in the Queen's office, and the next Leah was landing on cold sand, the night air filling her lungs.

Hands wrapped around her shoulder and pulled her up to her feet. "What the hell were you thinking?" Helen shouted.

Leah blinked, her eyes adjusting to the dark. "How did you . . . how did you know?"

"I saw that ghost of yours. I can't believe they got to Reginald," Helen said, brushing sand off Leah.

"No," Leah said, grabbing on to Helen's arm. "It's worse than that. He's Legion."

Helen shivered under Leah's grasp, her mouth falling agape.

"Leah?" a voice called. "Over here."

They both turned, spotting Sarah a few feet off, holding a flashlight and waving. "Come on, we're set up over here."

Leah glanced at Helen, then Sarah. "We have a problem. We need to get to the others, now!"

"Come on. They're over here," Sarah said, waving them down a path.

They traveled a short distance into the woods until they spotted a set of flashlights. Gabe, Isaac, Nick, and Zafirah stood within the circle with Nykima, who held open the black tome and was eying the circle. Leah spotted Eli behind Nykima, eyes closed and seated on the ground.

As Leah stepped over the circle, a density came down on her. She pushed through, her head aching, lungs straining against the force, and her knees feeling as if they were about to buckle before the sensation vanished altogether. She stumbled, gasping for air.

"Apologies, Pawn Ackerman. The circle took a minute to recognize you," Nykima said before looking up at Queen Helen. She sat upright in her wheelchair. "Pawns, your Queen is here!"

Isaac and Gabe stood at attention, but Helen was quick to say, "At ease," as she stepped through the circle.

"We have a problem," Leah said. "Legion is here already!"

"You are certain of this?" Zafirah asked, wearing nothing but leggings and a sports bra, seemingly unphased by the frosty night.

"Yes," Leah said. "He's possessed Black Rook Reginald Platt. I tried to attack him, but he attacked."

Helen joined Leah's side and said, "It was foolish to face him head on, but I got us both out of there before he attacked. Leah is telling the truth."

"And the others? Where are they?" Leah asked.

"Sandeep is on his way," Eli said, his eyes still closed. "I'm projecting myself to reach the others. However, Yuki is too intoxicated to see me, and I cannot find Nona. I sent Desmond to fetch Yuki. They should be here any—ah, here they come."

She turned and spotted two figures out through the trees and on the training grounds, coming toward them. The smaller silhouette stumbled while the other held her from falling.

Hear me! A voice boomed in Leah's mind. The sound

was immense, racking through her skull and forcing her to her knees.

"Leah?" Sarah asked, her voice muffled. "Are you okay?"

They've discovered us. Leah fell to her side, holding her head, as it felt like it was about to split in two.

"Isaac? What's happening?" Sarah shouted.

"Don't touch them," Nick urged.

Leah opened her eyes for a moment and saw her friend also holding his head as she writhed on the ground.

"They hear him," Queen Helen whispered. "We must—"

Do it now. We shall take them tonight.

CHAPTER 44
CHAOS

The pain stopped, along with the voice, and Leah slowly got to her feet. She eyed Isaac, whose scar had grown darker along his face.

A noise coming from headquarters sounded like hundreds of little thunderbolts striking. Sarah helped Isaac to his feet while the Sages and the Queen's eyes glowed yellow, staring at headquarters.

Warmth spread behind Leah's eyes as she called on *Tiferet*. A massive crack appeared in the sky, glowing with a sickly yellow light. An explosion sounded, then another, and with each one, the crack in the sky grew. Movement inside the break in the sky caught her eye. Something fell free, falling onto headquarters. Then another. She used *Tiferet* to focus in on one, spotting a strange rocky body with enormous claws diving free from the marred sky.

"Demons," Helen said.

"Coming from the Astral," Eli added.

A glass wall in an upper floor of headquarters shattered, and a person flew out, tumbling toward the ground before landing hard.

"No," Leah whispered.

Another loud explosion widened the opening, and the demons fell by the hundreds, like rain.

"They won't know what's coming," Zafirah said, speaking of those trapped inside headquarters and stepping toward the edge of the circle.

"No!" Nykima shouted. "We can't risk it. You'd be taken in seconds if you went in there."

"Hurry!" Eli screamed at Desmond and Yuki, who had only crossed half the field.

Demons washed over the headquarters, climbing along the outer walls and clawing into windows. Several landed on the ground, rearing their heads toward the group.

Desmond grabbed Yuki and leaped from the ground, using *Malchut* in his strides to lunge closer to the circle. Dozens of demons chased on all fours, snapping at his heels as he ran. With one last leap, he flew into the circle, only to tackle Eli to the ground.

The horde of demons collided with the edge of the circle as if it were some kind of super-heated fire. They barely had time to scream as they dissolved into wisps of smoke. Once the demons caught on, several stopped and backed up, circling the perimeter with glowing eyes.

Screams and gunshots sounded from inside headquarters as the demons continued to flood the building. Another wall exploded, and several demons flew out, likely forced by *Malchut*. Fire burst through another window as howls and screams grew louder.

"They're all going to die," Sarah said. "We have to help them. This can't . . . it can't happen again."

Nick pushed past Leah, stepping over the circle.

"No, Nick, wait!" Leah shouted.

"No," he said, turning back. "People are dying. You

brought us to the circle so we could fight together. We go now, or we lose everyone."

A demon lunged forward from the brush, eyes locked on Nick.

"Look out!" Isaac shouted.

Helen appeared behind him in a burst of air and cut the demon in half. Nick turned and sliced the air, sending a *Malchut* blade and severing its head.

Several more demons came at once, circling the two of them and leaping forward. Before Queen Helen had a chance to strike, a bright fire surrounded them, destroying each of the creatures.

The Black Queen eyed the heap of charred demon before holding up her katana. "We're not going to sit by while they possess everyone. They might have the numbers, but we have the strength. Sages, to me!"

The Sages didn't hesitate, crossing the circle and joining Helen and Nick as they cut down the remaining demons surrounding the circle.

Energy filled Leah's hands, and she looked at Nykima. "I'm going with them."

"Me too," Sarah said, puffing out her chest.

"Yeah, I'm in," Isaac said.

"Wait," Nykima said.

Sarah shook her head. "They'll need all the help they can get."

"That's not it," Nykima said. "Bring back any injured. The circle will stay strong through the night. Pawn Tate, stay with me."

"No, wait, but—They need me," Gabe protested.

"You're not bonded," Nykima said. "You'll be more of a risk. Stay here and help me keep the barrier safe. You three, go. Now!"

Leah took off her bag with the book and tossed it to Nykima. "Please, keep this safe."

"Leah," Gabe said, stepping forward.

Leah shook her head. "Tell me when we get back. Until then, keep her safe." She nodded toward Nykima.

Leah turned and joined her friends, chasing after Queen Helen. They rounded a corner in the path, and two black demons lunged out from the dark. Before the creatures could land an attack, Sarah pushed forward and unleashed a wall of fire. The demons screamed as they burned, racing off into the dark. The group broke free from the woods, and five more demons ran toward them, tearing into the ground before leaping into the air.

Leah heard a clap beside her, and the five demons froze in midair.

"Get them, quick!" Isaac said, his voice straining.

Leah fired off *Malchut* bullets at the first two, killing them in an instant, while Sarah rammed a *Malchut* fist into a third, tearing off its jaw.

The other two fell, *Hod* broken, and readied to attack. However, prior to Leah attacking, both demons flattened into the ground and Yuki landed on top of them.

"You're slow, better catch up," she said, grinning at Sarah.

"I thought you were drunk," Sarah said.

"Who said I'm not?" Yuki smirked.

"Come on, we can't fall behind," Isaac said, racing forward.

They followed the war path of the Sages and Queen Helen, stepping over the corpses of fallen demons, finally finding their allies in the courtyard just outside the lobby. Most of the lobby's windows had been blown out, and the scene was chaotic, with Mystics fighting other Mystics all around them.

She spotted Jaime in the middle of it, leading a group of Mystics toward them. Several demons lunged onto him, clawing at him, but their sharped boney claws flowed over him like water. He grinned and grabbed one of them by the throat, his hand bursting into flames as the demon screamed and grasped his hand.

Glass shattered above Leah, and a Mystic shrieked as they fell to the ground. Two more Mystics jumped out the window, landing on their feet next to the dead Mystic. One of them was an older woman Leah knew and had once thought was like a sweet old grandmother. Now her knit sweater was splattered with blood, and she stared back at Leah with bright yellow eyes.

"Nona?" Leah said.

Zafirah stepped between Leah and the woman. "Nona is gone." She shot a blast of fire at the old woman.

Nona gracefully moved out of the way, shifting quick on her feet as Zafirah sent more fiery bolts her way. "You're going to have to try harder than that, little one."

Sarah joined Zafirah, but Nona moved with grace, her eyes glowing yellow, predicting every assault.

Then Yuki lunged from the left, ramming into Nona's side with *Malchut.*

The woman collapsed in an instant.

Yuki stood over her, swaying. "Didn't see that one coming, did you?"

"Leah, watch out!" Isaac screamed.

Leah's left arm acted on its own, turning her around with its own force and grabbing the neck of an incoming Mystic. Mathew stared at her, his eyes wild as her hand squeezed involuntarily.

No, she willed, relaxing her hand. *Not him.*

A sharp pain blossomed on her side, and her breath caught in her chest. She looked down to see Mathew holding the hilt of a small knife, sticking out of her side. She let out a breath, and with it tasted iron.

You bastard, Asmodeus said, regaining control of Mathew.

"No," she wheezed as Mathew grabbed at her hand, his eyes bulging. "Stop."

But it was no use. She squeezed harder, crushing Mathew's windpipe. Then Asmodeus threw Mathew back and controlled both of Leah's hands to make the sign of *Samael.*

Leah slumped to her knees as Mathew's cheeks sunk in and blood vessels in his eyes popped. As he fell limp, the pain in Leah's side vanished, and the knife fell to the ground. She grazed her fingers over her wound, and only found her ripped T-shirt.

Do not stop me again! Asmodeus shouted in her mind. *We are at war!*

Before she could react, an invisible force rammed into her, throwing her away from the Sages and her friends and out toward the fields. She landed several feet back in a heap of mud and gasped for air.

A smokey haze filled the air as it billowed out from headquarters, flames filling the building. She pushed herself up, right in the middle of other Pawns, Bishops, and Knights. Yuki and Zafirah raced out from the courtyard, flanked by Sarah, Isaac, and a group of Mystics.

Fire burst from the hands of the Knight beside Leah. She was dark-skinned, and her eyes shone gold as she pulled Leah up from the ground.

"They're coming!" the Knight yelled, flinging streams of fire into the tree line.

The earth shook beneath Leah's feet, roots bursting through the ground and piercing through the Mystics ahead before slithering toward her, ready to tear her asunder.

The Knight jumped forward, using *Malchut* to rip the roots apart.

She's been here before. Seen this happen before.

Leah looked at the Knight. "No! Wait!"

Yet, the moment had already slipped away. The woman flew back, slammed by a *Malchut* force that flung her like a ragdoll right into the fire.

Energy flowed into Leah's arms, readying herself for the attack.

"Incoming!" Yuki shouted. Leah's training kicked in, and she called on *Netzach.* A thick ooze of energy covered her, just before the bullets peppered and bounced off her skin.

Leah unleashed a *Malchut* wave toward the two closest Mystics aiming guns at her, sending them flying through the air and back into the trees. A Black Bishop surged forward, and Leah sent another wave of energy, but it washed over him.

He's possessed and using Netzach, Leah said.

They, Asmodeus said, a shake in his voice. *They have complete control over them.*

The Bishop used *Malchut* to launch into the air, but roots leaped up from the ground and twisted around him, piercing and weaving through his legs and stomach.

"We need to regroup!" Zafirah shouted, gasping for air as the roots fell back to the ground. Yellowed moss sprouted around her, illuminated by the light above.

This is chaos, Asmodeus said. *He's going to collapse everything.*

From her vantage, Leah could see Nykima pulling Mystics into the circle as Gabe and Tom defended it. Bodies flew left and right as Gabe shot waves of *Malchut* and Tom, now a massive tentacled being, threw and tore demons apart.

"We need to protect the Queen!" Zafirah said.

Behind Zafirah, toward headquarters, a long chain burst out from the lobby, bouncing off Desmond before retracting back into the dark.

He's there, Asmodeus growled.

Leah clenched her jaw and spat through gritted teeth, "Legion."

CHAPTER 45
CHECK

The crack in the sky wavered and shrank as Leah looked up. Their efforts to stave off the demonic infiltration were working, and the fissure was faltering with each demon they killed. She slipped between fights, dodging a line of fire from a Black Rook, unsure if that was meant for her or only a misfire as the Mystics clashed with one another.

She reached the courtyard once again and ducked as a body flew toward her. So many Mystics were piled on top of each other in this small space, with energy flying left and right as those who were possessed protected Legion and others cut them down. He stood at the center of it, shadows creeping up along his black suit and covering his face, his crow-topped cane nowhere to be seen. No one would last long here, not with chains flying in every direction without care of who they tore through.

Helen appeared next to Legion, katanas glinting in the light as she swung them down at him. But each strike simply bounced off his flesh. She vanished again, appearing next to a demon and shoving her blade through its chest, her eyes still locked on Legion.

Desmond and Jaime propelled themselves forward, landing punches on Legion's shadowy face and gut, lifting him off his feet and knocking him back into a wall. Chains flew forward toward their heads, sparking as they glided off them without so much as a scratch.

"Cut them all down!" Helen shouted, cutting another demon down. "One of them is protecting him!"

Leah caught on to what she was doing. Helen couldn't get a hit on him because one of these demons was using their energy to protect him, same as what happened back at the academy. They needed to take them out if they had any chance of facing Legion.

She called on *Thagirion* to enshroud her, allowing the thick energy to wash over her as she moved along to the side of the building and away from the fight. She then called on *Tiferet* and studied the space around Legion. She'd seen his protection before; she just needed to trust her instincts and spot the . . .

A thin red line wisped off him, trailing up and into one office overlooking the lobby.

There! If she followed that she'd find the demon who was protecting Legion.

Leah crept along the wall, steering around the battle and slipping into the emergency stairwell. She raced up the stairs, crawling through the broken doorway. Demon corpses littered the ground, which she carefully avoided as Black Rook Skyler Barnes stepped out from the office.

He glanced up and down the hall, through Leah, before looking down at the carnage below.

There was no way she could take him head on, but if she was invisible . . .

She crouched, stepped over the bodies of demons, holding her breath and following the red line while energy flowed to her left arm. One demon stirred, and a clawed hand wrapped around her foot, yanking her to the ground. It crawled on top of her, clawed hands phasing through her chest as it attempted to possess her.

Asmodeus took over Leah's arm and cut the demon in half with a huge *Malchut* blade that sank into the stone walls. Leah pushed herself up to her feet, but before she could fully stand, something hit her hard in the head and she fell to the ground. She rolled on her back, looking up at the Black Rook.

"Clever, sneaking up to take out Legion's shield. Shame we didn't possess you sooner." Skyler smirked.

There was a ringing in her ear, and she spat blood. "Bastard."

Asmodeus attempted a call on *Samael*, but Skyler jumped back, sending a sent a wave of *Malchut* with his foot, throwing Leah across the corridor. She pushed herself up as he walked toward her with a spring in his step.

"You really don't know when to quit," he said.

A crash sounded behind Black Rook Barnes, along with a massive cloud of dust. A man dressed in an all-white suit adjusted his tie as he stepped over what looked like two dead Black Rooks.

White Queen Micah eyed Skyler and sighed. "I'm sorry it has come to this."

Barnes stood up straight, taking a step back. "Same to you, my Queen."

Skyler sent the first attack, multiple pulses of *Malchut*, which Queen Micah waved off with a hand. Barnes switched to *Gevurah,* thrusting a fist of fire that set Micah into motion.

Micah raced forward as columns of fire closed in on him. He didn't dodge as the flames burned at the edges of his suit, closing the space between him and the Black Rook.

Skyler crooked his neck to the side and arched his back,

bones protruding out of his hands into long claws. He swung at the Queen, but it simply slid off him without the slightest effect.

Micah closed the space in an instant and placed two fingers on Rook Barnes's forehead before shutting his eyes. One second Skyler was rounding for another attack, the next he fell to the ground, blood seeping from his ears.

Micah brushed at the edges of his singed suit, then looked toward Leah, his eyes a soft glow of yellow. "You have a broken rib, Pawn. Let me help."

He approached, the air around Leah growing warm as he hovered a hand over her. Heat enveloped her, and the bone inside her shifted and settled back into place.

"Much better. Come. We must join the others." Queen Micah offered her a hand and pulled her up.

"But Legion, he's here," Leah said. "We have to—"

"No, Pawn. The time for running has come and gone."

"No," Leah said. "That's not what I mean. There's a demon," she nodded down the hall, calling on *Tiferet* to trace the red line of energy. "Down there who is protecting Legion with some kind of magic. If we take him out, Legion will be vulnerable."

"Ah," Queen Micah grinned. "Glad we have someone like you on our side, then. Where is it?"

Leah pointed at the door. "There."

Queen Micah peered in the direction and sighed, his shoulders dropping. "Of course, Legion would employ a child to protect him."

"He's possessed more than that, my Queen. We can exorcise him; that will stop Legion."

"No," Micah said, stepping toward the office. "That child is gone. A mere shell of the demon that has consumed him." Micah raised two fingers and whispered. "Please, forgive me."

A single *Malchut* bullet was fired from him with such strength, it sucked the air of the corridor, the deafening sound cracking through the air. Leah invoked *Tiferet* once more, just in time to see the thin red line disappearing.

"Come," Micah said. "We have a demon to kill."

CHAPTER 46
VOID

Chains flew wildly through the air as Leah and White Queen Micah joined the fight on the training field. They joined Desmond, cutting down and deflecting the chains sprouting out of Legion like hydra heads. He was desperate; he had to be now that he was without his shield.

Leah cut down a chain as Micah propelled himself upward and fired a concussive set of *Malchut* bullets. One of them ripped through Legion's shoulder with such force it knocked him off balance. Legion thrust an arm up at Micah, sending a wave of *Malchut* that knocked Micah back, landing hard on the ground with *Netzach*.

Sarah and Isaac stood on Legion's other side, along with Yuki, cutting down demons and deflecting Legion's attacks.

Desmond jumped forward with an open opportunity to land a punch on Legion, but Nona stepped in his path, blackened scars tracing up her side. She clapped her hands together, holding Desmond with *Hod*. Legion threw several chains at Desmond, sending him flying toward the edge of the forest, where a group of possessed Mystics surrounded him.

Nona's eyes glowed a brilliant yellow as she swung her arm to her left, sending a blade of *Malchut* into a Mystic closing in on her and Legion, slicing him in two. She deflected everything that Legion missed, covering his blind spots as they cut down Mystics and stopped the Sages' and Queens' advances.

Leah braced for Nona's wave of *Malchut,* but it was too strong, and she went flying, landing hard in the rubble that was once the courtyard. She readied to leap back into the fight when a hand wrapped around her ankle. She spun around, fist clenched, ready to take out whatever demon was trying to wriggle its way to her.

Instead, she met the wide eyes of a Pawn, not much older than her, with freckles across his face. "Help me," he mouthed. She looked down at his side, peering through his ripped shirt and on skin that was a dark blistery green with black veins scattering and pulsing under his skin. She'd seen this before, when Isaac had been partly possessed.

"Medic! I need a medic!" Leah yelled, crouching down to his side. It was futile. Even with *Chesed,* he'd only be healed so much.

"It hurts," he whispered, tears streaming down his face. "I . . . I . . ."

Leah reached into her pocket, hand wrapping around the mandrake potion.

No! Asmodeus shouted. *We need that for Legion.*

"I have to help him," Leah hissed. "He doesn't deserve this."

There is nothing we can do for—

"Shut up!" Leah screamed, leaving the bottle in her pocket. "Somebody, help! Please!"

The Pawn trembled beneath her, his eyes rolling up in the back of his head.

She had the power to put an end to his pain right now. She could help him, but—

"Leah?"

She looked up and saw Nick running toward her from the Lobby, holding up a Mystic with a makeshift tourniquet around the end of a now missing leg.

"Help! He's partly possessed. *Chesed* will stabilize him," she begged.

Nick frowned, easing the other Mystic to the ground and kneeling next to her. He laid his hands on the Pawn. Immediately the Pawn relaxed in Leah's grip, and his eyes closed.

"That should give him some comfort. Help me move him out of sight."

"Thank you," Leah said, grabbing the Pawns arms and maneuvering him to the side of the building, out of harm's way. "Are there any left?"

"A few." He sighed, propping the Pawn up. "Go on, keep Legion distracted while I get them out and to Nykima."

Lean nodded. "On it."

She raced back into the fight, joining beside Eli, Zafirah, and the Queens. They all moved with incredible speed, cutting or melting away chains as Micah took another shot at him. A deep gash marred Reginald's face, making the man that once held Legion nearly unrecognizable.

Leah cut the air in front of her, sending a *Malchut* blade into Legion's arm. Eli seized the opportunity and landed a kick right at Legion's jaw. A chain snaked around Eli's leg, pulling him and knocking him down on his back as another chain readied an attack. But Zafirah lifted her arms and a root pierced through Legion's leg, and the chain wavered enough to allow Eli to escape.

Nona moved too fast, zipping past Leah before she could stop her, and landed a hit on Zafirah. She tried to counter, but with Nona's burning bright eyes, she easily moved out of the way of the fire the Zafirah threw at her.

Leah sent off another blade, but it was easily deflected by Legion. She then dodged a set of chains flying toward her.

Helen appeared at her side, pulling her up. "Stay back and try to get a few shots on him if you see an opening."

Whirring sounded high in the air. When Leah looked, several helicopters, illuminated by the yellowed light from the sky, descended on headquarters.

"That's our exit," Helen said. "In case this goes sideways, make sure you get on one of those. Understand?"

One of the helicopters hovered above the field, and soldiers streamed down, landing on the field and firing toward the possessed Mystics. They didn't fall without a fight, and a possessed Rook released a wave of *Gevurah* fire that crashed into the helicopter, throwing it teetering into the woods with a massive flash of fire.

Legion let out a scream and hundreds of chains exploded out of him. Helen swung her katana, deflecting the chains from both her and Leah. Others weren't so lucky, and several Mystics, both possessed and not, crumpled to the ground, torn to shreds.

"You've grown desperate, Legion," Micah said as the Sages flanked him and Helen appeared at his side. Leah raced over, joining beside Sarah and Isaac, who were still standing, but both looked like they'd taken a beating.

Reginald spat a wad of blood and smiled. "I'm just getting started."

Micah leaped forward, but a Knight lunged in his way, taking the brunt of *Malchut* and collapsing to the ground.

Legion laughed, eyeing the body on the ground. "I will consume you all!" His mouth stretched wide, the skin around his lips tearing, and an inky blackness spread out across his mouth and across his skin.

"Not a chance, fucker!" Yuki shouted, lunging forward.

"No!" Desmond grabbed onto her ankle in mid-jump, pulling her back.

Teeth broke free from the darkness surrounding Legion, turning both his head and his torso into one enormous mouth.

No, not again, Asmodeus said. He took Leah over and shouted, "Move back!" in a low, guttural voice.

Legion's chest puffed up, and the maw of teeth widened. He breathed in, and the wind drew in from all directions. He became a vortex, his mouth at the center of a force that lifted Mystics up from the ground and sent them soaring into him. Consumed by him.

Leah dropped to the ground, wrapping her arms around a hunk of metal debris as she positioned herself to withstand the pull.

Bodies flew by her, screams lost over the roar of the wind. It was as if he were a black hole, opened up right in the middle of the battlefield. Her grip slipped as the metal shifted.

"He's too strong!" Leah screamed. "I can't hold on."

Keep holding. Let me try something. Asmodeus called on *Nehemoth*, pulling in energy from the metal and the ground, forming a coating of ice that secured it in place as Legion pulled.

Other Mystics flew past her, lost in the void. She could see her friends and the other Sages holding on to anything they could get their hands on.

She couldn't just sit here anchored while others were sucked into their death. There had to be something that could stop him. Something that could stop him in his tracks.

Something like the mandrake potion. Now was her chance to get him to consume it. She tried to reach for it in her pocket, but as she shifted her arms, she nearly lost her grip.

Now's our chance, Asmodeus said.

She met Sarah's eyes, who'd wrapped herself around a tree, holding on tight as the trunk slowly bent toward the void, roots popping up out of the ground. Leah caught her eye and gave her a slight smile.

"I've got this," Leah mouthed.

Sarah frowned and shook her head, but Leah let go, lifting off the ground and tumbling toward Legion.

The world spun as she flew backwards. She clawed at her pocket, but the force was too strong.

I can't get it! she screamed at Asmodeus.

Leah's arm wheeled around and launched a *Malchut* blast that sent her to the ground. She clawed at the ground and the rocks, but the pull was too strong. Her fingernails dug into the earth, and Asmodeus called on *Nehemoth* once more, allowing Leah to use her other hand to slip into her pocket and grab the bottle.

Asmodeus let go as she pulled the cork out with her mouth, flying toward Legion. She held the bottle closed with her thumb until she was mere feet from his mouth, then let her thumb up and watched the globules of greenish liquid vanish in the dark.

But the pull didn't stop, and she had nothing else to grab onto as she slipped into the wide opening that was Legion's mouth.

CHAPTER 47

CASTLING

Leah fell into the void of complete darkness as it collapsed and pressed against her. She felt her shoulder pop and her chest creak against the force. This was it. She was going to die here, consumed by Legion.

No! Asmodeus shouted in her mind. *Fight back!*

She called on *Netzach,* a barrier forming around her and the pressure, but the force was so strong, squeezing her tighter and tighter.

"I . . . I . . . can't," she groaned.

Then the force quivered and undulated, and the pull reversed. One second, she was being pulled into oblivion, certain she'd be crushed to death, and the next she was flying backward, expelled from Legion's mouth and cast onto the soft earth, rolling over piles of bodies and debris. Her shoulder rammed into a rock, and her back surged bright hot as her arm fell limp, swinging as she rolled. Her other hand squeezed as she came to a stop, the potion bottle nearly crushed in her hand. She held it up, surprised she still had the thing, noting the small bit of thick liquid clinging to the sides. The smell wafted into her nose, and she gagged before stoppering it with her thumb.

Legion let out a horrendous scream that rattled Leah's skull. He'd fallen to a knee, heaving as black ooze purged from his body. His form shrunk, and the teeth hanging out from his mouth rippled. A possessed Mystic rushed to his side, placing a hand on Legion's shoulder. "Sir, Legion. How can we—"

Whatever else they were about to ask was drowned out as they screamed, teeth turning on them and clamping down on their hand before moving like little fingers, digging into the Mystic's arm and pulling them into Legion's black mass. As the Mystic vanished, the darkness encapsulating Legion rippled, and dozens of little slits opened along his body, revealing eyes with black irises that looked around wildly. Six wings burst out from his flesh, pinfeathers tearing through skin and glistening with black ooze as they unfurled. He fell to his side, screaming.

What the hell is that? Asmodeus asked in Leah's mind.

"Mystics, charge! He's wounded!" Micah shouted, taking lead as the group of Sages and Mystics trailed behind him.

Isaac flanked Queen Micah's left along with Jaime, leading Mystics to clash with a remaining set of demons. Isaac slammed his hands together, holding several demons with *Hod* as Jaime led the charge in cutting them. Leah pushed herself up and found an opening for Legion, aiming her good arm toward him and surging energy into her fingertips. She fired, piercing one of the many eyes on his calf and shredding it to bits.

Helen appeared next to Legion's side as he staggered and stabbed him in the chest with one of her katanas. He swung a fist at her, but she disappeared, reappearing a few feet back from him.

"You'll pay for this!" he shouted, gasping for air, his

voice strained and weak as his injured eyes dripped with ooze.

Helen readied her sword and stepped forward. "Not if I kill you first." She vanished once more, appearing next to him, swinging her blade toward his neck.

An explosion rocked through the battlefield, bursting from the walls of the academy and sending debris flying toward them.

Helen stumbled back as shards of glass and heaps of stone came flying at her. Leah covered her head, bracing for the impending assault, but it never came. Instead, the debris hovered in the air, frozen, as if waiting for the right time to fall.

Sandeep stepped out from the hole in the wall, hands clasped together, flanked by at least fifty Rooks.

"Took you long enough," Legion growled. "Kill them!"

Sandeep simply looked at the fight to his right, toward Isaac and the others, and the debris in the air descended on them with such force that a mist of blood and dust enshrouded them.

"No," Leah muttered.

Helen spun on her heel and teleported a few feet from Sandeep, sending a *Malchut* push. Nona landed beside Sandeep and deflected Helen's attack before sending a counter push toward Helen that missed by inches as she disappeared and reappeared next to Micah.

The dust settled, and Isaac still stood, hands together, holding back the rubble and glass that would have otherwise killed him.

"Enough!" Legion shouted, thrusting an arm out toward an injured Knight near Isaac. A thin chain shot out of his arm and wrapped around the Knight, dragging her in toward him. Isaac dropped his *Hod*, evading the debris and racing to grab her, only to be hit by another chain that sent him flying away. The Knight dug her hands into the dirt, her face bloodied.

"No! Please no!" she screamed as Legion descended on her. Long arms gripped her, tearing into her shoulders and lifting her up off the ground.

"Protect me!" Legion commanded as White Queen Micah broke free from the last bit of demons.

Nona raced past Legion, using *Malchut* to launch up rubble toward Micah and the others, crushing several remaining Mystics under the debris.

The Knight screamed, clawing at Legion's hands as he moved quick, using one hand to hold her up and the other to trace on the ground. "Your sacrifice will be remembered on this day," he growled, before slitting the Knight's throat.

Blood poured out from her neck, glowing on the ground as it fell onto the symbols. Then her body became rigid, floating suspended in the air. He looked back toward Micah and grinned. "One day. When you least expect it. I'll take you. I'll take all of you." He dug his hands into the Knights chest and ripped it open, red light beaming out from her insides.

"He's going to get away!" Leah screamed.

Red lightning crackled off the ground, striking at the feet of Micah and Helen. Leah aimed and shot a *Malchut* bullet at him, her knuckles aching from the blast, but the lightning seemed to catch the energy and glow brighter. Legion pulled his way inside the fallen Knight's body, and once the last of him was through, the red light vanished, and the Knight fell to the ground in a heap of flesh.

CHAPTER 48
JUST ENOUGH

Dozens of remaining demons turned and ran into the woods, and the remaining debris in the air fell like rain as Sandeep released *Hod*. Micah and the others chased after them, leaving Leah alone on a battlefield full of bodies.

"No," Leah whispered, groaning as she tried to sit up.

"Leah!" Sarah yelled, blood covering half her face as she and Isaac came running up to her.

They helped her sit up, stopping as she winced. "Wait! I think my shoulder might be broken."

Isaac and Sarah rested their hands on Leah, and a warmth spread from their palms. Memories flooded Leah's mind, from the moment they met at the Outpost to the late nights they spent together, the joy of passing exams. Her shoulder moved under their hands, popping into place. Feeling came back to her, and she opened and closed her hand. The warmth dimmed, and the memories faded, the pain a mere nuisance now.

"That's better," she said, smiling up at them. "You made it."

"Yuki helped. She saved our asses a few times," Sarah

said, clapping Leah on her good shoulder. "But you stopped him. How did you do it?"

Leah opened her hand, revealing the small bottle. "This did the trick."

"We need to get back to the circle," Isaac said. "Legion fled, but that doesn't mean any of his minions won't try to pick us off if we aren't careful."

Isaac and Sarah helped her to her feet, and they carefully made their way back to the woods, avoiding the bodies along the way.

Nykima was outside the circle, wheelchair knocked on its side while she hovered over a body.

Leah spotted the ashen hair first, and her heart dropped. "No. Gabe."

She pulled free from her friends and sprinted toward him, ignoring the pain and dropping to Nykima's side. "What happened?"

Black spidery veins traced up the side of his neck and his eyes rolled up into the back of his head.

"Tom couldn't stop them all," Nykima said. "He tried to help, but the demon still got him. *Chesed's* not working."

"No. No," Leah said. Squeezing her fist and feeling the glass still in her hands. She sat up straight, shocked she'd been clutching it this whole time. "Wait, I. I might have some left. It's a potion. It helped Isaac. There might still be enough."

"Leah?" Gabe grumbled, his eyes slowly opening and focusing on her. He smiled for a second before wincing in pain. "You . . . made it."

She brushed back his ashen hair and smiled. "Shh, it'll be okay. I've got—"

"Help!" a voice shouted behind her. "The Sage of *Chesed* has fallen. We need help!"

A Pawn emerged from the forest path with Nick's arm

wrapped around his neck, dragging the Sage toward them. Blackened veins covered him, and a black ooze dribbled out from his mouth.

"Someone, help! Please!" The Pawn begged, stumbling and falling to their knees.

Leah uncurled her fingers and looked down at the remaining potion. There was barely any left. Not for both of them. Maybe not even one of them. "No," she whispered. *Chesed* wouldn't save them, not without this.

Gabe shakily reached out and grabbed her hand. "Him," he said, his eyes welling with tears. "He. He needs it more than me."

"No," Leah said, leaning in close. Her stomach turned, and she could taste bile on her tongue. "You can't. Gabe. You'll—I can't choose him over you."

Gabe squeezed again, his hand trembling. "You have to." He looked up at the trees. "He'll help others. Save more people."

"Gabe," tears fell from her cheeks. "I—"

"Please!" he screamed, his voice cracking as he refused to look at her. "Go!"

She backed away and looked down at the bottle. He was right. There were others all around them. Injured Mystics lay all around her, the scent of blood heavy in the air. They needed the best healers they could get. They needed Nick.

She wiped away at her tears, pushing herself up off the ground and peeled her gaze away from Gabe. Each step away from him was a pain that beat in her chest and thrummed in her ears. By the time she reached Nick's side, it felt as if her heart were torn into thousands of shreds.

Leah kneeled next to him, cradling his head in her hands. She worked his mouth open and poured the remaining contents into his mouth, the gel-like potion plopping into his mouth.

"Swallow, please. Fight it."

His mouth moved and he the potion went down, his Adam's apple bobbing up and down.

Seconds later, he convulsed. Energy thrummed off him, and his back arched as he let out a groan. Veins receded with each pulse of energy. His back arched, and he gasped before collapsing to the ground. Color flooded his face, and the last of the blackened veins vanished, all but a long black scar on his side.

His eyes blinked open, and his breathing calmed.

"Nick?" Leah asked, grabbing onto his shoulder. "Can you hear me?"

He nodded. "Did we win?"

"He's gone," Leah said, looked back toward Gabe. "But there are a lot of Mystics who could use your help. Do you think you could—"

"Yes," he said, taking in deep breaths and blinking several times. "I'm the Sage of *Chesed*. It is my duty to heal." He sat up, wavering a bit as he got to his feet with the help of Leah and the Pawn. "Where are they?"

"Gabe," she said, pulling them toward her fallen friend. "He's half possessed. Like you were."

Sarah and Isaac were already circled around Gabe, beside Nykima as she shook her head, feeling around his neck. She looked up at Nick and shook her head. "He's gone."

Leah's knees buckled, and Nick caught her, his strength returning every second. He looked at her for a moment and frowned.

"He's not breathing," Sarah cried.

"Out of the way," he said, pushing past Sarah and Isaac. He laid his hands on Gabe, heat emanating from him for a moment. "No, no," he whispered, starting chest compressions.

"No," Leah said, siding up to Nick. "No. You can't. I—"

A Black Bishop ran toward them. "Sage, we need your help!"

"Give me a minute," he said, leaning into the compressions.

"Sir, there are Mystics still alive who need *Chesed.*"

"No!" Nick screamed.

Nykima grabbed his arm. "Nick. Stop."

Nick looked back at Leah, his eyes wide. "You saved me over him."

Tears fell freely and her voice caught in her throat several times before she croaked. "I. I didn't have enough. You. You were supposed to save him. I. I—"

Nick choked back a sob. "I . . . I'm sorry."

He pushed himself to his feet as Nykima leaned back and closed Gabe's eyes.

"No," Leah cried.

Nykima spoke over her, her voice straining as she held back tears. "Gabriel Tate saved many tonight defending the circle long enough for them to seek refuge. He may not have been one by name, but he died a Knight, and should be remembered as one."

FORTRESS

"We've got another one!" Leah shouted as she emerged out from the rubble, arms around a Knight with a crushed leg. She helped them through the tent and onto a cot that the Shadow Board helicoptered in a few hours after Legion escaped.

"Leah, you need to rest," Nykima said. "The Shadow can take it from here."

Leah shook her head, pushing down the emotions that were clawing to come out. "No."

"See any others?" Nykima asked, wheeling over with a thin blanket and a bag of saline.

"The rest of the sublevels are caved in," Leah said, sitting on an empty cot beside the Knight. "Couldn't see anyone else with *Tiferet*."

There were still dozens of empty cots, and a whole other tent ready to set up, but of the nearly five hundred Rooks and the nearly thousand Knights, Bishops, and Pawns, less than a hundred were accounted for. She looked over at Isaac, who'd joined Nick as they moved to each cot, performing *Chesed* where they could, and triage where they couldn't. Some people Leah had pulled out of the wreckage already had sheets over them, waiting for Sarah, Yuki, or one of the others to dig a grave for them.

The day had been a blur after Micah and the others returned, noting that the demons had run off completely. The Shadow Board came soon after, setting up tents, taking Tom's book, and assigning Leah to rescue any remaining Mystics in the rubble while nearly all the Sages left and the Queens vanished into a smaller tent.

The whole day nearly passed her by before Queen Jan Xie stepped out of the tent with two muscular guards trailing behind her. She paused in the center of the tent, and everyone fell silent save for the occasional moan or whimper.

"Thank you all for tending to our fallen Mystics. We will report our next moves soon, but for now, Nick, Yuki, Nykima Amana, Leah Ackerman, Sarah Turner, and Isaac O'Conner come with me." She turned and slid back inside the tent without another word.

"Doesn't she see we're busy?" Nick asked, loud enough for the whole tent to hear.

"We've got it from here," a Bishop at his side said, sweat glistening on their forehead.

He stood and gripped Isaac's shoulder. "Come on, let's go." He turned back to the others. "We'll be back. Don't do anything that might get you hurt. Understand?"

"Yes, sir," the remaining Bishops and Pawns said before leaning back over a Mystic with a piece of rebar sticking out of his side.

Leah pushed herself up off the cot, eyeing the pale face of the Knight she'd brought in.

"The tourniquet will hold," Nykima said, nodding down at the makeshift wrapping Leah had applied around the Knight's leg. "He might lose it, but he'll live as long as they get to him soon. Come on, there's nothing we can do now."

Inside the Queen's tent, laptops, stacks of papers, and a massive map of the United States with big red circles drawn with a marker covered a table. Sarah came up to Leah's side and nudged her shoulder, giving her a half smile as Isaac joined her other side.

Helen looked up from the table, marker in hand and hair slightly astray. "Thank you for all that you've done today. I've related some of what you told me before last night's attacks, but the Sages and Queens would like a recount from the source. If you please."

Nykima took the lead, recounting everything she'd been told, while Leah and the others filled in on the rest, ending with Leah showing the empty bottle that contained the mandrake potion.

"You saved countless lives," Desmond said. "All of you." He bowed his head to each of them.

"But I didn't know it would work," Leah blurted out. "The potion, I mean. It was just a guess."

"Guess or not, the four of you prevented Legion from taking over," Queen Helen said. "Your three Queens still stand, and Legion has been injured. He fled because of what you did."

"Five," Leah said.

Helen raised an eyebrow.

"Gabe makes five of us."

"Yes, of course," Helen said. "We've agreed to raise his title to Knight. He will be remembered as the bondless Knight that protected the injured until his last breath."

"Thank you," Nykima said, lifting her head. "But what now, my Queens?"

"We recuperate and tend to the injured," Queen Micah said. "They won't return here. Not yet. Not without their leader."

"No," Leah said, stepping forward. "We need a plan. We need to take him out now while he's weak."

"You will watch your tongue, Pawn," Queen Jan Xie spat.

Micah lifted a hand. "We have scouts out looking for Legion's location. But for now, the Mystics still on the Board must recuperate and prepare for departure."

"Departure? Where?" Leah asked.

"That is for us to still decide," Queen Micah said, turning to his fellow Queens and the Sages. "This place is compromised. There is no telling where else Legion and his demons have infiltrated."

Eli cleared his throat. "He broke a veil between the Material and the Astral. Even if he is weak, it's impossible to know what other tricks he may have up his sleeve."

Zafirah pointed to the map in the middle of the room. "It was a ritual. Had he done it on the night of the vote, when the solstice was at its peak, there's no telling what would have happened. Those markings, all those places they hit before here, they were calculated. He's been planning this for months."

Leah eyed the map on the table, spotting the circles that encompassed headquarters.

"Enough," Queen Jan Xie said. "Pawns, Knight, you are dismissed."

Helen nodded toward Leah. "Black Queen Jan Xie will provide us with an evacuation plan. Keep that book of yours handy, as we'll want a final confirmation before departing. And Nykima, now that your connections to the voodoo community are public, we may call on you for assistance."

"Yes, my Queen," Nykima said, followed by the others.

"Good, now go and rest. Tough times lie ahead."

A Small Request From Us, The Authors

Thank you for continuing Leah's journey. We hope you've enjoyed it, so far.

As independent authors, reviews are so important to spread the word and reach new readers.

If you have a few seconds to spare, would you please consider leaving an honest review on the website you bought this book?

Your support helps so much in continuing Leah's story and the many others we plan to write in this world.

All the best,

A.B. Cohen & JP Rindfleisch IX

DIRE QUEEN
LEAH ACKERMAN SERIES BOOK FIVE

The story continues:

https://abcohenwrites.com/dire-queen

THE ASTRAL LAYERS
SHORT STORY

Go beyond Leah Ackerman

Delve into a secret world, an impending alliance, and a common enemy. From the shared universe of the Leah Ackerman series, check out this short story now!

https://BookHip.com/QQTLNDW

CURSED JADE
AN ERIC MIZRAHI NOVELETTE

Get it free using the link below:

https://abcohenwrites.com/cursed-jade

Acknowledgments

As you may have noticed, we dedicated this book to three very special people: Claudia, Chris, and Nissim. They have been our beta readers for the past four books and counting, and they deserve a special mention because we know how much time and effort they have selflessly put into our books. For *Dormant Rook* in particular, we were on a really tight schedule and they were able to read and give feedback in a week. They surpassed all expectations and went above and beyond to help us achieve the story you now hold in your hands. To you three, thank you; we couldn't have done it without you.

A special shout-out to our wonderful and steadfast team of editors, proofreaders, and designers, including Zach Bohannon, Lori Diederich, and Getcovers.com. Your ongoing assistance and dedication to Leah Ackerman's story have been crucial in bringing this series to life.

We remain grateful to the multiple author communities of which we are a part for their ongoing support, as well as to our friends and family who have been with us every step of the way. Even when we wake you up with our loud keyboards in the early mornings, you stuck with us. Thank you for being understanding and awesome.

Lastly, we want to thank you, our incredible readers, for joining us on Leah's adventures. We hope you've enjoyed *Dormant Rook* as much as we've enjoyed writing it, and we can't wait for you to see what comes next in *Dire Queen*, book five of the Leah Ackerman series!

Thank you all.

A.B. Cohen & JP Rindfleisch IX

About the Authors

A.B. Cohen is an author of freaky stories for weird people. He focus mainly on thrillers, horror and urban fantasy tales. Originally from Caracas, Venezuela, today he lives in Berkeley, California. Along with his passion for writing, he also loves dancing, soccer, and traveling. You can find out more about A.B. Cohen's upcoming writing projects using the link below:

www.abcohenwrites.com

JP Rindfleisch IX is a horror, urban fantasy, and science fiction writer. They live in Rockford, Illinois, with their partner of eleven years, and a menagerie of animal children including a Siberian husky, miniature dachshund, African grey parrot, Quaker parrot, and a run of the mill cat. They love creating art, nerding out over science, video games, tabletop RPGs, and spending hours in the kitchen crafting delectable vegan grub. You can learn more about JP Rindfleisch IX by following the link below:

www.jprindfleischix.com